WANDERERS

WANDERERS

stories by

Edward Belfar

STEPHEN F. AUSTIN STATE UNIVERSITY PRESS
2012

Wanderers
Copyright © 2012 by Stephen F. Austin State University
All rights reserved.
Printed in the United States of America.

Permissions
Stephen F. Austin State University Press,
1936 North Street, LAN 203,
Nacogdoches, Texas, 75962.
sfapress@sfasu.edu

Book Design: Laura McKinney and Kristi Warren
Cover Design: Laura Davis
Copy Editor: Kristi Warren

LIBRARY OF CONGRESS CATALOGING-IN-PUBLICATION DATA

Belfar, Edward

Wanderers: stories / Edward Belfar. - 1st ed.
p.cm.

ISBN-978-1-936205-47-9

I. Title

First Edition: April 2012

for Kathleen

ACKNOWLEDGEMENTS

The following stories appeared in these publications: "Mistaken Identity" in *Shenandoah*; "Roman Honeymoon" in *Confrontation*; "Visitations" in *Snake Nation*; "The Peacock" in *Colere*; "The Ruined House" in *Natural Bridge*; "Leaving the Chesapeake" in *On the Page*; "Errors" in *Aethlon*; "Eviction" in *Open Spaces*; "Something Small" in *Tampa Review*; "The Rule of Law" and "A View of the Fireworks" in *Silent Voices*; "Ashes" in *Rive Gauche*; "Departure" in *Imagination and Place*; "Matters of the Heart" in *The Baltimore Review*; and "Wanderers" in *Front Range Review*.

CONTENTS

MISTAKEN IDENTITY

In Karen, people still talk about the American who chose the wrong sister to be his bride, though it happened several years ago. Well, Karen is that sort of place. Though it is only a half-hour's ride from downtown Nairobi, it still has, in parts, the transient look of a trading post. Not a whole lot has happened there since Karen Blixen left. And so, when something does, people talk, and they talk some more, and they embellish. And when I come to town, I try to set them straight. I have an interest in the matter, you see. The sisters in question are mine.

The man who came between them was an American—an "African American," as they call themselves over there, an appellation that I have always found a bit baffling. Here, one identifies oneself first and foremost as a Kikuyu or a Luo or a Kallinjin, and no self-respecting Kikuyu would ever join a club that admitted Luos or Kallinjins. But Dr. Malik Wilson appeared to have made a nice career of being African American, for he taught African American Studies at UCLA, where my sister Faith had first become his teaching assistant and then his fiancée, and he had also found time to record a hip-hop CD, entitled African Undaground, copies of which he dispensed as gifts at every opportunity. A tall, slender man in his late thirties or early forties, he had a long, narrow face with round owl eyes and a goatee that came to a sharp point. He favoured knit sport jackets and brightly colored shirts and always wore a black leather beret.

It was owing to my parents' conservatism that Professor Wilson became my roommate for a time. Not only had he shared a maisonette with Faith for more than a year, but, by the time the two of them landed in Nairobi, they were legally man and wife, having taken their wedding vows in an office of a justice of the peace, beneath a mock trellis lined with plastic vine leaves. Nuptials of that sort carried little weight with Mum and Dad, though, who decreed that here in Kenya, at least, Faith and her beau could not abide under the same roof until they had "whitewashed" their vows in church. Thus, as soon as she and Malik reached the sidewalk outside the main terminal at Jomo Kenyatta, their paths diverged. After much confusion over which piece of luggage would go in which car, a swarm of aunts, uncles, and cousins bore Faith off to Mum and Dad's house in Karen, while I drove Malik to my flat in Nairobi.

As one might expect, the sudden, enforced separation from Faith, whom Malik described, disconcertingly, as "a sweet, ripe fruit" of which he always craved a mouthful, did not entirely please him, but it did offer him certain compensations. Kikuyu weddings tend to be chaotic and interminable affairs, full of impromptu speeches and professions of faith by guests unknown to anyone in the wedding party and maybe even a chorus or two showing up unbidden to serenade the bride and groom. In typical Kikuyu fashion, our family had planned not one, but two extravaganzas: a traditional ngurario to celebrate the engagement with at least a few hundred guests and, a week later, an Anglican ceremony and an even larger reception. Many of the wedding invitations had yet to be sent out; the bridesmaids' dresses were not complete; the caterer was demanding more money; and Faith, a bubbly sort by nature, had grown tense and, on occasion, even snappish, blaming her fiancé for his nonchalance, if not for the sloth of the dressmaker or the greed of the caterer. While she, Mum, and the bridesmaids haggled with caterer, florist, photographer, and dressmaker and held stormy meetings that sometimes dragged on well past midnight, Malik and I made the rounds of the Nairobi pubs. I put his conscience at ease—not that it required much easing—by telling him that such a division of labour accorded perfectly with Kikuyu tradition.

One evening, a few days after his arrival, I drove Malik out to Karen for his first formal meeting with his future mother- and father-in-law. My parents and my younger sister Lucy still lived in the house in which I had grown up, a broad, single-story stucco dwelling with a maze-like interior of narrow corridors intersecting at bizarre angles and ideal little nooks for games of hide-and-seek. The vast grounds provided a home and sustenance to several dairy cows—all that remained of my father's herds since he had sold off his land and cattle up in Muranga and settled, more or less, into retirement.

Dad, a dark, compact man, with stubby fingers and a large, square head, greeted us at the door, wearing his customary red and white checked flannel shirt and blue jeans.

"So you've come to bring the dowry," he said, with a sly grin, as he grasped Malik's hand and squeezed it hard.

The usually loquacious professor, finding himself, for the moment, bereft of words, meekly offered up the coffee table book that he had brought with him from America.

I answered for him: "He would have, but he couldn't get the goats through customs."

Dad led us through the long foyer into the dining room, where the rest of the family awaited us. Mum, Faith, and Lucy were there, along with two cousins, Wanjiru and Wanjiku—dour, hefty women both—and their husbands and assorted off-spring.

Once we had seated ourselves, we all joined hands as Mum, a plump woman with a broad, flat face, thanked our Lord and Saviour Jesus Christ profusely and at great length for the many blessings he had bestowed upon us: good food and good health, the rare pleasure of having the entire family present at the table, the love that Faith and Malik had found in one another.

Servants came and went with muffled steps, emerging from the shadows into the dim yellow light cast by the globular ceiling fixture and then vanishing again, leaving behind dishes heaped with roasted lamb, curried fish, and lentil stew. Permeated by the fragrance of the curry, the room grew steamy. The children laughed and squealed. Faith, seated at the far end of the table, reminisced with Wanjiru and Wanjiku about long hours spent together snapping open pea pods and picking stones from rice. Lucy, our enfant terrible, unattainable object of desire of every friend I had ever brought to the house, drummed her long violet fingernails on the table, looking bored and sullen. Tall and lithe, her physique all sharp curves and angles, she had large, luminous eyes, a complexion like dark chocolate, and rosebud lips. She kept her hair straightened and pulled back from her face, the better to accentuate her impressive cheekbones. On this night, she wore skin-tight jeans and a red and blue flowered blouse, revealing sufficient cleavage to evoke the occasional furtive glance from Malik, as well as some censorious looks from Faith, who did not miss much. I had no doubt that Lucy had chosen both her outfit and her place at the table beside Malik to provoke just those reactions, for she and her older sister had never got on well.

Mum, passing along a bowl of sweet potatoes, asked, seemingly in all innocence, though Malik is a common enough name around here, "What kind of name is Marik?"

"I told you, Mum," snapped Faith, "Malik is not a Muslim."

I wondered which had caused Faith greater mortification,

the question itself or Mum's country Kikuyu mispronunciation of Malik's name.

Turning to Malik, Lucy added, mockingly, "This is a 'Christian' house," forming quotation marks with her fingers around the word Christian lest he miss her sarcasm. "No Muslims allowed."

Once, such a remark would have earned her a slap, but she had come into her majority, and now my parents could manage only a resigned silence. Some time before, Lucy had become engaged to a Muslim and had even gone so far as to convert and adopt the name Rania because his parents, he said, would not allow him to marry outside the faith. "Will we have to go to Mecca for the wedding?" Mum had wailed. In the end, the wedding had not come off, in Mecca or anywhere else, thanks to the ever-multiplying demands of the prospective in-laws. While Lucy could as easily mouth one prayer as another, she did not intend, as she said, with her admirable Kikuyu pragmatism, to give up her nascent modeling career or "to walk around dressed like a ninja or stop going to pubs."

At length, Malik, recovering his voice, assured Mum that, no, despite his name, which his parents had bestowed upon him at a time when many African American parents were giving their children Muslim names, he was not of that faith.

"You mean you weren't named after one of your relatives?" asked Mum, incredulously.

"No," he said, shaking his head, "My parents just liked the name Malik." Of course, he added, he liked it, too, and he had enormous respect for Islam, one of the world's great religions. He then launched into a long disquisition about the many ways of approaching God, during which he referenced not only Islam, but also Buddhism, Shintoism, Hinduism, Jainism, Judaism, and Christianity, while taking care not to slight the traditional animist beliefs that he hoped to learn more about during his stay in Kenya. His speech left Mum goggle-eyed.

We all trooped into the living room for coffee and dessert. Malik gazed in rapture at the batiks on the walls depicting fierce spear-wielding Masai warriors. His eyes lit upon the animal carvings that lined the shelves, skipping over the bibles and hymnals. Seating himself on a sofa, beneath a massive, gauzy, highly stylized portrait showing Jomo Kenyatta wearing skins as he never did in life, Malik proclaimed, "I like this room. This is a real African room."

"I'm very glad to hear that," Dad deadpanned, a mischievous twinkle in his eye.

As often happens in real African living rooms, the women gravitated to one end and the men, to the other—except for Lucy, who again contrived to settle herself alongside Malik.

The women spoke of the final preparations for the ngurario two days hence.

The ceremony appeared to fascinate Malik, who had bombarded me with questions about it ever since his arrival. Was the ngurario as performed today authentic? Why was the girl so reluctant to go with her new husband to his home? Why did she and the other members of her party hide their faces to confuse the groom? Did she want to get married or not?

As one of those effete, deracinated modern Kikuyus that our famous pop singer John Kamaru has made a very remunerative career out of satirizing—I live in the city, work for an American hotel chain, and, if forced to converse in Kikuyu, can barely hold up my end—I could not enlighten him very much. Generally, I told him what I thought he wanted to hear, assuring him that the ngurario we had planned would hew very closely to tradition.

Now, he had a curious thought. Leaning close, he whispered confidentially, "What happens if the groom chooses the wrong woman?"

"The idea," I answered, "is that you're supposed to know your bride so well that you'll pick her out even if you can't see her face." Then, as I saw his gaze drifting once more toward the parting in Lucy's blouse, I added, "There are two things you should keep in mind. One is that Faith has a temper. Two is that the ceremony involves a rather large carving knife."

He replied with a nervous laugh, but his eyes remained glued to my sister's cleavage.

Wanjiku's husband spoke of the trials he had encountered while trying to buy steel rods for reinforcing concrete.

"So I told the chut," he said, employing the common East African derogation for Indians, "that I'd prove to him that the rods were nowhere near fifteen millimeters, and I took out my calipers and showed him. He said my calipers were defective, and he chased me out of the shop."

Even Malik's admiration for all things African had its limits. "Man," he said, shaking his head, "they could never get away with that in America."

"They get away with it in Kenya," said Lucy, with a touch of bitterness, "because everyone's too beaten down to put up a fight."

The blame for our abject condition, Malik assured us, lay with the white men who had colonized and exploited us and continued to do so from afar. "When they say globalization," he intoned, recycling a line from the title track of his African Undaground CD, "they mean colonization."

"Our good Dr. Wilson," observed Dad, who I thought, until that moment, had fallen asleep, "has spent three days in Kenya and already diagnosed all our ills." Then he yawned, closed his eyes, and began to snore.

Lucy, having got started on one of her favourite subjects, began to expound at length upon the maladies that plagued our poor Kenya: the crime, the corruption, the tribalism and general backwardness, and—most grievous of all, from her point of view—the paucity of nightlife options. Naturally, Faith felt compelled to defend the land she had forsaken, which she regarded as the most beautiful place on earth and the home to the kindest and warmest people. The argument grew quite heated until Dad emerged from his slumbers once more to say, "You're both right. Daughters are always right." Everyone laughed, except Lucy and Faith.

Lucy, at least, had Malik's rapt attention to sooth her bruised feelings, and she quickly turned to her other favorite subject: her recent photo shoot for a Sunday supplement of the Daily Nation. Across the room, meanwhile, Wanjiru and Wanjiku were compiling a lengthy list of all the Kikuyu marriages made overseas that had broken up when the couples had returned to Kenya and the men had begun acting like typical African males. All African men were louts, the two cousins concluded, with Kikuyu men the most loutish of all.

"African women do have to put up with a lot," said Faith, a bit too loudly.

Oblivious to her baleful glare, her fiancé and her younger sister exchanged chuckles and confidences.

≈≈

The resplendent afternoon sun threw its light upon pink bougainvillea, scarlet roses, white orchids, yellow rhododendrons, purple bellflowers. It kindled the orange blossoms of the Nandi flame tree near the outer wall of the property. It pressed its molten mass upon the necks and shoulders of the guests in the yard, causing skin to glisten and collars to stain.

From Nairobi, Nyeri, and all points in between, the guests had come, wearing outfits as vari-coloured as the flowers. When they had filled their plates at the buffet table, they retreated to the shade of two blue and white striped tents, arranged perpendicularly to one another on the lawn, and gorged themselves on mutton and reminiscences. Uncles and aunts whom I had last met when I was in nappies, if I had met them at all, smothered me with hugs and kisses.

Faith, the beaming bride-to-be, the focus of all camera and camcorder lenses, wore sandals, a brown t-shirt beneath an ocher dress that was cut to look like an animal skin and hung off one shoulder, and a brown cap with faux earrings made of cloth attached to the sides. She floated about the lawn exchanging pleasantries with the guests, while her bridesmaids, wearing the same outfit as she, minus the cap, orbited around her. Only Lucy, whose antics at the dinner party a couple of nights before had very nearly cost her her place among the bridesmaids, kept her distance.

The time had arrived for the ceremony to begin. The women of the bridal party went to stand on the veranda to await their part, joined by a company of young girls and old women. Malik and I sat down in two folding chairs set up in front of the buffet table, and my father, holding a cordless microphone, emerged from one of the tents and shuffled out onto the lawn.

"Karibu!" he cried, above the murmuring of the crowd and the incessant chirping of mobile phones. "Welcome. Welcome, everyone."

Then, switching to Kikuyu, he introduced some of the legions of the Nairobi-area aunts, uncles, and cousins. Customs may change over time, he said, but in one respect, at least, the ngurario remained what it always had been: an occasion for the families of the bride- and groom-to-be to meet, mingle, eat, drink, and have a good time. And that was all he asked of his guests.

From the other tent, the jovial, pear-shaped Uncle Mwangi came out to join him. Uncle Mwangi introduced several members of the Nyeri branch of our family, which, on this day, would have to stand in for Malik's. Beckoning Malik to come forward, he draped his arm over the younger man's shoulders and welcomed him to the family. Uncle Mwangi explained that he had come all this way from Nyeri to negotiate the dowry on Malik's behalf, since everybody knew what a hard bargainer my father was. Peals of laughter rose from both tents.

Then, Uncle Mwangi asked my father to bring forth the bride. Half a dozen girls came scampering forth from the veranda, none older than ten. The spectators guffawed and yelped with glee. Malik, warming to his part, grinned and shook his head, and Uncle Mwangi asked again. Dad looked toward the veranda and smiled. Now came the grandmothers and great aunts. Again, Malik shook his head. Toothless old Aunt Elizabeth, full of mock outrage at being spurned, wagged her finger and gave him a stern lecture in Kikuyu, to the delight of the assembly. Uncle Mwangi asked a third time. My father stroked his chin as if thinking the matter over and once more turned his gaze toward the veranda. Now came the bride and the bridesmaids, with their heads and faces hidden beneath identical brown shawls. The women circled around Malik—too closely, I feared, for while I could clearly see Faith's telltale ankle bracelet from where I sat, he searched in vain, looking more and more panic-stricken with each passing second. I cringed when I saw his hand hover above and then, for just an instant, alight upon the shoulder of the woman with the long, sleek calves, for, even with her face hidden, no one could mistake Lucy for any of the others in the party. The crowed emitted a collective gasp. Faith, shoving her sister aside, dealt her fiancé a sharp kick to the ankle. Wincing, he nevertheless embraced her, and, to the cheers of the guests, she pulled away her shawl to reveal herself. Her smile, though, appeared more strained than triumphant, and Malik looked as though he had eaten something that disagreed with him.

Now the waiters brought out a great silver tray, lined with banana leaves, upon which rested the goat's shoulder that Malik had to cut through to seal the marriage contract. They set the tray down upon the buffet table. But where was the knife? Dad pleaded with Faith. She shook her head. He drew out his wallet and offered her a fistful of notes. In the rehearsal the day before, she had quickly relented, accepting the money and fetching the knife from the veranda, but now, she pivoted about and stomped off across the lawn. She reached the veranda and kept going, slamming the back door behind her as she disappeared inside the house.

"Something's wrong," I heard one of the waiters whisper.

Beneath the tents, the crowd buzzed with apprehension. Dad stood with his mouth agape, still clutching his wallet in his left hand and the notes in his right, wondering, perhaps, why fate had decreed that he must live in an age when Kikuyu daughters brought nothing but heartache to their fathers instead of a century ago when a man could marry his girls off to whomever he liked and grow rich off their dowries. Uncle Mwangi whispered something in his ear. Dad nodded, said something in reply, and then he, too, went inside the house. Malik sat down beside me once more and slumped forward in his chair, shaking his head and muttering, "I never even touched her. I swear it."

Uncle Mwangi addressed the crowd again, this time in English, so that all the generations could understand him. "The ngurario is a bittersweet occasion for the bride," he said. "On the one hand, she is happy because she is becoming engaged to marry the man she loves. On the other, she is sad because she knows she will be leaving her village and going to live with her husband's clan, and she may never see her own again. And so, she hides herself, and even when she is revealed, she hesitates."

Always a great talker, he now put his gift to good use, saving the day by filibustering for the next twenty minutes or so. He spoke of the role of tradition in keeping us anchored in this ever more bewildering world. Extolling the joys of marriage, he quoted from St. Paul's hymn to love, that staple of wedding vows so often honoured in the breach. He talked until, at long last, my father reemerged from the house, clasping the knife in his left hand and Faith's wrist in his right, as he pulled her along behind him.

Malik, making a great show of shedding his sport jacket and beret and rolling up his sleeves, took the knife and set to work on the shoulder. Some of the women began to sing and others—mostly those of my parents' generation—to ululate, their shrill cries piercing the air. Malik hacked and sawed, but to little effect. Panting, he paused in his labours and wiped his brow with the back of his hand. Furtively, I made my way over to the table.   While he resumed cutting, I held the shoulder down—a breach of decorum that some of the older guests would mutter about afterwards. Contrary to some of the stories that would emerge later, I did not take the knife from Malik and finish the job for him.

After the ceremony, he and Faith shied away from one another. While the guests lingered around her and offered hearty congratulations, they spoke much more perfunctorily to Malik. Eventually, I found him sitting alone beneath one of the tents, still sweating profusely and appearing slightly dazed.

"Are you all right?" I asked, sitting down beside him. I told him that I had seen others struggle just as much as he had in trying to cut through the shoulder and assured him that he had no reason to feel embarrassed at his efforts. I thought it best not to mention his more serious faux pas; only Faith could offer him absolution for that. "Now that you're an honorary Kikuyu," I said, "we'll have to think of a Kikuyu name for you."

He gazed at me blankly without answering.

≈≈

The most absurd version of the story I've heard had Malik and Lucy eloping after the ngurario. Actually, the wedding went off the next week without a hitch, albeit without Lucy in the wedding party. A baby boy and then a divorce followed in relatively short order. Faith could forgive Malik Wilson for botching his part at the ngurario but not, alas, for the philandering that followed. Had she been a superstitious village girl, she once remarked rather ruefully, she would have seen what the ngurario portended and called the whole thing off. Eventually, she came back to live in Karen with Mum and Dad, who, with Lucy having departed for Paris and become the supermodel Rania, welcomed the company.

I have a wife and a daughter of my own now, and on Sundays, we often drive out to the house in Karen. My three-year-old Wairimu gambols in the yard with Faith's four-year-old Maina, just as the two of us once did. We talk of those times and of many other things besides—but never of Malik Wilson, the American who chose the wrong sister to be his bride.

ROMAN HONEYMOON

Though he had yielded to almost all Salma's demands during the planning of the wedding and even let her drag him all the way from Pittsburgh to her former hometown of Jersey City for an interminable Coptic Orthodox ceremony, David had finally prevailed in his choice of Rome as their honeymoon destination. At twenty-six, he had never before ventured abroad and had longed for such a trip for years.

Nothing he had read or seen in the movies, though, had quite prepared him for the splendors of the Eternal City. He marveled at the Trevi Fountain; at the dome of St. Peter's, the twisting bronze columns of the baldachin above the altar, and Michelangelo's Pieta; at the miraculous capture of light on canvas by Caravaggio in his "Rest on the Flight into Egypt"; and at the wonders wrought by Bernini in marble throughout the city. Guidebook in hand, he left Salma far behind as he wound his way through the ruins of the Coliseum, the Palatine and the Foro Romano. His imagination labored to restore the glories of temples of which only broken columns remained, to re-build the crumbling walls of imperial palaces, to refurnish the chambers where emperors once trod on marble floors but where children now played on the grass.

"You're more interested in a pile of old bricks than me," said Salma through pursed lips one afternoon as she sat herself down on a marble slab before what remained of the colonnade of the round Temple of Vesta. Removing her pumps, she rubbed her feet. Sweat beaded her olive skin. Having lived the first twelve years of her life in the shadow of the pyramids at Giza, she had seen all the ancient ruins she ever cared to, and for the second time that day, she let him know that she worked very hard all year and needed a rest, not a forced march, thank you very much, and would rather have spent the two weeks on a beach in the Bahamas.

He rolled his eyes—a response that she immediately gave him cause to regret as she began a lengthy recitation of all the things that irritated her about Rome: the crowds; the traffic, which made the simple act of crossing the street a death-defying feat; the cease-less buzz of motor scooters and the two-note drone of police sirens, which gave her tension headaches; the litter and graffiti; the lack of toilet seats in the public bathrooms; the price of meals and of the closet of a hotel room that he had booked for them; and the rat that she had seen scurrying across the floor of the restaurant at dinner the night before. Moreover, she did not appreciate his habit of walking out alone at night after she had fallen asleep. Just what was he up to? She saw the way he looked at the local sluts with their tight jeans and purple lipstick.

Irritated, he turned his back on her and walked away. It's simple jealousy, he thought. She could not allow him to derive pleasure from a source outside herself. In her perverse way, she had come to see Rome as a rival for his affections.

Once he had found even these fits of pique endearing, for while the world saw a brisk, efficient, self-possessed Salma, Chief Resident in obstetrics and gynecology at the largest teaching hospital in western Pennsylvania, to him she exposed her vulnerabilities—and her terrible need. Of late, she had been out of sorts a little too often for his liking, but he still had the consolation of knowing that her anger, like a summer squall, would soon spend itself. Indeed, when, after fifteen minutes or so of exploring the House of the Vestal Virgins, he returned and sat down beside her, she placed her head on his shoulder and lightly ran a finger over the back of his hand. Upon returning to their room, they shared a frenzied lovemaking session.

That night, though, he wandered out again, first to the gelato shop two doors down from the hotel and then to the nearby Spanish Steps. Salma never stayed awake past 9:00, while he could seldom get to sleep before 1:00, and he could not bear to sit in the dark in the tiny hotel room.

Descending the steps halfway, he leaned against the balustrade, drew his camera from his knapsack, and sought to frame within his lens the life that surrounded him: the caricaturists and artisans; the vendors selling puppets, roses, and tin models of the Coliseum; the knots of spiky-haired adolescents playing guitars and singing Beatles' songs in English; the young couples seeking out the darker corners on the steps and feverishly kissing and embracing and the middle-aged lovers strolling hand-in-hand on the piazza below; the laughter and the music of the Italian language; the smell of roasting chestnuts. An unaccountable sadness filled him, and without taking the picture, he replaced the camera in the knapsack and turned back toward the hotel.

Entering the room, he saw Salma in silhouette, sitting up in bed and tugging at her hair. When he called her name, she did not respond. Dropping his knapsack and jacket onto a chair, he sat down on the bed beside her and reached for her hand. She snatched her arm away and buried herself in the blankets, her back turned to him. The sound of her sobbing soon filled the room, and he lay on his back and listened in torment.

She had cried, too, the night before the wedding, when she had revealed her pregnancy and he had responded in a distinctly ungallant manner: "Pregnant? But how?" Though he had not given voice to his suspicion that that an all-too-deliberate memory lapse on Salma's part had facilitated the supposedly accidental conception, she must have sensed his thoughts. Hardly a day had passed since when she had not cried.

"I'm sorry," he said to the ceiling.

They ate breakfast in silence the next morning, but afterwards, on the metro, as they embarked upon their long-awaited excursion to the Sistine Chapel, she whispered, "I love you so much," and clasped his right hand in both of hers all through the ride.

Hand in hand, they drifted through the Statue Gallery, the Tapestry Gallery, the Map Room, and the Raphael Rooms, each chamber more dazzling than the last, but as they prepared to enter the Sistine Chapel, she began to cry again.

"Don't," he whispered, and he brushed her tears away with his hand. "I'll surprise you yet. I'll be a good father."

"You'll be a wonderful father. And the only one who'll be surprised will be you."

Inside the Chapel, the surging tide of bodies pulled him and Salma apart. With his eyes turned upward to the wounded visage of Adam expelled from Eden, David slowly became aware that the shouts that resounded throughout the venerable sanctuary, site of the election of popes and the flowering of Michelangelo's genius, came from Salma.

Fighting his way through the crowd to the far wall, David found her standing just outside the exit door, by turns wailing, begging and screaming in English and Arabic at a security guard, whose eyes, when they met David's, showed utter bewilderment.

"She go out-eh. She no can come back in-eh," said the guard, throwing up his hands. "Mama mia! Che stronza!"

With broad gestures and a jumble of Italian words and English phrases, David begged the guard's pardon, took hold of Salma's shoulders, and tried to guide her off, but she would not move. Her pupils were fixed and glassy; she did not seem to recognize him. Suddenly, she let loose a sustained scream, a sound as sharp and piercing as a dentist's drill. He stood frozen as the buzz of hundreds of murmured conversations died out, and all eyes in the vicinity bored in upon the two of them. Then he turned and ran.

Leaving St. Peter's Square without even a look back, he hurried across the Ponte Sant' Angelo, over the brown waters of the Tiber. For the next three hours, he lost himself repeatedly amid a maze of narrow cobblestoned streets and even narrower alleyways, many without names. Cars and scooters darted out from all directions, sometimes missing him by inches. Even when he could comprehend the directions people gave him, he could not remember them long enough to follow them through to the end.

Sweaty and aching, he returned at last to the hotel room and, to his relief, found Salma there. She was still seething, though, sitting on the bed plucking single strands of wiry hair from her scalp and writing lists of groceries to buy and errands to perform upon their return to Pittsburgh three days hence. To all his questions and entreaties she replied in monosyllables or not at all, her mouth tensed, her eyes narrowed, her face bathed in shadows. She had put on weight; she looked fat and lumpish. For the first time, he hated her—and hated the life inside her that promised to bind the two of them perpetually in fetters of recrimination and contempt.

While she stayed in the room, he ate dinner alone at a pizzeria, then began his nocturnal wanderings. At the Trevi Fountain, he removed his jacket and stuffed it into his knapsack, for the night was a warm one. Closing his eyes and turning his back to the fountain, he tossed two coins into the basin, each bearing a wish: the first, in keeping with the tradition, for an eventual return to Rome and the second, that time might yet prove wrong his growing apprehensions about Salma's stability and about his own capacity to bear the burden of steadying her.

He did not remain long at Trevi, for the revelry there did not suit his mood. Continuing southward as far as the Piazza Venezia, he then reversed direction and started back toward his hotel.

As he turned from Via del Corso onto Via del Tritone, he stepped aside to avoid bumping into a man who stood on the corner peering at a map.

"Signore," said the man, looking up from his map. "Dove il Piazza Barberini?"

Short and paunchy, the man had a rounded face, with narrow,

glinting eyes, thick jet-black hair brushed back from his forehead and a Van Dyke beard. He wore a maroon sport jacket and tie and a gray shirt.

In the course of his travels that afternoon, David had become well acquainted with the words "destra"—right—and "sinistra"—left—but to tell the man that the piazza lay straight ahead, he could only point and say, "There. That way."

"Ah, English."

"American. I'm going toward Barberini."

"I've visited America on business," said the man as the two began to walk, side-by-side, toward the distant Fontana del Tritone. "Boston, Chicago, Washington, New York."

"I'm from Pittsburgh."

"Ah, the Steel City. I haven't been there yet. Is there much to see?"

"It hasn't been the Steel City in a long time. It's probably best known now as a center for liver transplants."

The man laughed loudly, revealing a set of nicotine-stained front teeth.

"I'll remember that. I might need a new liver some day."

"Other than that, it's not very exciting. It rains a lot. It'll be hard to go back after two weeks here. Rome is so much more…alive. I think I'll miss the piazzas most of all."

"Yes, one thing I've noticed about American cities is the lack of places where people can gather, especially at night."

His name, he added, was Hans. He had come from Zurich on business, but with the day's work completed, he wanted to relax. Someone had told him of a nice piano bar near Piazza Barberini, but ten years had passed since his last visit to Rome, and he no longer remembered where anything was.

"And you? What brings you to Rome? Business or pleasure?"

"I'm on my honeymoon."

"Well, then, congratulations. I used to be married, too, but it's something I'd rather forget. Where is the beautiful bride tonight?"

"She was …kind of tired from walking around. She felt like staying in tonight."

When they reached the piazza, David halted and pointed to his right.

"You want to go that way. My hotel is in the opposite direction, toward the Spanish Steps."

"Why don't we have a drink together?"

David hesitated. After the events of the day, he did not wish to add to his list of real and imagined offenses that of staggering in after midnight with alcohol on his breath.

"I would, but I have to get up early tomorrow. We're going on a tour of Florence."

"Your wife won't mind, will she?"

A mocking half-smile played upon Hans' lips.

"No," David snapped.

The marquee above the door read "Piano Bar The Pussy Cat." Blue light, smoke, and a smell of hairspray suffused the interior. The piano player, a slight, balding man in a black tuxedo and a ruffled white shirt, crooned, in heavily accented English, an up-tempo version of "Mack the Knife." Several young women, wearing the scantiest of outfits, sat around the piano, nursing drinks and smoking. On a sofa to the left, a large man with jowls and a bad comb-over nibbled at the ear of his much younger female companion, who looked utterly bored.

A hostess in a navy-blue blazer and a mini-dress that showed off her long legs to maximum effect led David and Hans across a parquet dance floor to a black leather divan set against the rear wall and fronted by a low, lacquered table. Hans ordered a gin and tonic; David, a beer.

"Cigarette?" asked Hans, drawing a pack from his jacket pocket.

"I don't smoke."

"Not too many people smoke in America anymore, do they? It seems to be banned in most places. What pleasures are you still permitted, aside from shooting one another and invading smaller countries? Yours is a very strange country—the strangest I've seen so far. But it's a young country yet. Maybe it will grow up one day."

"On the other hand, we fought the Nazis. We weren't their bankers."

"Touché!" replied Hans, laughing.

Now, two of the women joined them. The one who sat beside David was tall and lean, with skin as dark as Salma's, black hair cut short as a boy's, and black eyes. She wore a sky-blue tank top, white shorts that concealed very little of her thighs, and open, high-heeled pink sling-backs with matching pink polish on her fingernails and toenails. On her right arm she had a tattoo that looked like two intersecting curves of razor wire. A powerful scent, pungent yet faintly sugared, wafted in the air about her; he wondered whether Salma would smell it on him. The woman's partner, who perched herself on the sofa next to Hans, appeared older, a bit shopworn. Blonde, busty, heavier of build than the other, she wore a sequined scarlet sweater and matching mini-skirt.

They introduced themselves, respectively, as Mimi and Violetta, evoking a guffaw from Hans.

"Oh, that's good. That's what I love about you Italians. Even when you're picking my pocket, you do it with such charm. I'm Alfredo, and this is my friend Rodolfo." Turning to the befuddled David, he added, in a stage whisper, "Let's hope they don't give us consumption."

"That's not nice," said Violetta crossly, folding her arms across her chest.

"Will you buy me a drink?" asked Mimi, leaning close and placing her hand on David's left knee.

As if on cue, the hostess reappeared with four wineglasses and set them down on the table.

"Is it all right if we open bottles for the ladies?"

David nodded but began to sweat when a waiter stepped forward with an ice bucket and a massive champagne bottle wrapped in a white napkin and poured out four drinks.

Raising his glass, Hans said to the still sulking Violetta, "Cheer up, my dear, and have some champagne. Libiamo!"

Drink they all did, Mimi finishing her glass in one long gulp. Almost immediately, the hostess returned with a second bottle.

Mimi asked for a cigarette, and finding that David had none to offer, prevailed upon him to buy her a pack, plying him with a second glass of champagne.

"Your English is very good," he said. "Have you been to America?"

No, she hadn't, but she hoped to visit next year, perhaps even to live there someday. At twenty-five, she wanted to see more of the world. Like most of her unmarried friends, she still lived with her parents. That was the way things were done in Italy, but she wanted her independence—like an American. She wished she could afford her own flat. By day she drew caricatures for tourists on the Piazza Navona, chiefly to provide an outlet for her love of drawing.

"But it's not…How do you Americans say? It's not making a profit."

Some days, she added, she sold nothing at all.

"I started college as an art major," said David. "I thought I had some talent. But when I went away to school, I was in a much bigger pond, and I wasn't the big fish any more. Maybe I gave up too easily. I ended up with a degree in information science, which is a more impressive way of saying computer programming. Now I do Web design. It pays pretty well."

"Sometimes we're most profligate when we think we're being practical," said Hans. "Squandering one's youth is a grievous sin. That's why I've decided to live mine over again. But somewhere in my attic, there's a portrait that's growing old."

"Are you here on business?" Mimi asked.

"He's on his honeymoon," interjected Hans.

Mimi's eyes narrowed.

"Really? You're a bad boy. Where's your wife? Did you have a fight?"

"We've been fighting ever since we got here."

"I bet she has a bad temper. Is she Sicilian? My father is Sicilian. That's why I'm dark. But I don't have his Sicilian temper. I'm just a little pussycat. Just like the name of the bar."

Refilling their glasses a third time, she leaned close, put her head on David's shoulder, and begin to hum along as the piano player segued into "A Kiss to Build a Dream on."

Fat droplets of sweat rolled down the sides of his face.

"Why don't we dance?" she asked in a husky whisper.

Looking up, he saw Hans and Violetta on the dance floor, pressed together, barely moving. He shook his head.

"I should be going. My wife will be waiting up for me, pulling her hair out. I found out the other day that I'm going to be a father. Can you imagine me as a father?"

"You look so young."

"You ought to take it as a warning when a woman tells you she wants twelve kids. But still…I ought to be happy. I'm in Rome. I'm on my honeymoon. I'm going to be a father. If I could be happy, then she'd be happy, and she wouldn't dissociate in the Sistine Chapel. There's a memory to take home with me."

"Why don't we dance?"

"Two weeks ago we were very happy. So why not now? I'll just go back to the hotel and be happy."

"When you dance, you can forget for a while."

"I'm no good at dancing."

"It doesn't matter. Nothing matters. You're in Roma. You're far from home."

She stood up and took his hand. Draining his glass, he rose unsteadily.

As they swayed along the perimeter of the dance floor, she sang softly, her chin resting on his shoulder:

Give me what you alone can give,
A kiss to build a dream on.

Her slim and supple body, brushing against his, promised erotic delights that he had yet to encounter in his limited experience. When he kissed her, he breathed in the spicy scent of her perfume.

"Oh, you are a naughty boy," she murmured.

≈≈

In the glow of the hostess's flashlight, he saw the sum total of his folly: € 221. He poured himself another glass of champagne, which he promptly finished off in two gulps. Sweat began to seep through his shirt. "How will I explain this one when my wife sees the Visa bill?"

he said to no one in particular. He laughed mirthlessly and reached for his wallet.

"What? You're leaving so soon? We just got here!" cried Hans, settling himself upon the divan once more, this time with Violetta in his lap. "But maybe you have the right idea. If we stay here too long, we'll go bankrupt."

"We can get you a taxi," said the hostess, casting a furtive glance at Mimi. "To go back to your hotel. It's complementary."

"I can walk," said David, shaking his head. "My hotel's not far. And I need some air."

"A smart businessman never refuses something offered for free," said Hans. Turning to the hostess, he added, "Are the girls complementary, too?"

She answered with an enigmatic smile.

David raised the champagne bottle once more but finding it empty, let it drop onto the table. The bottle tottered, fell, rolled to the edge of the table and fell again, coming to rest at last on the carpet.

"Now I'll go back to my wife and be happy," he said.

Grabbing Mimi by the shoulders, he kissed her again, then rose, hitting his thigh against the edge of the table.

He stumbled out into the darkness, stepping off the curb without pausing to check the traffic. A scooter whizzed past. In the middle of the street, he stopped, immobilized by the lights of the little red sports car that bore down upon him, its engine snarling, wheels screeching, horn blaring. Arms outstretched, he closed his eyes and waited, holding his breath, each heartbeat a hammer blow. He felt a hot gust of wind; then the noise of the car's engine was behind him.

"Imbecille!" cried the driver, and the word seemed to hang in the heavy night air long after the car had vanished.

VISITATIONS

I can still read faces. That much I know. The blank countenances of my attending physicians, who flit about me, moth-like, for a few minutes each morning amid the light of the overhead fixture, hint at horrible truths withheld. I rage inwardly at the young residents, interns, and med students who gape at me as if I am a frog awaiting dissection. The beneficent smiles of the nurses who wash and change me induce both shame and gratitude, while the mournful looks I get from friends and relatives unnerve me. I feel, somehow, a sense of obligation to put my visitors at ease, though not strongly enough to attempt speech with a ventilator tube down my throat. When I see the fright in my daughter Rebecca's eyes, my own eyes grow moist. That life can be unforgiving I have known for a long time; that it would demand such a fearsome price from a ten-year-old in payment for my own carelessness and stupidity is almost too much to bear.

Of all the faces that come within my view during the course of a day, the hardest one to decipher belongs to my wife. Pale, drawn, distended, it hovers above me for what seems like hours at a time, and the dark, almond-shaped eyes in which I could once lose myself as I lay beside her in bed rain down their tears upon me. But what do those tears signify? Grief? Remorse? Sorrow? Self-pity? Rage at me? Rage at herself? All of these and more? Salma Said was her name before she took mine—in Arabic, Peaceful Happy. But for a long time, she has been neither.

"I'll always love you," she vows.

I've heard that one before. Still, I suppose that she'll remain on her best behavior for a little while at least, if the old patterns hold true. Let me catch so much as a sniffle, and she becomes a ministering angel, bearing soup, tea, Jell-O, cold capsules, aspirins, nasal sprays. Only when I get well again—well enough to wish, to hope, to desire—does the trouble begin. Aside from the fact that I can't give her any more kids, I am now her ideal husband.

Every evening after work, she brings Becky, and the child reads to me a chapter from Treasure Island—as I used to read to her. Salma's mother has come to stay, and she watches Becky when Salma returns to the hospital late at night to keep a vigil by my bedside. A doctor herself—an ob-gyn specialist—she keeps a wary eye on the doings of the nurses and doctors, sometimes questioning the latter a little too assertively for their taste, as evidenced by their occasionally snappish responses. Despite my carping, which is, after all, purely internal, I wish I could find a way to express my gratitude to her, to give and receive absolution for years of strife and strain. If only I had the use of my arms, I would embrace her.

Gratitude is precisely what my brother, who comes to see me wearing a lab coat over his suit and a stethoscope around his neck, thinks I lack.

"I don't know if you know this," he remarks with studied casualness, as he fiddles with his pager, "but your airbag didn't deploy. I made an appointment with a lawyer. I think we can make some money off this."

We? But I suppose I shouldn't judge him too harshly. He simply can't help himself. The spirit of the age has infected him.

Something I do—an inadvertent roll of the eyes, perhaps—must provide a clue to my thoughts, for suddenly he bristles.

"You know, I was the one who made sure you were brought here once you were stabilized. It's because I'm on staff here that you have a private room and the best care you can get. I went and found the lawyer. I've done a lot of things for you over the years. And you haven't always shown much appreciation."

Abruptly, he pivots and exits the room, leaving me with only the whirring ventilator for company.

Across the ceiling, the shadows and light advance and retreat. Doctors and nurses come and go. Practiced hands poke and prod, shift me about, replace catheters and waste bags, take vital signs.

By the second week—or so I estimate, though it matters little, for I exist now outside of time—Salma's demeanor has changed considerably. One evening, unaccompanied by Becky, she bursts into my room, brandishing a letter.

"Look at this!" She holds the document to my face, the paper almost touching my nose. Amid the blur of print I can distinguish only the orange letterhead that reads, "TotalCare—We've got you covered."

"This wonderful hospital that your brother got you into is not a preferred provider. TotalCare says it will only pay 50 percent!"

Salma begins to pace the floor, disappearing and reappearing with dizzying rapidity. She is a large woman, and her steps resound throughout the room. Pausing by my bedside, she plucks a single wiry hair from her scalp and flicks it away—a long-time habit of hers.

"Does your brother want to see Becky and me begging on the street? Is that what he wants? Is that what you want? Mujrim! Ibn al kalb!"

Over the years, I have developed a variety of strategies for tuning Salma out, no matter her volume. I replay in my mind a song that Becky loved as a three-year-old:

Six little ducks came out to play.
Six little ducks from far away.
But the one little duck with the feather on his back,

He led the others with a quack, quack, quack.

One thought does trouble me, though: my ability to see Becky will now hinge on Salma's moods.

Salma's emotional state has not improved at all by the following evening. She does bring Becky, but only in the capacity of a corroborating witness.

"Now your daughter is being stigmatized at school, thanks to you!"

"Mrs. Crane asked me if I wanted to go to the school counselor," says Becky, summing up her view of the matter with the induced vomiting gesture so beloved by her cohort. "I'm like, 'I'm not mental.'"

My sweet pea. Becky no longer holds adults in awe, and her spunk just might enable her to surmount the parenting of a lunatic and a vegetable. A tall, big-boned girl with honey-brown eyes, she brings home flawless report cards, stars on her junior league soccer team, and solos at Suzuki violin recitals, but those accomplishments seem to bring her little joy. For the last year or so, I have strained to recognize, in the often distant and occasionally sullen child before me, the chubby little elf-girl who used to sing "Six Little Ducks" as I carried her on my shoulders. What I would give to carry her that way one more time, big as she is now, though she would find the idea appalling. Her chief satisfactions these days derive from her displays of independence: laundering and folding her own school uniforms, preparing her own lunches, putting her room in order. She has become a premature adult.

"They want me to put her in therapy. Because her worthless father got drunk and crashed his car! Thank you soooh much. Thank you soooh soooh much."

Girded for battle, Salma glowers at me, her arms folded across her chest, her shoe tapping against the floor.

"Well? Well?"

The tapping ceases. For a moment, she appears nonplussed.

"Why do I even bother? The sad thing is nothing has changed. Talking to you was just the same before the accident. Come on, Becky.

Let's go. Now! Yellah!"

Salma stomps out of the room. The child sighs and rolls her eyes as if thinking, "Eight more years of this." Scooping up her backpack, she follows her mother out.

Ever mercurial, Salma brings a dozen roses the next night as a gesture of reconciliation. She bends over me, kisses my forehead, and strokes my hair, while Becky reads two chapters from Treasure Island. Briefly, the routine of the first week—readings from Becky, bedside vigils from Salma—resumes.

Winter must have descended, for outside the wind wails, and ice-encrusted branches tap against the windowpane. On the ceiling, the shadows drive out the light more quickly every day. My guests come attired in heavy coats, scarves, and hats.

And here in room 5806, another cold blast from TotalCare quickly ends the false spring. One evening Salma shows up alone, her parka caked with snow. In her right hand, she clutches another missive bearing that unmistakable orange letterhead.

"Your wonderful insurer says that only your first four days on the respirator were medically necessary. Mujrim!"

Salma stamps her foot, her boot heel striking sharply against the linoleum. As the snowflakes that had settled atop her hair began to melt, tiny wisps of steam curl ceiling-ward.

"You're bankrupting me with every useless breath you take. You can't even destroy yourself without destroying Becky and me. Every dream I ever had, you've killed." Without appearing to feel any pain, she uproots from her scalp and tosses away one, two, three, four, five, six strands of hair in rapid succession.

I call on the ducks again:

Down to the river they would go.
Wibble, wobble, wibble, wobble, to and fro.
But the one little duck with the feather on his back,
He led the others with a quack, quack, quack.

"I wanted a family. I wanted children all around me. I had so much love to give. I had so much life in me. You just drained it all out of me, day after day, week after week, year after year. I gave, and you took. May God forgive you. May God forgive you."

A fat lot of good His forgiveness would do me now. Maybe He should ask for mine instead. I recall the lines from King Lear:

As flies to wanton boys are we to the gods;
They kill us for their sport.

I try to recall other Shakespearean passages, snatches of movie dialogue, song lyrics, even commercial jingles. Before Salma leaves, I run through two more renditions of "Six Little Ducks." Her outbursts, I learned long ago, come and go like summer storms. The cold rage that she displays when she returns the following night, again without Becky, alarms me far more.

"I want another child," she says, her eyes dry and her mouth rigid. "I'm going to have one, whether it's by you or someone else."

Perhaps, getting drunk and flipping my car was an entirely rational thing to do, given the circumstances.

In vain I try to recall the cause of the altercation that precipitated my ill-fated flight from the house. After eleven years, neither Salma nor I require causes any more. The existence of the other suffices.

For two weeks or so—though it could as easily be one or three, as one day blurs into the next—Salma stays away, tormenting me only by proxy. The nurses now bring me my correspondence from TotalCare and my auto insurer, as well as my credit card bills, none of which interest me in the least. Imprisonment within a broken body has, paradoxically, freed me of money worries. Why fret over something that has no value anymore? The envelopes, most still sealed, a few torn open, begin to pile up on the little table beside my bed.

One day, a nurse, squirming with embarrassment, holds up for my inspection an envelope from the bank that has the lien on my car. The envelope is open, and on the outside Salma has scrawled, "This is yours! It's overdue! You pay it!!"

Or they'll repossess the wreckage?

The nurse sets the letter down on the table and leaves. Perhaps I have not become quite so indifferent to money as I had thought, for suddenly, my left shoulder begins to twitch, and then my whole arm. My entire body jerks violently. Unable to get a breath, I try to scream, but emit something closer to a quack. Then, as quickly as it came on—but for a few aftershocks—the attack subsides, and the air from the ventilator fills my lungs once more.

A few days later, I experience a less severe and less frightening attack subsequent to a visit from my brother, who had come with a bone to pick: "The lawyer said we have no case. You weren't wearing your seat belt, and your blood alcohol level was .25. That's more than twice the legal level for DWI."

When Salma next appears, she brings with her a man I do not recognize. Trim and fair-haired, he looks like a young Dan Quayle. Wearing an expression of ennui, he stands by, his cerulean eyes surveying the room, while Salma drops several more envelopes onto the growing pile on the table. She embraces and kisses the young man, then steps back, smiles, and strokes his cheek. He still looks bored.

More the dispassionate critic than the volcanic Pagliacci even when I was whole, I cannot quite summon the murderous rage that a cuckold ought to feel. Yes, you play your role to perfection, my dear, but your directing and the male lead don't measure up, and the production falls flat. You're not as good as you think. You're pushing forty, overweight, overworked, overstressed, overtired. You have varicose veins, stretch marks from carrying Becky, an appendectomy scar, debts, disappointments. You desperately want another child, because the one you have has become an adult at ten and can manage quite nicely without you. All your bedroom tricks won't keep Frat Boy around for a month. This will end badly, and you'll have to make someone pay, as you always do. Not Frat Boy, of course. His kind never suffer. That's a law of nature. That leaves Becky and me, and what can you do to me that I haven't already done to myself?

I do not have to wait long for an answer. A week or so later, Salma appears alone. She advances slowly toward the bed and bends over me, panting heavily. Her parka is soaked, and her hair matted to her scalp, but for an area above her right temple, about three-fourths of an inch in diameter, which is nearly bald and covered with dried blood. Streaks of black mascara line her cheeks. Through fixed pupils she stares at me without seeming to see me.

She's going to pull out my breathing tube.

My face begins to burn, and my heart pounds against my ribs. I close my eyes and wait, steeling myself. If now, so be it. Why cling to this life when, for all intents and purposes, I am already dead? Above the whir of the ventilator, I hear a plea in Arabic for God's help, repeated five, six, seven times. Then she falls silent. If now, so be it. But the silence howls and keens and roars as it sits like an elephant upon my chest. When I can endure no more of it, I open my eyes again—and find myself alone.

≈≈

But for the boredom and the fact that I miss Becky, I experience mainly relief at having no more outside visitors for the next few weeks—aside from my brother, who occasionally stops in for a minute or two on the way to his office in another wing of the hospital. Much of the time, I sleep. If I could read, I would feel as content as one can in such circumstances, but having only the television for diversion, I often fall to brooding, more about the past than about the future, which I can hardly bear to contemplate at all. I think sometimes of women I might have known, but for a lack of nerve, and of some I have known; of the all-consuming lust that Salma and I shared in our early days together; of trips abroad not taken and of one I did take, and the magical Irish countryside that I saw then. I remember one night in Rome, on our honeymoon, when Salma and I had quarreled and I wandered out alone, and a man who may or may not have been a tout persuaded me to accompany him to a piano bar, where a hooker coaxed me into buying her a $200 bottle of champagne. Never could I have dreamed that there would come a time when I would long for the chance to go back to that same piano bar and get snookered again.

I remember so many things: a blazing sunset over the Gulf of Mexico, viewed from a beach on the west coast of Florida; the warmth provided by a cup of coffee that I drank while sitting on a fishing boat and watching the rising sun melt away the cottony fog that spiraled skyward from the surface of the water; the games of skee ball I played as a boy at a boardwalk arcade and again with Becky many years later; the hikes through the woods, amid the splendors of the changing leaves; the nights of bar hopping with my brother, enlivened by his wickedly precise impersonations of so many of our acquaintances.

I recall, too, my displays of pettiness and spleen, for which I can now never make amends, and the acts of kindness I could have performed but chose not to; the people I let drift out of my life; my multitudinous failings as a son, older brother, friend, husband, father, the last of which gnaw at me most of all. How carelessly I have squandered the gift of thirty-seven years as a whole human being.

As if to compensate for my loss of physical sensation, my emotions have developed a hair-trigger sensitivity. The sappiest human-interest story on the six o'clock news can prompt copious tears, which I can no more control than I can my bladder or bowels.

My spirits rise a bit when I awake one morning—or, perhaps, afternoon—to find a that a smaller tracheal tube has replaced the bulky monstrosity that has been both the preserver and the bane of my existence since I have taken up residence in room 5806.

Each day now, a woman comes around to teach me to breathe again. Her nametag says, simply, "Esther Maina, Respiratory Therapist," but to me, she seems quite an exotic creature. Cheery but a bit formal in her bearing, she has a mocha complexion, with a high forehead and cheekbones that taper down to a full, luscious mouth and narrow chin. She speaks in accents that I imagine must have prevailed at Oxford during the Edwardian era.

Under her tutelage, I progress quickly, and soon I can breathe for several minutes at a time without the aid of the ventilator. I take pride in these modest accomplishments, but my favorite part of each session comes at the conclusion, when Esther sits on the edge of my bed, writing her progress notes and humming or singing snatches of arias and show tunes in a lilting soprano. Sometimes I manage to convince myself that she lingers a bit longer than is strictly necessary, but in my more lucid moments I dismiss the thought. If I am to live on, I must recognize my physical limitations and not torment myself by wishing for the impossible.

Unfortunately, Salma seems to have decided that she will not let me breathe. One afternoon, a large, rotund man strides into the room, carrying a bulging briefcase. He has thick, tawny hair, turning to white at the temples, and a walrus moustache.

"Art Kerry," says the man, extending a meaty hand. The hand hovers above me until its owner withdraws it. He smiles sheepishly, revealing two rows of yellowed teeth, with a large gap between the two front uppers. Shedding his coat, beneath which he wears a sport jacket of a color approximating that of a rotten pumpkin, he sits down beside the bed—a little closer than I would like.

I gaze at the ceiling, hoping he will leave soon. Mistakenly, I assume that my brother, having turned over enough rocks, has at last found someone—or something—willing to take on the absurd lawsuit against the manufacturer of my car. Art Kerry, though, has come on a different mission. Opening his briefcase on his lap, he removes several folders and a legal pad.

"The issue is this," he says, loosing upon me gales of hot, bitter tobacco breath. He speaks in a deep rumble, interrupted by frequent pauses for breath and occasional attacks of wheezing. "Your wife wants more kids. She argues that, as your wife, she has the rights to your sperm."

No longer do I look at the ceiling. He has my attention now.

"They have this new technique for harvesting sperm. It's called electroejaculation. They take a probe, and…Well, never mind the details. The point is that that can cause you all kinds of trouble. From what your brother told me…" Kerry rummages through one folder and then a second.

"Must have grabbed the wrong file," he says, appearing perplexed. "Oh, well. Anyway, from what I remember, your brother indicated that your marriage was pretty well on the rocks. Now, if your wife were to conceive a child this way, and then file for divorce…She could claim abandonment. Technically, you have moved out of the house. She could ask for child support. Garnish your disability pay. Well, I guess she could do that already, since you already have…You already have a kid, don't you? But if you have another…"

Two resounding coughs interrupt the disquisition. From Kerry's nostrils there issues a sound like that of a boiling teakettle.

"If you have another kid, you'll be even farther up the proverbial creek. Now, your brother wants to stop her. He sees the whole business as sort of ejaculation without representation. Heh, heh. Now, I'm going up before Judge Kallas tomorrow. I'm going to ask for a restraining order, and I think he'll give it to us. Your wife will go postal. She'll appeal. Sometime in the next three or four months, there will probably be a hearing…."

The shadows advance across two complete rows of ceiling tiles before Art Kerry completes his exposition, to which I attend raptly at first, then intermittently and, in the final stages, not at all. He outlines various strategies, hypothetical counter-moves that the other side might employ, and his possible responses. He relates tales of past triumphs, as well as a bawdy joke or two, which he punctuates with snorts, guffaws, and wheezes.

"Now, if you have any questions," he says, as he rises, "you just give me a holler. The important thing now is that you keep your spirits up. Just remember: we're gonna win this thing."

He gives me a vigorous clap on the left shoulder, then draws back, startled, as my arm shoots upward as if I were hailing a speeding cab. The arm lingers for just a second at the apex of its arc—perpendicular to my body—then falls and lies inert on the mattress once more.

Late one night, a burst of light from the overhead fixture awakens me from an uneasy sleep. But perhaps I am mistaken. Perhaps I am not awake at all, for the scene that unfolds before me has the surreal quality of a nightmare, as though Art Kerry's words, having undergone some grotesque mutation in my cerebrum, have become animate. Into the room strides Salma, carrying a specimen cup. Close behind her come two other women. One, a slightly built Indian who wears a lab coat and carries in her right hand a rather ominous-looking cylindrical appliance, I recognize as a colleague of Salma's, having met her once or twice at parties. The third woman I do not know. Short and slender, with coarse black hair, she wears a gray business suit and carries a large briefcase. Her pointed tongue, continuously darting in and out of her mouth as though to catch flies, and her olive skin with its oily sheen lend her a certain reptilian quality. Salma's lawyer?

Wordlessly, the women pounce. Salma and the reptile pull me up onto my left side, while Salma's colleague circles behind me, lifts my gown and strips away my waste bag. Salma unscrews the lid of the specimen cup, yanks out my catheter, grips my limp penis, and holds the cup beneath it.

"No!" I gasp, as the vibrations begin to radiate outward from somewhere deep within.

My body shudders violently, falls slack, shudders again, and begins to thrash wildly all about the bed. Plunging me into darkness once more, the three women slip out the door, leaving my gown bunched at my waist, my bottom exposed, my waste bag at my ankles. I feel a stabbing pain in my throat. Frantically, I try to draw in air, but something impedes the flow. The overhead light switches on again. Above, I see a blurry form in blue hospital scrubs. A pair of hands reaches for my throat. I feel another sharp pain, and then my lungs fill with air. A nurse appears with an infusion pump. I watch the needle pierce my right forearm and feel nothing. The doctor and nurse draw back, lingering at the edge of my field of vision, and then I see no more.

More than the pain in my throat, the presence of Art Kerry at my bedside when I awake the next morning or afternoon confirms that what I thought I experienced last night did in fact happen. From love—or whatever one chooses to call that state of intoxication that Salma and I shared in our first months together, when I could spend entire afternoons running my hand through her hair and kissing her eyelids, her nose, her lips, her chin, her neck, and even the tiny mole in the center of her forehead—through successive stages of ennui, regret, resentment, to violation with a cattle prod is a common enough progression in a metaphorical sense. It takes a Salma, though, to make such a metaphor a reality. One lover wants; the other withholds, whether out of spite or incapacity; and the one who wants will not be denied. When the lovers have finished disemboweling one another, the maggots come to feast on the carcasses. Enter Art Kerry.

"I was wondering if you were ever gonna come around. That was a nasty trick they pulled last night. Violating Kallas's restraining order. I'm heading right to the courthouse after this, and I'm gonna ask that your wife be held in contempt. I wouldn't want to be in her shoes the next time she has to go up before Kallas. I don't know what he'll do. Give her a stern talking-to, if nothing else."

Despite the pain in my throat, I try to speak. My words—"I want to see Becky"—come in a sepulchral whisper.

"Ah, but I did need to talk to you about one other thing. Not a very pleasant subject, I'm afraid. The retainer your brother gave me has almost run out. As long as your wife has power of attorney, he can't draw money from your account so that you can pay him back. I indicated to him that I'd be needing another retainer soon, but he's been a little…" He breaks off in mid-sentence to let loose a window-rattling cough. "He's been a little, ah, evasive."

"I want to see Becky."

"What's that?"

"Becky. My daughter. Becky"

"The heck with him, 'eh?" Kerry frowns. "Well, er, I don't want to take sides here between brothers. The sooner you can get this straightened out with him, the better off we'll all be. When you hire Art Kerry, he'll go to the wall for you. But he can't afford to work for free." He clasps my shoulder. "Now, keep the faith. We'll beat 'em yet."

≈≈

On the ceiling now, the shadows are in retreat, but my mood has remained unremittingly foul ever since the Night of the Long Probe. One day, I hear a twittering outside and see a sparrow hopping about the window ledge, and the sight fills me with bitterness. Even an insentient creature such as that one has full use of its limbs and can bask in the afternoon sun.

Almost daily, it seems, my brother brings me a new invoice from Art Kerry.

"I paid him another retainer for you, but I can't keep that up forever. The guy's a bottomless pit."

The judge fixes a date for a hearing on the motion to hold Salma in contempt, but scheduling difficulties cause a postponement. I learn that Salma has filed for divorce and custody of Becky and that the court has granted Salma's request for a hearing on child support. My brother shows me a subpoena that threatens me with "bodily attachment" should I fail to appear. Out of all the punishments that the legal system could inflict upon me, that one worries me the least.

Of Becky I hear nothing. I have one keepsake: a three-by-five-inch photograph in a cheap pine frame that stands on the table beside my bed. Taken a couple of summers ago, the picture shows Becky and Haley, my brother's daughter, a slight, sad-eyed little beauty, standing in an open field. Tanned and robust, beaming at the camera, Becky wears pink shorts and a sleeveless white blouse with pink polka dots and holds three dandelions in her left hand. Shy Haley, her gaze fixed upon the grass at her feet, presses herself against Becky's chest as though seeking shelter there. Becky happily obliges. Her right hand is draped over Haley's right shoulder, and her right cheek rests atop the younger girl's head. Will I ever see my lovely sweet pea again?

Only Esther Maina seems aware of my deepening depression. Gamely, she tries to puncture the shroud of gloom in which I have enveloped myself, accompanying her entrance each day with bows and salaams and ever more elaborate salutations: "Greetings, your lordship most high, doyen of the SCI ward, fearless tamer of the Shrew of Araby, wise and loving guardian of the beauteous Rebecca…"

At times I cannot suppress a smile. Still, I fight her, for some perverse quality always leads me to bring grief to those who show me the most kindness. My respiratory therapy proceeds in reverse, from stagnation, to regression, to active sabotage. With the air off, I simply refuse to breathe. Never once, though, do I win the test of wills with Esther Maina; never do I refrain from inhaling long enough to force her to restart my airflow. And never does she grow cross or scold me. Sometimes I want to ask her, "Why do you make the effort?"

One afternoon, following a particularly trying session, she sits at the edge of the bed writing her progress notes and humming the Barcarole from Tales of Hoffman. Wistfully and sweetly, she begins to sing, beseeching the fair Venetian night, the "night of love," to smile upon our revels:

Belle nuit, ô nuit d'amour,
Souris à nos ivresses!
Nuit plus douce que le jour,
O belle nuit d'amour!

Try as I might to concentrate my attention on counting and re-counting the ceiling tiles, I grow agitated. Tears roll down my cheeks. Those damn tears again! Why can't I control myself?

"Oh, oh, my goodness," says Esther. "I've upset you. David, I'm sorry." She places her hand upon mine, and I grope for a memory of the gentle pressure and warmth that I once would have felt.

"No," I whisper. "Please sing. Please. You have a beautiful voice. You are…" My own voice fades out, and, as she averts her eyes, I cannot tell whether she hears my last word: "beautiful."

"Oh, I…Well, O.K., If you like." She laughs nervously. "I'm not used to command performances." Still hesitant, she finally draws in a breath and begins anew:

Belle nuit, ô nuit d'amour,
Souris à nos ivresses!
Nuit plus douce que le jour,
O belle nuit d'amour!

THE PEACOCK

So pitted and cracked was the road to the Masai Mara that, at times, Peter, the driver, found smoother going in the dry grass on either side. By the third hour of the drive, backs had grown stiff, necks ached, and a coating of brown dust had settled upon the sweat-stained clothes of all the passengers in the minibus.

In the rear sat the Martins, both wearing khaki safari jackets and pants. Mrs. Martin, a slender woman of about sixty with the stooped posture and the hooded eyes of a vulture, clucked and gasped with each new jolt and kept up a steady whine in between. "This is appalling," she repeated over and over. "I've never seen such a road." Her husband, a plump, round-faced man with oversized glasses, maintained a stoical silence and a blank grin as he leaned back into his orthopedic neck pillow.

"God, I hate my fellow 'muricans," muttered Jonathan Coleman, seated by the window in the third row. Removing his glasses, he wiped the narrow rectangular lenses with a handkerchief. An unprepossessing, slightly fleshy thirty-nine-year-old, he had an ovular face, indistinct features, and near-shoulder-length blond hair that had begun to retreat up his scalp. "I come all the way to the other side of the world to get away from them, and here they are."

Anneke, his companion, did not acknowledge him. Delighted to have found a compatriot on the bus, a large, loud, vulgar fellow named Everhart, she had been conversing animatedly with him in Dutch since the beginning of the drive. Recently, she had become a bit too welcoming of other men for Jonathan's liking, and he feared that she might be tiring of him. He could not help but notice that the Dutchman's gaze often strayed toward her breasts, lightly concealed by a flimsy turquoise tank top that clung to her sweat-moistened skin. Within the last couple of hours, Jonathan had concluded that he did not at all care for the throaty, harsh sound of Dutch.

He had met Anneke upon the Spanish Steps in Rome one sunny afternoon, while on the last leg of a European journey that had seen him meander through the U.K., Portugal, Spain, France, and Italy. She had settled herself on the one of the steps to compose a text message on her cell phone. Beside her lay a massive backpack covered with a collection of flag decals that encompassed most of the European Union. He had very nearly tripped over that backpack—a most fortuitous near-accident, for it evoked repeated apologies from her and gave him a pretext to strike up a conversation.

A five-foot-two-inch sprite, several weeks shy of her twentieth birthday, she had full, pink lips, a gently curved chin, and eyes as blue as the Mediterranean. Her left eyebrow had a slight arch to it, which gave her a perpetual air of mischief. Her hair, curly and wheat-brown, fell below her shoulders, the bangs spun into symmetrical pairs of dreadlocks, around which she had wound green ribbons.

In his hotel room the morning after their encounter on the Spanish Steps, as they lay entwined on the narrow bed, swathed in the pinkish-gray light of dawn, Anneke said to him, "You can go all night like a lumberjack, ja?" What a splendid gift she had seemed to him then, the culmination of a summer of well-deserved idleness after so many seasons of striving and a year-and-a-half of celibacy. Because of her, he did not conclude his travels in Italy, as he had intended, for she yearned to see other continents, and he did not want his idyll to end. They set off eastward. To her collection of flag decals, she added those of Turkey, Jordan, Egypt, and Kenya. His credit card debt rose to new and alarming heights.

Once more, the driver of the minibus in which they were now traveling veered off the road, this time to avoid a road crew that consisted of four young men listlessly filling in potholes with sand.

"That will last until the next rain," chortled the big Dutchman.

Stupid, condescending, racist bastard, thought Jonathan.

"You see how it is with our road tax," said Peter, a squat, very dark man of about forty, as he steered the minibus back onto the road. "The money goes into the pockets of the big men, and we get sand for our roads." As if on cue, the minibus hit a bone-jarring pothole.

When, at last, Peter brought the bus to a stop before the entrance gate of the Masai Mara, a crowd of Masai women closed in, bearing wood carvings, beads, necklaces, and bracelets. Tall and gaunt, wrapped in frayed, dusty red blankets, they had shaven heads, lined, weathered faces, slender necks wrapped in beads, and dangling earlobes with vast holes in them.

"This is an example of what I was telling you about the other night," said Jonathan.

Anneke gave him a puzzled look.

"Here you have a proud people reduced to selling trinkets to Western tourists. This is the 'passport to development' we've given them."

Genuinely indignant, he could not help thinking nevertheless of how he might put that indignation to use. The editors of the prestigious Journal of Transcultural and Transgender Studies and the committee that had finally awarded him tenure, redeeming his six years of struggle, had both been most impressed by his article "Cultural Imperialism and Post-Colonial Tourism: Hegemonies, Spatialities, Geohistories, and Disembeddings." Now he had visions of expanding that piece into a book, one which might well include a chapter on these abject Masai women.

Those visions quickly evaporated as the aggressive peddlers thrust their wares at him through the windows of the minibus. The oldest of the lot, a toothless, wizened woman with concave cheeks and stringy limbs, dropped into his lap a carving of a fierce-looking Masai warrior poised to throw a spear. "Five hundred," she croaked.

Everhart slammed his own window shut in the face of another of the peddlers. In the rear of the bus, Mrs. Martin rasped, "No, Arnie. You tell her we don't want it." But Jonathan, beset by post-colonial guilt, reached for his wallet and drew out a thousand-shilling note. Slack-jawed, he watched the Masai woman walk off with his money.

Everhart let loose a window-rattling laugh. "You got taken to deh cleaner's!" he cried.

Gently, Anneke stroked the back of Jonathan's head. "I sink my little Johnny is too soft," she cooed. "He has to be tougher."

His body stiffened, and he withdrew from her touch. The minibus began to move again, slowly making its way over a bumpy dirt road. Silent, jaw clenched, he gazed out at the arid landscape. Suddenly, he hurled the unwanted carving out the window.

"Dere goes a thousand shillings," needled Everhart.

The "tent" that Jonathan and Anneke shared at the Zebra Lodge did not resemble any he had ever seen. It did have a canvas and mesh exterior on three sides but also a queen-sized bed; two end tables with battery-powered table lamps; a bathroom in the rear that included a shower; and even a little concrete patio, complete with two chairs, where one could lounge in the shade provided by the overhang of the shingle roof.

The tent had one major drawback: its proximity to those of the other guests. Jonathan could hear the Dutchman singing in the shower, delivering a resounding but badly off-key rendition of the Rolling Stones' "Start Me Up." From the opposite direction came the sounds of a one-sided quarrel.

"Arnie, why didn't you get a receipt from the driver when he collected the money from us at the gate?"

"He didn't give anybody a receipt."

"Of course not. He probably collected twice what he needed and pocketed the difference. As soon as he said we had to pay cash to get in, I knew he was up to something."

Hot, dusty, weary, and beset by a vicious headache, Jonathan lay down on the bed and closed his eyes. Even if he could have shut out the discordant human noises on either side, he could not do the same with the eardrum-shattering screech of the peacock that circled among the tents in pursuit of an ever elusive peahen. With each cry from the bird, he felt a fresh stab of pain above his right eyebrow.

Anneke, shedding her clothes, lay down beside him, undid his belt, opened his jeans, and slid her hand inside.

Aroused, he nonetheless said, doubtfully, "Everyone will hear us." Of late, he had become a hesitant lover. Though he had always been capable enough, going all night like a lumberjack had never been the norm for Jonathan, and that first night in Rome had proved impossible to duplicate. The harder he had tried, the more erratic his performance had become and the more his confidence had waned.

"Who cares what day sink? We'll never see dem again. Don't be so bourgeois, Jonathan."

For Jonathan, perhaps no other insult could have cut so deeply. Wriggling free of his jeans, he pulled Anneke on top of him. But the Dutchman's unmusical baritone, the peacock's cries, and Mrs. Martin's wails nearly spoiled the moment. The bird emitted yet another shriek, and Jonathan's aggrieved neighbor lamented, almost as loudly, "Will we have to listen to that thing all day and all night?" Jonathan began to wilt, and only some frenzied stroking and extraordinary contortions by Anneke saved the day.

≈≈

Later in the afternoon, the group boarded the minibus again, this time for a game drive. Much to his chagrin, Jonathan realized he had come poorly equipped. His compact Minolta, barely adequate to take in the monuments of Rome, could hardly do justice to the Serengeti Plain. By contrast, Mrs. Martin's camera had a massive 400 mm zoom lens, and her husband and Everhart both carried camcorders.

The minibus bounced along over a stark landscape of high, tawny grasses and widely spaced thorn trees. A smell of manure and, here and there, of rotting animal flesh, hung in the air. Zebras grazed, elephant herds lumbered about, and giraffes munched on spiny leaves. Vultures perched ominously atop the trees. A pack of the scavengers, accompanied by a hideous marabou stork, tore with their beaks at an antelope carcass until chased off by a couple of spotted hyenas—depraved-looking beasts with arched backs and fur that seemed to stand on end. Thousands upon thousands of wildebeest ran hither and thither, bouncing as they went as if they had springs beneath their front hooves. A large male baboon approached the minibus from the side and turned his red rump to the passengers, evoking a guffaw from Everhart. And the King of Beasts simply slept, much to the dismay of Mrs. Martin, who seemed to think that her park entrance fee entitled her to see a lioness on the hunt. Still, everywhere that one of those regal creatures lay, minibuses and Range Rovers gathered around it, the vehicles battling one another for position. Passengers poked cameras out the windows and popped up through apertures in the roofs. As if to show its disdain for its two-legged subjects, a very large, grizzled lion with a white chin and a wild, dark mane suddenly emerged from the grass and lay down right across the dirt road, directly in front of the minibus.

From the back, there came a lamentation: "Arnie, how could you have missed him? He was right there. Now he's just laying down again."

Everhart rushed to the front of the minibus to film the lion through the windshield. Standing in the aisle, Jonathan adjusted and readjusted his retractable zoom lens until Anneke, crying, "Jonathan, you're too slow," grabbed the camera out of his hands. She stood up on her seat, her upper half disappearing through the open roof hatch. Snapping several pictures of the lion, she then executed an abrupt about-face to photograph a female elephant wandering the plain with its calf. Everhart, on the way back to his seat, froze in the aisle in mid-stride, staring ravenously at Anneke's buttocks, crescents of which were visible where her scanty white shorts ended.

Jonathan, who had also observed well the creep of those shorts and noted Everhart's reaction, silently sulked through dinner that evening, while Anneke and her countryman resumed their conversation in Dutch. Afterwards, in the tent, rebuffing all her attempts at conversation, he sat up in the bed reading a book he had purchased in the Nairobi airport. It was a memoir, or purported memoir, by an English anthropologist who had set out to do fieldwork among the Masai but, attracted by the apparent freedom offered by a nomadic life lived in harmony with the rhythms of the seasons, had stayed on in the village and become the fourth wife of one of the tribesmen. The freedom had proved chimerical, but the loss of status and the daily drudgery all too real. The narrative traced the woman's gradual disillusionment, which culminated in her flight from the village. Though she had entered willingly into a polygamous marriage, she now viewed the custom—and others practiced by the Masai, such as female circumcision—with contempt. Her superior tone irritated Jonathan.

"The usual Eurocentric crap," he said, tossing the book aside. "The usual incomprehension of the Other. The usual condescension and ill will. The usual sensationalism. It's about what you'd expect to find in an airport bookshop."

Anneke, absorbed in a video game that she was playing on her cell phone, did not answer.

Though earlier he had snubbed her, he thought it somehow unjust that she should respond in kind, especially now, when he wanted an audience for his deconstruction of the Englishwoman's book. At times, he found her lack of interest in ideas—his ideas in particular—maddening.

"Everhart certainly seemed to like your shorts," he added petulantly.

She looked up in surprise. "My shorts? What are you talking about?"

"They don't leave much to the imagination."

"I've worn dem many times. You never minded before." Laughing, she threw her arms around his shoulders. "I sink my poor Johnny is jealous. Don't be jealous, Johnny."

He pulled away from her. "The word is think, not sink. Sinking is what a ship does. And please don't call me Johnny. I've never liked that name. And I'm certainly not jealous of that half-wit Everhart."

Far from being put off by his display of temper, she leaned close and began to fondle him. "I don't want my Johnny to be angry," she murmured. "I want him to be happy."

Indeed, his anger melted away at once. Unfortunately, his potency, already put to the test earlier in the day, proved almost as ephemeral. Half-erect and barely inside her, he came with a sorry little twitch.

Afterwards, having dragged the blankets to her side of the bed and cocooned herself inside them, she quickly fell asleep. For a long time, he lay on his back, gazing absently at the roof of the tent and listening to the cackling of the hyenas and the desolate cries of an owl: two long hoots followed by four short ones, the pattern repeated endlessly. Why, he wondered, at just thirty-nine and paired with a woman more beautiful and more sexually voracious than any he had ever known, could he manage only so feeble a performance? Had his virility had somehow seeped away during the parched year-and-a-half that had preceded Anneke? The gods are cruel, he thought.

In the middle of the night he awoke, shivering. The owl was still hooting. Jonathan rose and groped vainly in his valise for a sweatshirt. Still shivering, he returned to the bed and lay down on his stomach, covering his head with his pillow.

≈≈

In the morning, Anneke donned another microscopic pair of shorts, along with a purple tube top.

"You can't visit the Masai village dressed like that," Jonathan cried in alarm. "They're a traditional people. You're their guest. You can't go barging into their home and impose your mores on them."

"Oh, shut up, Jonathan," she replied in a contemptuous tone that he had not heard from her before.

At breakfast, she again lavished her attention upon Everhart. When she began to massage the Dutchman's neck and shoulders, Jonathan rose and left the table.

He boarded the minibus before any of the other guests.

"Where's your lady friend this morning?" asked Peter, yawning and stretching in the driver's seat.

"She's coming."

"She's a handful, eh?"

Jonathan did not answer.

The Masai settlement, just a few miles beyond the gates of the game park, lay on a flat, dusty, windblown patch of dry grass and sandy soil. The village consisted of no more than a dozen low but broad huts arrayed in a circle.

A hundred yards or so outside the village, the visitors disembarked from the minibus. As they approached the huts, a ram's horn sounded a single harsh note. Suddenly, Jonathan and the others found themselves surrounded by a band of chanting, leaping Masai, young men in their late teens or early twenties. Tall, lithe, dark-skinned, with the same slack, dilated earlobes as those of the women peddlers who had ambushed the minibus the day before, the young Masai wore red blankets, some plain and some tartan-like, and brandished wooden staffs.

Closing in a tight circle around their guests, the Masai herded them into the village. Despite Jonathan's apprehensions, the men paid no notice to Anneke's attire. Nor did his own Che Guevara t-shirt arouse their curiosity. Rather, they gazed in wonder at the outsized tattoo of the World Trade Center towers emblazoned across Everhart's upper right arm. Several hesitantly touched the image, as if, not quite trusting their eyes, they required confirmation by other means that it was indeed real. The Dutchman explained that he had acquired the tattoo as a gesture of solidarity during a visit to his favorite city in the world in late 2001. A gruesome thing, thought Jonathan. Nowhere in his summer travels had he encountered so thoroughgoing an American as this Dutchman.

Droning ceremonial songs that all sounded identical, the young warriors performed several dances. One of the men grabbed Arnie Martin by the wrist and, from a standing start, bounded two feet into the air, a feat he repeated several times. Arnie, wearing a bemused grin, gamely tried to match him. "Go, Arnie, go!" shouted the delighted Mrs. Martin, snapping picture after picture, but her husband never rose more than a couple of inches off the ground.

Meanwhile, another of the Masai had chosen Jonathan as his partner. Jonathan tried to beg off.

"Go ahead, Johnny," Anneke urged. "Don't be so stuck in the mud."

"The expression is, 'Don't be a stick in the mud.'"

She looked at him crossly, and for the first time, he considered the possibility that correcting her English diction, especially in public, might have an effect other than the desired one of enlightening her.

As a gesture of atonement, he yielded to the Masai's entreaties. He made little effort, however, to conceal his disdain for the whole sorry spectacle. The three half-hearted jumps he attempted barely matched Arnie's in height.

Meanwhile, Arnie, panting and sweaty but still giving his all, landed awkwardly at the end of his best jump and stumbled, his glasses falling to the ground. Only the swift reaction of his Masai partner, who yanked Arnie's arm to draw him close and then caught him in a bear hug, prevented Mrs. Martin's luckless husband from plunging headlong into the dust. Wisely, the Masai decided to terminate the audience participation phase of the entertainment.

A Masai named Kamite, shorter and slighter of build than most of his mates and with better command of English, led the guests through a narrow doorway into one of the huts. Dark inside, the hut smelled of burnt wood. In the center lay a pile of ashes—the remnants of an extinguished fire. Soot covered the hut's walls and the wooden posts that supported them. On either side of the hearth lay a sleeping area—one for the mothers and children, the other for the father—with beds made of dry grass or straw covered with animal skins. The women of the village built the huts, Kamite explained, out of the materials they had at hand: cow dung and urine, twigs, and dried grasses.

"Where are deh women?" asked Anneke.

"The women?" The question appeared to take Kamite by surprise. "They're probably busy in the huts or out gathering water." Then, with an awkward little laugh, he added, "They're very shy. They don't like to show themselves to strangers."

Anneke eyed him skeptically. "Maybe it's not so good to be a Masai woman, ja?" she replied, causing Jonathan, his feminist sympathies notwithstanding, to squirm.

When Kamite had finished his talk, he led the guests back outside. Aided by one of his comrades, he set out to demonstrate the Masai way of starting a fire. On the ground, he lay a knife and a handful of straw. His confederate handed him a narrow stick, which Kamite held perpendicularly to the knife, one end resting on the blade. He rubbed his hands together, causing the stick to rotate and to scrape against the blade more and more rapidly. A single spark shot up from the blade. Another quickly followed, and then there came a burst of them. The straw ignited.

True to form, Everhart posed a quintessentially American question: "Why don't you just use a match?"

Kamite, who must have heard the query countless times before, had a ready answer, albeit one that elicited a groan from Jonathan: "People who live in grass houses shouldn't throw matches."

Next, he and his partner led the guests across the field to another hut, in front of which sat a long table laden with blankets, beads, bracelets, sandals, and carvings. There were spears that one could disassemble into three pieces and undersized leather shields. The spears might fly apart in battle or on a hunt, and the shields would offer little protection, but both would fit snugly inside a suitcase.

Jonathan absently picked up a club from the table. Its wood surface adorned by neither varnish nor stain, the club nonetheless felt surprisingly smooth. It had a handle of roughly two feet in length, narrow at the bottom, wider and heavier toward the top, with lines and pyramidal shapes carved into the upper portion. The head of the club—blunt, bulbous, and menacing— was angled at about forty-five degrees to the handle.

"It's an orinka," said Kamite. "You use it to keep the leopard away from your cattle." Taking the club from Jonathan's hands, he pantomimed a sidearm throwing motion. "You throw it at him. You break his ribs. Then you finish him off with your spear." He handed the weapon back to Jonathan. "Two thousand shillings."

Jonathan frowned. "Well, I haven't run into too many leopards in downtown Madison."

Nevertheless, the club did have a certain appeal, a solidity and an authenticity that the spears and shields lacked. When Kamite dropped the price to 1,500, Jonathan was ready to yield. Before he and Kamite could complete the transaction, though, Everhart intruded. "Fifteen hundred shillings for dat? You don't know how to negotiate, man. A hundred fifty is too much."

While Kamite and Everhart amused themselves and Anneke by haggling over the orinka, the would-be purchaser stood by, silently fuming. Eventually, the Dutchman and the Masai settled at 300 shillings.

"I just saved you 1,200 shillings," crowed Everhart, as Kamite handed Jonathan the orinka.

Far from feeling any gratitude, Jonathan had to fight off a powerful urge to brain the Dutchman with the club.

≈≈

Though the humiliation was still all too fresh in his mind, Jonathan resolved not speak of Everhart when he and Anneke returned to their tent after lunch. He expounded instead on hegemonies, spatialities, geohistories, and disembeddings, and how degrading those young Masai warriors must find having to earn their livelihoods by putting on shows for tourists.

As he talked, Anneke wrapped him in the red and blue checked blanket that she had purchased in the village, handed him his club, thrust her tongue in his ear, and whispered, "I've never fucked a Masai before."

But the peacock was shrieking, the Dutchman snoring thunderously, and Mrs. Martin wailing, "How could you forget your Hytrin? No wonder you can't go." By the time he got his clothes off, Jonathan had gone limp, and this time all Anneke's exertions proved futile.

"Poor Jonathan," she murmured. "Poor, poor Jonathan. And poor Anneke. When I go home, I'll have to find a randy Dutchman."

In another moment, she had fallen asleep. Rising to gather his clothes, he stood over her for a moment. The equatorial sun had browned her skin, now glossy with perspiration, and lightened her hair. She lay sprawled across the bed in loose-limbed abandon, a vision now reserved for him alone but soon to be granted to Everhart or some other randy Dutchman. She was a sumptuous banquet set out before a man who had lost his sense of taste.

As he reached for his t-shirt at the foot of the bed, Jonathan nearly tripped over the orinka. Cursing his now-unwanted souvenir, he dealt it a violent kick with the side of his foot. The orinka went skittering across the floor with such velocity that it barely slowed as it punched its way through the narrow space beneath the front flap of the tent. Wincing from the pain in the joint beneath his big toe, Jonathan heard the club whack against something—a chair leg or a post—on the patio.

Now seated in one of the patio chairs, the orinka by his feet, he watched the peacock woo the peahen. The male was a magnificent creature, with a long sapphire neck and eye-like dots of the same hue ornamenting its emerald tail feathers. The female was a nondescript brown. The peacock, tail feathers spread wide and rustling, slowly advanced upon his quarry. Nonchalantly, the peahen poked in the grass with her beak. The peacock moved still closer. His fan, towering menacingly over the female, vibrated with ever greater speed, thrashing the air around it, the sound like that of an outboard motor. Turning her back to him, the peahen walked away. For a moment, the peacock stood still, his fan contracting. Then, as he began to follow her, the motor revved up again.

Half an hour later, with the peahen still paying him no mind, he skulked away in defeat.

Picking up the orinka, Jonathan slapped the head against his palm several times. He drew back his arm and, just as Kamite had shown him, flung the club—aiming it directly at the peahen. The orinka grazed her head crest as it flew past, striking the ground several feet beyond and bouncing end over end in the grass. The bird glowered at Jonathan and then waddled off toward the Dutchman's tent.

THE RUINED HOUSE

The Volvo had seen better days. Its front grille had fallen off, and where the right headlight once had shone, only a black hole remained. The hood and the roof looked as though someone had turned a sandblaster on them; in some places, the white paint had peeled away down to the metal. Even routine stops caused the brakes to screech, and the exhaust pipe spewed out billows of blue-tinged smoke. When Njeri Mwalimu tried to crank open the rear window on the driver's side, the handle popped off in her hand. The car, a late-1970s model, had once belonged to her father. Mwangi, her younger brother, had not kept it purely out of sentiment.

"I'd like to get a newer car," said the plump, moon-faced Mwangi, stretching his a's and flattening his r's, his East African lilt having remained intact through his undergraduate years in America. "But with the roads in Nairobi as they are…"

His brother completed the sentence for him: "Even a brand-new car would look like this one after six months."

Slouched across the front passenger's seat to Mwangi's left, Thomas, the eldest of the three, did not much resemble either of his siblings. Tall and slender, he had a lighter, mocha-colored complexion, concave cheeks, and lazy, hooded eyes. Next to Mwangi, who wore beige chinos and a white polo shirt, Thomas looked a bit shabby in jeans and a tattered t-shirt with a map of the London underground on the front. Yet Thomas was the one with the perfect BBC diction, his consonants gem hard and clear. "A decent car will also make you a target for carjackers. I never even bother to wash mine anymore. Not that it would stay clean, if I did."

"Things are this way because you allow them to be," said Njeri, sounding thoroughly American in her exasperation. "Nairobi used to be the jewel of East Africa."

The three had barely begun their journey, but the heat, the exhaust fumes, the constant jostling, and the jarring two-note horns and booming stereos of the passenger vans that careened through the traffic, often with riders perched precariously on the running boards, had already begun to take their toll on her. So, too, had the view from her window—of rooftops peeking over walls topped with razor wire and broken glass; of plywood and tarpaulin curbside stalls stocked with CDs, luggage, mangoes, whole chickens, goats, and roasted meats; of rutted streets lined with piles of rubbish and clogged with pedestrians who had nowhere else to walk. A coating of soot and dust clung to her white sleeveless pullover and beige skirt.

"What you remember is the pre-capital flight Nairobi," said Thomas.

"We can thank Mr. Daniel arap Moi for all this," said Mwangi, blasting his horn at three women who had stopped to converse in the middle of the street. "He's finally gone, thank God, but things don't change overnight."

"He's gone from the Statehouse," added Thomas, cackling, "but his spirit remains in all of us. 'L' État c'est Moi.' Did you know that when he was still in office, there were stolen cars being driven onto the Statehouse grounds? If he could have, he would have moved Mt.

Kenya to the Swiss Alps."

"When she dropped me off at Dulles," said Njeri, shaking her head, "Catherine Wanjohi told me, 'Nairobi will break your heart.' But I had no idea." She sighed dejectedly. "Still, I hate the thought of leaving."

Her holiday was nearing its end. Save for brief excursions to the coast and the Masai Mara, she had had a month full of reunions—a month spent with aunts, uncles, and cousins, some of whom she had not seen in more than twenty years, and with nieces and nephews of whose existence she had not known. They had welcomed her home with kisses and embraces; with feasts of goat ribs, mutton curries, and lentil stews; and with gifts of dresses and jewelry. Her time in America had not changed Njeri a bit, everyone insisted, pretending not to notice that she had grown stout or to remember that when she had last visited, eleven years before, with her new American husband in tow, she had come not as Njeri Kariuki but as Mrs. Christine Clarke, using her Christian name and his surname.

On occasion, when the conversation touched on those not present, the family gatherings had grown a bit melancholy. Mummy and Daddy were gone, buried on the grounds of their sprawling country house in Muranga. Njeri had not returned home for their funerals, for the first had followed her own miscarriage by a mere two weeks, and the second had come later the same year. She had yet to see the graves, and only today had she run out of reasons to delay the trip to Muranga. Uncle Maina and Auntie Margaret had also passed away. Cousin Muthoni had died in a car crash in Langata. John Ndereba, a childhood friend, had succumbed to AIDS. The once jovial Uncle Wahome, who had suffered a stroke, did not recognize Njeri when she came to visit.

≈≈

North of Nairobi, the road smoothed out, the traffic thinned, and walls no longer hid the lush greenery from view. In Thika, Njeri and her brothers stopped at a hotel renowned for its outdoor buffet and for the two waterfalls that flanked the grounds.

A maitre d' in a white jacket and bow tie led the three of them out onto a spacious lawn adorned with poinsettias, azaleas, orange-blossomed flame trees, and neon-purple bougainvillea. A peacock with a magnificent fan of jade and sapphire strutted about among the tables. Bright yellow umbrellas, emblazoned with the Tusker beer elephant head logo, shielded the diners from the fierce equatorial sun. The occasional breeze carried the enticing scent of barbecued meats.

For the guests' entertainment, the hotel had supplied a folksinger/guitarist, whose all-too-predictable verbal miscues revealed him to be one of Njeri's tribe, but not the sort with whom a Nairobi Kikuyu would want to acknowledge kinship:

Rike a mbridge over troubled wa-tah,
I will ray me down...

Thomas roared with laughter. "Now, where else but in Kikuyuland could you hear singing like that? How it makes me yearn for the old hut."

Njeri tossed a bread crust onto the lawn and watched with amusement as the peacock's hunger overcame his feigned indifference.

"The last time we were all here together," she said, "I think Mwangi was still in primary school."

Even after a month back in Kenya, she still marveled at the fact that the one-time cherub with the dimpled thighs, whose fat little toes she had loved to pull while reciting "This Little Piggy Went to Market," now had two girls of his own. She regretted that the exigencies of the academic calendar had kept her from flying back to Nairobi for his wedding and that such communication as the two of them had had in recent years had chiefly consisted of laconic e-mails from Mwangi with family pictures attached.

"It must have been the late seventies," said Thomas, absently, pouring himself his fourth Tusker. "That was back when it was still possible to live in Kenya."

Mwangi, sufficiently provoked to set aside the rib on which he had been gnawing so avidly, replied, "It is still possible to live in Kenya, even with all the hardships. Once you get outside Nairobi, it's still the most beautiful country on earth. And people here still make time for one another. In America, I rented the same flat for four years and never even saw my neighbor. Who wants to live that way?"

"People are kinder here in Kenya," added Njeri, with a touch of wistfulness, as she threw the peacock another crust.

She had lived in America for half her life, become a citizen, taken advantage of the many possibilities offered by that dazzling and sometimes infuriating land—had done everything but call it her home. Njeri Kariuki had become Christine Clarke, and then metamorphosed again into Njeri Mwalimu, taking the Kiswahili word for teacher as her new surname. She had attained a tenured faculty position at Georgetown; won the acclaim of her colleagues with a massive tome entitled The Female Moran: Feminism(s) and the (Re)Shaping of Female Identity in the African Diaspora; and surrounded herself with throngs of adoring young female acolytes, one of whom she had allowed to seduce her. Banishing the conservative outfits that she had once preferred to the farthest reaches of her closet, she had donned billowing head scarves and patterned dresses of canary yellow, emerald green, and violet.

In America, though, love, in the person of the philandering Jerome Clarke, had failed her, and her womb had brought forth only death. Then, after more than three years of grief, divorce litigation, and celibacy, she had admitted the foul-mouthed sophomore LaKeisha Hawkins to her bed. For Njeri Kariuki, such an encounter would have been inconceivable; even for Njeri Mwalimu, it proved barely endurable. All throughout, she had endeavored to keep herself and her lover safely hidden beneath the comforter, though from whose eyes she could not have said. Later, LaKeisha, a C+ student, had extorted an A with threats of exposure. There were more tears, therapy, medications, and, when the school year mercifully came to an end, a ticket for the first available flight that would bear Njeri back to that benighted land she had departed so long ago. She had left the colorful new dresses and scarves back in Washington, and when her relatives here called her Njeri Kariuki, she had not bothered to correct them.

"I would still be in London," said Thomas, "if Nyambura had not had her breakdown. But one marries for better or for worse. Or so

I thought at the time. It never occurred to me then to ask myself, 'Which is worth more, a degree from the London School of Economics or a dysfunctional wife?'"

Ahr-most heaven, West Vah-ginia,
Mbru Ridge Mountain, Shenandoah Live-ah…

"I was too civilized. Instead of giving up my studies to bring the poor, fragile little thing back home, I should have exercised the prerogatives of a Kikuyu man and taken a second wife to look after Nyambura."

"I would come back here in a heartbeat, if the chance came along," said Njeri, the discomfort of the ride out from Nairobi seemingly forgotten amid these enchanting surroundings.

"You would make a lot of people very happy if you did," said Mwangi. "Everyone misses you so much."

She smiled but did not meet his gaze, keeping her eyes on the peacock instead.

"It's one thing to come back here on holiday," said Thomas. "It's quite another to have to live here. What would you do here? Your mind would decay. You would grow bored with game drives. You would miss the galleries, the museums, the bookstores, the conversation, to say nothing of reliable water and electricity and the rule of law. You can't get anything done here without bribing someone."

Raindrops keep farring on my head…

"They've sacked a lot of the corrupt judges," countered Mwangi.

"How daft can you be, man? Where in Kenya will the government find honest judges to replace them?" Draining his glass, Thomas set it down on the table with a loud thwack. "This place is hopeless. We need to be re-colonized!"

"Are you mad?" cried Njeri, glowering at him across the table. "How could you say such a thing? There were people in our family who fought for our independence. Uncle Maina was a Mau Mau."

"And what exactly did the Mau Mau accomplish besides butchering a handful of British civilians and a couple of thousand Kikuyus? Somewhere in the course of acquiring all those academic credentials of yours, you should have learned how to distinguish between myth and fact."

A waiter wearing a crimson blazer approached with the bill.

"Another Tusker!" cried Thomas, a bit too loudly, holding his empty bottle aloft. "I'm not nearly drunk enough."

The waiter glanced at Mwangi, who shrugged and looked away.

≈≈

The Volvo sped north, into the heart of Kikuyu country. Njeri exulted as the rich, undulant landscape that she remembered so well spread itself before her once again. Sisal plants that had taken root in the red soil by the roadside stretched out their broad, flat leaves to catch the sun. To the right, at the bottom of a gentle declivity, lay vast fields of maize, and every now and then, Njeri could discern the outlines of a human form hunched over amid the stalks. To her left, she saw banana orchards.

The traffic on the periphery rivaled that on the road in volume if not in speed. Bent beneath the bundles of firewood strapped to their backs, women in brightly colored kerchiefs and dresses—figures who had stepped out of a painting by Jean François Millet and into a modern world where power lines loomed overhead—trudged ever onward. Men perched precariously upon bicycles piled high with boxes and bales of hay. A bulging parcel tied in a plastic supermarket bag balanced easily atop a young woman's head as she walked along the shoulder. A donkey cart inched its way along some ten paces behind the young woman, its driver sporting a New York Yankees' cap. A girl of no more than ten struggled mightily with her outsized load, fastened to her back by leather straps around her midriff and her forehead.

"I finally got around to reading that book of yours," said Thomas. "What was it called again? The Female Oxymoron? A tad tendentious, don't you think?"

She wondered what had ever possessed her to send him a copy.

When she had mailed him drafts of some of the early chapters, he had offered little help and much derision.

Mwangi switched on the radio. An American pop diva was singing a dirge for her failed romance.

Thomas began to shout over the music: "And when did you start calling yourself Njeri Mwalimu? What kind of name is that? You could scour this godforsaken continent from Cairo to Cape Town and never encounter such a name. And what's with that picture on the jacket? You're dressed like a Nigerian, for God's sake."

Mwangi turned the volume higher.

"At one time," she replied acidly, "your opinion would have mattered to me. You've never been an easy person to get on with, but you used to be someone I could respect."

"'I yam what I yam, and that's all that I yam,' said Popeye the Sailor Man."

"You are what you've chosen to be."

"And you've chosen to take on the ways of your adopted land and become a sanctimonious old cow."

She did not reply, and Thomas soon began to snore.

"He gets nasty when he drinks," said Mwangi, switching the radio off again. "And he drinks a lot these days."

They passed through the town of Muranga, with its dirt sidewalks and ramshackle wooden buildings fronted by hand-painted signs. But for the addition of a mosque, the town had not changed noticeably; its air of impermanence had endured. When staying at the house, Njeri and her family had rarely ventured into Muranga proper.

North of town, Mwangi left the highway and then made two quick turns, the second of which led him onto a stone-studded dirt road. They did not have far to go now. Njeri felt her stomach tighten.

"I should warn you," said Mwangi. "The house is not the way you remember it. There have been several break-ins. We had to remove everything that was left."

Cautiously, he guided the Volvo over dips and swells, swerving between the middle of the road and the shoulder, raising clouds of red dust. He and Njeri both grimaced when they heard the muffler scrape the ground. Thomas never stirred.

A high stone wall, overgrown with creepers, rose up on the left. Mwangi steered the car to the left, halting in front of a black iron gate. The gate hung open, but behind it, the way was blocked by a formidable log, suspended between the low-hanging branches of two red hot poker trees proudly showing off their incandescent blossoms. Mwangi tapped twice on the horn, waited for a full minute, and then sounded a sustained blast.

"Bloody useless caretaker," he muttered, switching off the ignition. "I should have given him the sack long ago."

He stepped out of the car and approached the red hot poker to his left. Grasping the log at one end, Mwangi tried to wrestle it free of the branches that held it up. There was a loud cracking noise as the thickest of those branches gave way and then a succession of snaps as the weaker ones followed. Mwangi jumped backwards as the end of the log on which he had been tugging just seconds before crashed to the ground, narrowly missing his feet.

"Are you all right?" cried Njeri, jumping out of the Volvo.

"I'm fine. Stay back!"

"Should I wake Thomas?"

"I don't see how that would help matters."

The log now stood at a forty-five-degree angle, with one end on the ground and the other still caught in the tree to the right of the driveway. Circling behind the two red hot pokers, Mwangi pushed against the still-suspended portion of the log with his shoulder. As the other end fell from the tree, he nearly tumbled to the ground in its wake, his body tilting far forward, his arms spread like wings. Somehow though, he remained upright.

Now lying across the drive, the log blocked it off just as effectively as it had before Mwangi had freed it from the trees. Lifting one end of the log a foot or so off the ground, he sidled counterclockwise, letting go, pausing for a breath, and then beginning again, until, at last, he had cleared a path for the Volvo. Panting and sweaty, with the front of his shirt stained brown and covered with dirt and bits of bark, he returned to the car.

Halfway up the driveway, the house where Njeri had spent so

many of her school holidays came into view. A single-story white stucco dwelling, it stood atop a grassy plateau, with a separate dwelling for servants set some distance behind. As if to compensate for its lack of height, the house had spread itself far and wide over the property. It had grown out in stages, as indicated by its odd angles and mismatched roofing—black shingles here and orange Spanish tiles there. The stucco had taken on a grayish cast; some of the Spanish tiles had fallen away. Crab grass and weeds clotted the flower beds on either side of the front door. Once, the lawn had provided an ideal surface for afternoon games of croquet; now, dried leaves lay scattered amid the foot-high grass. Somewhere back in the woods behind the servants' quarters, an owl sounded a sorrowful chant: Hooo, hooo, hoo-hoo-hoo-hoo.

Near the door, a man seated in a white plastic lawn chair listlessly watched over a young boy who was rolling about in the leaves. When he spied the Volvo, the man grabbed the broom that was propped against the wall and frantically began sweeping leaves from the walkway onto the lawn.

From the trunk of the car, Njeri retrieved the two bouquets of intoxicatingly fragrant lilies she had bought that morning. Leaving Thomas to his slumbers, she followed Mwangi up the gravel path to the house.

The caretaker nodded at them but did not stop sweeping, too busy now to brook any interruptions. His slight frame and pinched nose suggested Somali origins. He had bulging eyes, smooth cheeks, and a wisp of a goatee. He wore sandals, dungarees that ended several inches above his ankles, a wool coat better suited for a Washington winter than a sunny day in Muranga, and a sweat-stained white skullcap with green stripes.

The boy's t-shirt and jeans had reached such an advanced stage of disintegration that they appeared best suited for consignment to a paper mill. Crouching, Njeri smiled at him. The wall-eyed child answered with a bashful smile of his own, then jumped up and scampered away, hiding himself behind the caretaker, to whose right leg he clung.

While Mwangi, gesturing angrily at the lawn, berated the caretaker in Kiswahili, Njeri wandered out onto the grass. The lawn sloped downward as it approached the outer wall, and at the bottom of the decline lay the graves. Each had a low horseshoe-shaped sandstone barrier at its head, which framed a plain wooden marker shaped like a cross. Mrs. Sarah Wanjiru Kariuki, 1937-1998, read the marker on the left. The other, lying face up on the ground, had had its inscription worn away.

Njeri had come to say goodbye and to seek a pardon. Surely, she would be forgiven now for missing the funerals. There had been too many deaths that year, and a person could only face so much at one time. But Mummy and Daddy, lying beneath an impenetrable tangle of grass, weeds, leaves, and twigs, would not or could not speak to her now. Squeezing the lilies to her chest, she heard only the owl's desolate call: Hooo, hooo, hoo-hoo-hoo-hoo.

With tears gushing down the sides of her face, she strode back up the slope and crossed the lawn again, the dead leaves crunching beneath her shoes.

"Here!" she cried, thrusting the bouquets at Mwangi, startling both him and the caretaker. "Give them to Theresa. They'd be wasted here."

She went inside. Stripped of furniture, as well as rugs, stove, refrigerator, and plumbing and lighting fixtures, the house appeared much smaller than she remembered. Someone must have dragged a sideboard or, perhaps, one of the missing appliances through the dining room, for the wooden floor had two long grooves etched into it. Muddy boot prints covered the white carpeting in Njeri's former bedroom. Wires poked through gaps where wall sockets and overhead lights had hung. The air was dank and heavy, and the narrow hallway off of which lay the toilet and the washroom reeked of urine. In the dim light of the living room, Njeri could trace the outlines of the mirror that had hung on the eastern wall. Try as she might, though, she could not envision the room filled with people, with Mummy and Daddy, Uncle Maina and Auntie Margaret, Uncle Wahome, Cousin Muthoni, and John Ndereba.

Outside, she found Mwangi leaning against the wall, his head and shoulders bent forward, his arms clasped about his midsection as though he were in pain. The bouquets lay on the ground to his left.

"I have to give this chap credit for inventiveness, if nothing else," he murmured. "He insists that all the leaves and debris came from elsewhere. A strong wind deposited them here."

"When? A year ago?" cried Njeri, her voice choked with rage. "If you don't watch him, of course he won't do any work. How could you have let this happen? I blame you for this. I expect nothing more from Thomas. But you…How could you?"

He shrugged, his puffy eyes still fixed upon the ground. He had done a careless job of shaving, she noticed now. Tufts of salt-and-pepper stubble sprouted from his chin. He looked worn and, suddenly, old, and that made her sadder even than what she had seen inside the house.

"I can't get up here very often. I do what I can. I've kept Kariuki, Ltd., going, which has not been easy, times being as they are. It's not as if I get much help." He turned his gaze toward the Volvo, where Thomas peacefully slept on. "If I'm lucky, Theresa and I might get to take the girls to the animal orphanage one or two Sundays a month."

He tried to brush away the debris that still clung to his shirt but soon abandoned the effort. "If Mum and Dad weren't buried here," he continued, "I'd gladly sell the property to anyone who would take it off my hands. I can't rent the house out because it's not safe to live here. I can't even keep it clean inside because the water supply is so erratic. But I have to take the long view. I expect to be buried here too, someday."

Njeri sat down beside him in the lawn chair that the caretaker had occupied so contentedly until their arrival. The latter, having taken refuge at the far end of the lawn where the descent to the graves began, languidly stirred up the leaves with his rake. Nearby, the boy, arms spread like wings, ran round and round the trunk of a bottle-brush tree resplendent with red brush-like flowers. Hooo, hooo, hoo-hoo-hoo-hoo, cried the owl.

"This was such a lovely place," she said, reaching into her handbag for a tissue and her compact. "Remember how Mumbi, the maid, would serve us our tea and sandwiches under that bottlebrush? Sometimes, I would sit out here all day with a book in my lap, while you and Thomas and John Ndereba were kicking a football around and kicking one another in the shins. You would laugh at me for being such a bookworm, but I was perfectly content. Far more content than I've ever been since." She paused to dab at her eyes with the tissue. "Why must everything fall to pieces?"

Gently, Mwangi squeezed her shoulder.

"I'm sorry," she said, leaning her head against his right side. "I've been terribly unfair. It was foolish of me to come back here after so many years and expect things to be just as they were. I know you're doing the best you can in an impossible situation. You're the only responsible one among the three of us. You're the only good one."

"All this time, I just thought I was the daft one."

"I'm sorry. I'm so sorry."

"I promise you, I will have those graves fixed up. Uncle Maina and Auntie Margaret don't have headstones yet either. Mwangi Wanjohi and I have been going around talking to some stonecutters. We're trying to see if we can get a good deal if we do all four of them at once."

Even as she wiped a tear from the bridge of her nose, she began to chuckle. "A package deal on headstones! What typical Kikuyus you are."

Grinning, Mwangi answered, "We are a pretty crass lot. But we keep what's left of poor Kenya running."

Out on the lawn, the caretaker, having at last assembled a small mound of leaves, paused in his labors. No sooner had he turned his back, though, than the boy, arms and legs awhirl, came dashing through the pile, scattering the leaves once more.

"Things will get better," said Mwangi, with a shake of his head and a resigned half-smile. "They have to get better."

LEAVING THE CHESAPEAKE

The Chesapeake Hotel, a dusty, brown-brick structure that stood a couple of blocks to the southeast of Baltimore's Penn Station, had a gabled roof, large frosted windows, and few other residents during my month-long stay. Far more common were the transients who used the rooms by the hour: whores and their clients—the former skeletal and hollow-eyed, with needle tracks lining their arms and legs; the latter an even more forlorn lot, most seemingly born before God invented dust. I had heard that the girls sometimes stole the Viagra from the befuddled old gentlemen and fetched a rather decent price for it on the black market.

My room, with its peeling, pea-green walls illumined only by a bare light bulb on the ceiling, had one window, sans curtain, that, no matter the weather, stubbornly remained one-quarter open, in defiance of all my efforts to force the sash up or down. A thick coating of grime covered the pane. The room had a "queen-sized bed"—a straw pallet and a box spring—that covered most of the floor, and no other furnishings.

Having lived in Europe, I had known Spartan accommodations before but nothing like these. I could imagine a television ad for the hotel: "Enjoy your getaway at the Chesapeake. Offering a unique combination of European space constraints and American urban squalor." The dim hallways reeked of mildew, tobacco, soiled linen, and every kind of human secretion and excretion. The building had neither showers nor hot water. One could take a cold bath if he dared to immerse himself in a tub encrusted with orange and black fungus. I scrubbed my body with wet towels instead. The toilets at either end of the hall had signs above them enjoining the user to flush but were perpetually stopped up, leaving one to wonder how. More than once I had defecated in plastic supermarket bags, which I had disposed of in the Dumpster behind the building.

Without iPhone, computer, television, or even radio, I had too much time for rumination and too few ways to divert or console myself. Most of my books I had placed in storage, but I did have with me a 1912 translation of the Discourses of Epictetus that I had picked up at a yard sale for fifty cents. When the heat and humidity made reading impossible, I would turn off the light and try to meditate, to focus on my breathing and filter out the sweat, the smells, the nausea, the chronic pain in my right knee, the tumult in the hall. Rarely did I succeed.

Rarely, too, did I trouble to answer the summons of the pay phone just outside my door. I made few calls, received even fewer, and knew my neighbors only by sight. On occasion, though, the ringing persisted so long as to become a torment and draw me out of my hole, and, invariably, the impatient voice at the other end of the line belonged to my brother Peter.

"What kind of a shithole are you living in, where you don't even have your own phone?" he would bark. "Why don't you get yourself a cell phone?"

"I can't afford one and don't need one," I would answer. "Nobody calls me but you."

Inevitably, either he or I would hang up in exasperation.

One night, though, he called with an invitation: "Listen, April and I are having a party tomorrow night. Why don't you come up to Long Island? It'll do you good. You haven't even seen the new place yet."

"I'd like to, but I have no money. I didn't leave my apartment by choice. They evicted me. I couldn't pay the rent."

"What? What's wrong with you? Why didn't you tell me? I would have helped you out."

"I know that."

From somewhere down the hallway, there came a piercing female shriek: "Everybody know what d-i-c-k mean."

Several bursts of harsh male laughter followed.

"Listen, we'll talk about it tomorrow. I'll buy you an Amtrak ticket."

"I'm working till six tomorrow. And Saturday, too."

"Call in sick. The hell with those bloodsuckers. It's not as if they pay you enough to live on. Why don't you look for a job up here? You can stay with us till you get settled. Why are you still in Baltimore anyway? You have nothing there anymore. What are you trying to do to yourself?"

I might have hung up at that point but for the brawny young man with the shaved head and goatee who hovered about me, glowering, edging ever closer, his right hand fidgeting with some change.

"You about done, dude?"

I ignored the man.

When he repeated the question, more loudly and with more menace in his tone, I turned to him and replied, "I'll be done when I'm done."

"You been on there a long time, dude. It ain't your phone, you know."

"It ain't yours either, dude. And I would finish a lot more quickly if you would leave me alone."

I turned my back to the man, my body tensing as if expecting a blow.

"Order me the ticket," I shouted into the mouthpiece. "I'll see you tomorrow."

≈≈

I knew that over the course of the weekend my brother would try to prevail upon me to see reason and not return to the Chesapeake and, when reason failed, would try to bludgeon me into submission. Nonetheless, I did not relinquish my room key before I left the next morning for the station, and I did take the precaution of calling out sick from work. Whether the latter would guarantee a job to return to, though, remained an open question. Because I would be calling out on Saturday as well as Friday, I would need a doctor's note. Taking two consecutive sick days without one could be a firing offense.

I sold newspaper subscriptions over the telephone, and I sold them to people who did not want the paper, people who couldn't read, people who couldn't see, to senile shut-ins and children whose parents weren't home. Yet, more often than not, I failed to sell enough to augment my salary—the legal minimum, minus "fines" for tardiness or failure to meet weekly or monthly quotas—with a commission.

That I would find myself in such a situation seemed proof to my brother of my perversity—a self-destructive impulse born of a desire to spite him. To me, though, brooding my way through Maryland, Delaware, and New Jersey on the Acela that morning, and in the afternoon through Manhattan, Queens and the suburbs on a Long Island Railroad commuter train, my stay at the Chesapeake had come to seem as though preordained.

I had completed my coursework toward my Ph.D. and, too slowly, my comprehensive exams and was trying to flesh out an inchoate idea of basing a dissertation on an ethnographic study of just such a place as the Chesapeake, when the walking corpse that was my marriage keeled over at last. Faced with a divorce and custody fight, I put scholarship aside—the world did not lose much as a result—and went to work. My new employer peddled hourly, daily, weekly, monthly, and yearly planners—both paper and software versions; books, CDs, and DVDs, on managerial techniques, team building, and time and stress management; and mugs, pens, stationery, etc., adorned with pithy sayings guaranteed to motivate and inspire. I put on time management seminars for middle- and upper-level managers, instructing my charges in how to use their planners with maximum efficiency. The wisdom I dispensed encompassed far more than mere tips on multitasking, though. Indeed, I offered an entire philosophy of life, a way of clarifying one's values, missions, goals, and means, and my eager pupils, who prided themselves on their hard-nosed managerial styles, lapped the swill right up. I closed each presentation with the words of William Ernest Henley, later made infamous by Timothy McVeigh: "I am master of my fate; I am the captain of my soul." Eventually, I tired of Henley and began culling inspirational bits from the words of literary and actual villains: Iago, Lady Macbeth, Hitler, Stalin, Charles Manson. Though Harvard Business and Wharton School grads abounded in my classes, none ever guessed at the provenance of those quotations, questioned the wisdom contained therein, or imagined that I did not offer them up in a completely earnest spirit.

The job paid well, and though three years of divorce and custody litigation left me buried beneath a landslide of debt, I managed to stay out of bankruptcy court for an additional two-and-a-half years. Unfortunately, by that time, heavy drinking had become necessary to numb me to the point where I could get through a week of my presentations, each identical to the last but for my specially selected quotation. Driving drunk one night, I hopped the curb and slammed into a tree, cracking a couple of ribs, shattering my right kneecap and tearing the medial meniscus. I needed two operations to put the pieces back together, and, even so, remained a semi-invalid for the better part of a year. Just when I had begun to walk again without a noticeable limp, my masters decided that an employee like me, so unproductive for so long, did not exemplify their values and could have only the most deleterious effects on their mission and goals, and let me go. My income from freelance editing, when available, and telemarketing—a trade I took up when faced with the possibility of becoming a street person or going to jail for nonpayment of child support—did not stretch far enough to pay the bills. In quick succession, there came bankruptcy, eviction, and the Chesapeake, in which environment I began to live the life of one of those people I had hoped to make the subject of my study. A nasty little irony.

≈≈

Peter met me at the station, clasping me in a bear hug. Burly and slightly bowlegged, with a graying beard and a weathered visage, he had the look of a mariner, though he had never shown much interest in boating, and even at the beach, he preferred the sand to the water. We wound our way slowly in his SUV past stone mansions set far back behind high walls, hedgerows, and pickets of oaks and beeches, Peter narrating the tour in his husky baritone.

"This whole section in here once belonged to the Vanderbilts. That house on the right belonged to a guy named Cliff Roberts or Robertson or Robinson. I forget which. His father had made a fortune mining bauxite in Utah and left him all his money. He wanted nothing to do with bauxite or Utah, so he came east and settled here, and a few years later, he went and shot himself. That smaller house, behind and to the right, was his caretaker's. Even his goddamn caretaker lived better than we do. How could he go shoot himself? It makes no sense."

"Every man has his reasons."

"What does that mean?"

"I suppose there are a lot of ways to make a hash out of your life, even if you do have money."

Peter shook his head. "It makes no sense."

Peter's own house, a colonial, though newer and not of the same gargantuan proportions as some of the legendary dwellings nearby, nevertheless provided ample comforts: high ceilings from which slowly spinning fans depended, a parquet floor in the dining room, a fireplace with marble mantle piece in the living room, and several bathrooms—one, containing a Jacuzzi. All of Peter's bathrooms were as large as or larger than my cell at the Chesapeake. A plank deck looked out over a vast yard, in the middle of which lay a fenced in area that surrounded a doghouse inhabited by a family of ducks. Beyond the property line lay marshland and cattails, and farther on, the

Great South Bay.

April, lounging on a beach chair on the deck, kept a wary eye on Adam, a scrawny nine-year-old, who was kicking a soccer ball back and forth with a friend at the far end of the yard. A tall, slender woman, she had a scattering of freckles on her cheeks and tawny hair held back from her forehead by pink barrettes. She rose at once when she saw me and greeted me with a kiss, ignoring my shouted warning—she wore hearing aids in both ears—that she ought not to get near me until I had showered and changed. Despite her broad smile and the time she had spent in the sun, she appeared wan and tired, with dark patches beneath her eyes and her skin stretched tautly over her cheekbones.

A moment later, the plate-glass door that led into the den slid open, and a gangly, slouching, sullen-looking adolescent with electric-blue hair stepped out onto the deck and murmured, "Mom, I'm going now. Be back tomorrow afternoon. Bye"

"Hey," growled Peter. "You're uncle's here. Don't you even bother to say hello?"

"Hi, Uncle Bobby," answered the boy, already retreating into the house.

"Where the hell is he off to now?"

"If you took the time to ask him, you would know," replied April.

"Last time I saw Eric," I said, "his hair was bright red. Is he going through all the primary colors first?"

"Bad subject," answered Peter.

"Did you ever think," I wondered aloud, "we'd get this old?"

≈≈

The party began in the early evening, and the house filled quickly with guests. Muted arrangements of "Autumn Leaves" and other jazz standards played on the stereo, while lawyers talked shop or debated investment strategies. Flitting from room to room like a ghost, I settled myself at last in a corner of the deck, relishing the cool breeze that wafted in from the bay, and half-hypnotized by the chorus of the crickets. High above, a three-quarter moon glowed in a slate-black sky.

As I reached into a cooler for another beer, I noticed April standing beside me.

"I was wondering where you were hiding," she said with mock severity. "This is Karishma Mathur," she added, placing her hand upon the shoulder of a petite woman in a sleeveless red and white flowered dress that fluttered in the wind. "Karishma works with me at South Shore. And works, and works, and works. She's the best nurse we have. The I.C.U. would fall apart without her."

"Oh, please," the smaller woman answered, with an expression that wavered between a smile and a grimace. "I would work less if I got paid more."

"Beer?" I asked, sticking my hand in the cooler again.

Karishma shook her head.

"What do American beer and making love in a canoe have in common?" she asked.

"What?"

"Both are fucking close to water."

The punch line left me sufficiently discombobulated that I spilled beer down the front of my shirt. No shrinking Indian violet was she, this beauty with the honey-brown complexion and eyes as big and dark as the night sky.

"Bobby has two girls. "How old are they now? Twelve and…?"

Even as she spoke, April had begun to drift back toward the house.

"Amanda's thirteen now, and Leah's eleven. Though it might be more appropriate to say I had two girls. I don't . . . I haven't seen them in a while. Mine was one of those divorces that only a lawyer could love."

"Your brother handled my divorce."

"And you're still on speaking terms? He's grown soft, my brother."

Karishma had a girl of her own, an eight-year-old. The story was one I had heard variants of before. Born in Hydarabad, Karishma had grown up in London, and she spoke in the accents of the latter city. She had come to the States to live with her boyfriend, who had resigned himself, finally, to marriage and even to fatherhood but not, alas, to monogamy.

Of him she spoke softly, so that her words sometimes got lost amid the song of the crickets. Only once did a note of bitterness creep into her voice, when she said, "He's a man, after all. You can only expect so much."

My ex had often expressed such sentiments, though in much more pungent language. Wisely choosing not to bring her into the conversation—a rare display of forbearance on my part—I remained silent. Looking sheepish, Karishma apologized at once. When she turned to gaze out over the bay, the moon draped her slender neck and shoulders with silver, and for the first time in many months, I had cause to wonder at and regret having allowed myself to grow so accustomed to solitude and celibacy.

≈≈

On Saturday, following an afternoon at the beach, Peter took me out for dinner and some bar hopping. As the muggy night wore on, what began as a slight ache in my knee steadily intensified. Peter's attempted flirtation with a pretty but harried young waitress evoked no response other than careless service, and during our subsequent wanderings, he grew surlier with each successive drink. Eric had not yet returned when we left for dinner, and though Peter tried to call home several times on his cell phone, nobody answered.

"My kid's a goddamn lowlife!" he shouted to the sky, from the parking lot of the last bar we visited.

During the drive back home, when I told him that I could not spend the whole of Sunday at the beach because I needed to return to Baltimore at a reasonable hour, he smashed his fist against the dashboard.

"What the hell are you going back to? Your kids? When was the last time you saw them? You're living in a goddamn whorehouse. If you don't get knifed, you'll get some disease that should have been wiped out a hundred years ago. Just what is your objective here? You couldn't finish yourself off in your car, so now you're trying to get someone to do it for you? If that's what you're up to, I can call half a dozen shrinks right now, and any one of them will be perfectly willing to put you in the hospital."

Neither of us spoke again for the remainder of the drive.

"Why do I bother?" Peter hissed, as we entered the house. "It's not as if I get any appreciation from anyone. Everything you do, you do out of spite and envy."

"I don't envy you. Not in the least."

I went straight to my room. Peter, however, continued to fume, to stomp, to curse, to shout—but now at April. Eric, it seemed, had returned earlier in the evening, hidden himself away in his room for two hours watching a movie on his laptop, and then had run off again.

"Why can't you tell him no?" cried Peter. "Just once."

"Why don't you go to hell?" shouted April.

There followed the sound of her footsteps, rapidly ascending the stairs, and then a door slamming. I fell into a doze, only to be awakened by Peter's final salvo, this one directed at Adam. Someone had fouled up the DVD player.

Though Peter had quieted down by the next morning, he remained sulky and shut off all through breakfast and the drive to Fire Island. The day was ideal, the air warm but dry, the water temperate, the sky a perfect dome, a trompe l'oeil masterwork, deep blue overhead and paling in the distance, with puffy, white cumulus clouds arrayed in a semicircle above the horizon. Swimming out beyond the crowds, I spent most of the morning and early afternoon bobbing with seagulls atop the waves or diving beneath. I floated on my back, suspended between ocean and sky, trying to ward off the Sunday dread and forget that there existed such a place as the Chesapeake Hotel. The previous night's histrionics notwithstanding, I knew I could not face a return to the coffin of a room that I had occupied for the past month. About that, at least, Peter had been right. I stayed in the water until my fingers grew blanched and as wrinkled as prunes, and when I swam back to the shore and tried to stand, my legs turned to jelly, and I fell forward onto the wet sand.

Still dripping, my body coated with sand, salt, and seaweed, my hair matted to my scalp, I sat down beside April. She lay on a blanket beneath a blue and white striped umbrella, flipping through a copy of

Town and Country filled with glossy photos of English topiary gardens and villas overlooking the Amalfi coast. Below us, at the edge of the water, Peter and Adam were tossing a football back and forth.

"I hope you're planning to call Karishma," she said, smiling mischievously.

"I don't know. I haven't had much interest in women lately. And I can't imagine, really, what she'd want with me, given my present circumstances. But it is a rare and wonderful thing to meet someone here in America who shares my abiding love of Asterix comics."

"Call her."

She touched my forearm gently.

"I had to leave my Asterix collection with the girls when I moved out. I used to read it to them at bedtime. All the furniture and everything else I was happy to leave behind, but that grieved me."

"You never see the girls anymore?"

"No. It's two, more like two-and-a-half years now. I send them birthday cards. Whether they get them or not, I have no idea."

"That's not right what she did, turning the girls against you like that. If Peter and I ever got divorced, I wouldn't do that, no matter how angry I got at him. It's the kids who suffer."

"I made the decision to stop seeing them. Hostile as they had become, it seemed the thing to do at the time. Not that they were to blame of course . . . Ah, what are kids anyway? They're Hobbesian creatures. Nasty, brutish, and short."

"You will see them again. I can promise you that. They'll come looking for you."

My eyes began to tear up then. I turned my gaze toward Peter, watching him backpedal, lunge to his right to evade an imaginary tackler, coil his body, whip his arm forward, and launch the football far down the beach. He was at least partially right about me after all, I had to concede. I would not have wanted to be him, but I did envy him in some ways. Whatever its frustrations, his was a substantial life, anchored by work, home, family, friends and colleagues. Mine, on the other hand, had broken up into so much flotsam, drifting hither and thither with the tides.

"Peter and I used to play football on the lawn when we were kids,"

I said. "One-on-one, tackle, no pads or helmet. Usually, I got the worst of it—broken finger, pulled neck muscle—but I got my shots in, too. He ended up with a broken elbow when I tackled him and he landed on the driveway. Do you think it's odd that I remember those games fondly? More fondly than I remember just about any other time we've spent together in the last twenty-five years or so? He's my brother, and I love him, but I find it hard to be around him for very long. He'd make me go deaf, too."

April's mouth tightened.

"I blame him for a lot of things but not for that."

"I'm sorry," I answered, feeling my cheeks start to burn. "That was an incredibly stupid and crass thing to say."

"It's all right. Anyone can see that we have our problems. We still go to counseling. Sometimes it gets better. Sometimes it gets worse. He's a good person, basically."

"A fact that, for reasons known only to himself, he's always tried his best to conceal. But he is a very good person. And he's been a far better brother to me than I've been to him. He's lucky he never needed anything from me."

"Every day at work he sees human beings at their worst. He has to be a certain way to do his job, and he can't just turn it off when he comes home."

"Sooner or later, we all become what we despise."

"I know he could have been more tactful about it, but he really does want you to stay until you get back on your feet. We both do."

Suddenly, the doubts that I thought I had shed in water assailed me once more.

"I would like to. But it's difficult, things being as they are. Given my recent employment history, my job prospects can't be very bright. I have the child support. I couldn't even pay the rent in Baltimore, and here everything costs three times as much. I don't want to be a charity case. I'm not even very good at being a guest."

"It's not charity. Right now, when you're having a bad time, you're better off being with family than being alone. You don't belong in that dump in Baltimore. You can't go back there."

I leaned far over to my right, scooped up a handful of sand, and let it run out between my fingers. Adam, I saw, had grown tired of playing catch. For the third time in succession, he let an eminently catchable pass slip through his hands, and, looking quite morose, trudged after the ball yet more slowly than before, kicking sand as he went. Peter, waiting with his hands on his hips, his shoulders and neck cooked by the sun to a blazing red, spit into the ocean.

"No, I can't go back to the Chesapeake. Whether or not I belong there is another question entirely.

"I had a little hot plate to make coffee or tea, but that got stolen. As I discovered one day when I locked myself out and banged on the door in frustration, you can open any door there without a key. The other day, someone stole my toothpaste and toothbrush. I can't imagine why, considering the general level of personal hygiene there. Whoever it was left me my Epictetus, though, so I can't dismiss the possibility that the thefts were a pedagogic technique, a lesson in the virtues of detachment.

"Whatever romantic notions I may have once had about the lives that people live in a place like Chesapeake are long gone. Even my academic interest is gone. It vanished with my academic career."

Adam, summoning all the strength he had stored in his spindly frame, punted the football far over Peter's head and began walking toward us.

"I'd better go make my peace with him. Let's hope it lasts."

As Peter went to retrieve the ball, I ran toward the water, narrowly avoiding the startled Adam. Without pausing to look up, Peter whirled and threw—a perfect spiral aimed at the spot where he assumed his son still stood. I leaped, plucked the football out of the air, and began to run it back the other way, defying the throbbing in my knee. Peter, crouching and gimlet-eyed, closed upon me, and I faked to the right and then veered left, toward the ocean. He dove, wrapped his arms around my thighs, and we slid through wet sand, seaweed, and salt water. Panting, I rose, brushed the sand and debris from my chest, legs, and swimsuit, and scooped up the football.

"My ball," I said. "First down. Count to five Mississippi before you rush. The lifeguard's chair is a touchdown."

ERRORS

My search for Billy Kapanka had led me as far west as Columbus, Ohio, where, until a few weeks before, he had worked in a Denny's as a fry cook and rented a furnished room. He had departed without leaving a forwarding address. I then visited a warehouse in Butler, Pennsylvania, where I had heard that he had driven a forklift. No one there remembered him.

By that time, I had already done quite a bit more traveling than was strictly necessary for one interview. Still, I persisted. I had my reasons: his story intrigued me; I was well compensated for my efforts; and, like Billy, I tended to get restless if I stayed too long in one place.

I followed the trail eastward—and backward in time—to Jersey City, New Jersey, where, in the mid-1980s, Billy had rented another room, fathered a now-grown daughter, and spent thirty days in jail for being drunk and disorderly. By way of another old girlfriend, a second estranged daughter, and an employee of the New York City Child Support Enforcement Bureau, whom I had managed to convince that I was the ex-girlfriend's lawyer, I finally traced Billy to a decaying yellow-brick structure called the Cross Bronx Hotel. I thought it best to drop in unannounced.

The lobby of the Cross Bronx Hotel was an airless phlegm-yellow room furnished with an end table, upon which stood a flickering table lamp with a tattered yellowish shade, and a frayed brown and yellow sofa. Above the sofa hung an enlarged photograph of a pre-9/11 New York City skyline. A bulky air conditioner, set into the rear wall, wheezed mightily but provided little relief from the July heat. Behind the front desk sat a heavyset black woman with a mottled complexion and half-closed eyes. Dressed in purple spandex pants and a matching, though sweat-darkened, tank top, she was leafing through a magazine. When I asked for Billy's room number, she eyed me warily, tapping on the desk with her inch-long purple fingernails.

"What you wanna see him for?" she huffed. "He owe you money? Tell him he got to pay for his room before he can pay you."

"No, he doesn't owe me anything. I've just come for a visit."

"You the first person to visit him since he been here."

"He's kind of funny that way."

"He funny all right. He funny in the head." Rising slowly from her chair, the woman let out a long, languid sigh and waddled out from behind the desk, her flip-flops slapping against the floor tiles. "I'll show you where he is. I got to talk to him anyway. He ain't paid his rent this month."

I followed her down a dim and stiflingly hot corridor where haggard men in undershirts lingered about, idly watching, wondering, perhaps, what business the stranger wearing the beige chinos and knit sport shirt and carrying the laptop case could possibly have there. A smell of ammonia, soiled linen, and insect spray hung in the muggy air. I had sniffed that odor before—in jails and VA hospitals.

My guide stopped in front of room 117, knocked on the door, and waited. From behind the adjacent door of room 119, a couple screamed oaths at one another in Spanish.

"I know he in there," she confided. "He does this every time."

She knocked on the door again—harder than before. "Kapanka!" she bellowed. "They's someone here to see you. I know you in there, Kapanka." Now she smashed her fist and forearm against the door, the blows echoing through the corridor.

I heard the creaking of bedsprings, a heavy footfall, and the sound of a lock turning. The man who opened the door had the slightly dazed, disheveled look of someone who had just awakened from a sound sleep. His uncombed hair, streaked with black and gray like a string mop in desperate need of a rinse, hung halfway down his neck. His pallid, pitted cheeks wanted shaving. Tall, lanky, stoop-shouldered, he was barefooted and dressed in torn dungarees and a black t-shirt, the pocket of which held a pack of cigarettes. He looked nothing like the puckish young man of the archival photographs I carried around with me. Had I found the right Billy Kapanka?

"Kapanka, you better pay your July rent. Two more days, Kapanka, and you out on your sorry white ass."

Standing a step or two back of the doorframe, his arms folded across his chest, the man maintained a cold, petulant silence. I sidled past him and slipped into the room—an instant before he slammed the door in the woman's face.

"Kapanka, you don't ever shut the door on me. I can have you out on the street right now. You hear me, Kapanka? You hear me?" Three more resounding blows shook the door.

"Welcome to Ida's Whorehouse and All-Night Crack Emporium," he growled. "Now who the hell are you, and what do you want?"

"Rich Bowen, Boston Herald," I said, extending him my hand.

He did not extend his.

I was working, I explained a tad breathlessly, lest he throw me out before I had a chance to finish, on a feature for the Herald: a thirty-year retrospective on a plucky but undermanned Red Sox team that had played far above expectations and challenged the Yankees for the division title all season long only to fall agonizingly short in the end. Naturally, I wanted to interview him. In fact, I had spent quite a bit of time trying to track him down. As one of the central players in that season's drama, he must have some great stories to tell.

His mouth constricted as if he had bitten into something bitter.

"Just when I was thinking things couldn't get any worse," he said, and then he sat down upon his unmade bed, and covered his face with his big, gnarly hands.

In the absence of any other available seating, I settled myself at the opposite end of the bed, opened my laptop case, and drew out the computer and switched it on. The front pouch of the case held a pocket-sized digital voice recorder and a folder of printouts from the Herald's archives. I took those items out as well and set them down upon the bed beside me.

Hotter even than the corridor, the room, a roughly 10' by 10' square, smelled of mildew and cigarettes. The walls were of the same putrid yellow as those of the lobby and completely bare. The bed stood against one wall, opposite a pine dresser with a clouded mirror. In the near corner, at the foot of the bed, sat a compact refrigerator, atop which rested several crushed McDonald's cups, some balled-up wax paper wrappers—one of which Billy now picked up and flung at the mirror—an ashtray, and an unplugged hotplate. The room had no bathroom attached. Its sole plumbing fixture was a sink—fouled with a wooly orange and black fungus and lacking a hot water handle—that jutted from the wall beside the dresser. The uncovered ceiling fixture featured two empty sockets; a single bulb shone weakly from the third. The lone window, which looked out onto the side wall of the adjacent gas station, allowed in precious little additional light and no breeze at all.

"Let me take a wild guess," said Billy, lighting up a Marlboro. "You're gonna ask me about that fly ball."

"Among other things." I replied nonchalantly, pressing the record button.

Already, I envisioned my lead: "In his mind's eye, Billy Kapanka can still see that fly ball descending." Though long forgotten by most, that botched play, which had brought such a painful end to such a promising season, had endured in the memories of Red Sox fans of a certain age.

I was eleven when I witnessed the event on television, and at that age, I did not take disappointment well. My poster of Billy—captured by the photographer in mid-swing, lips pursed, eyes narrowed in concentration, arms extended, the ball a white blur flying off his bat—had not survived that day. I had yanked it from its place of honor on the wall above my bed and torn it to shreds.

In time, I would recover, but I wondered whether for Billy the bleeding had ever stopped. His career had followed a trajectory like that of the space shuttle Challenger: the rocket-propelled ascent and then the sudden disintegration. Agile and swift, a three-sport star at New Rochelle High School, Billy had begun that season in Double A, but by mid-July he had become the everyday centerfielder for Red Sox. With the fluid left-handed swing that produced a .344 batting average, his dexterous outfield play, and his affable manner and fondness for locker room pranks, Billy had contributed as much as anyone to the team's surprising success. Then had come that blustery early-October afternoon at Yankee Stadium—the season's final day.

"There's not a whole lot to tell about it, really. I just screwed up. It's as simple as that. Is the Herald gonna pay me for this?"

Twenty-one years old, playing centerfield in that fabled ballpark against the team he had grown up rooting for, in front of three-dozen friends and relatives, Billy had driven home the first two runs of the game with a first-inning double. The Red Sox had grimly hung on after that, entering the ninth with a 3-1 lead, needing to hold the Yankees for one more inning to tie them for first place in the division and force a one-game playoff. But with two outs, the home team loaded the bases, and Reggie Jackson strode to the plate. Ball one. Ball two. Fifty thousand people stood on tiptoes. Fifty thousand voices cried out in rapture as Jackson connected and the baseball streaked toward the right field bleachers. But at the last instant, the ball curved foul. The crowd let out a collective moan. The pitcher fidgeted with his cap awhile, then stepped up onto the mound again and went into his windup. The sound wave crested again, but suddenly dissolved, for, on this occasion, the feared Yankee slugger could produce only a pedestrian pop fly. Billy had but to move in a dozen feet or so and wait for the ball to come to him. For some unfathomable reason, though, he retreated instead and kept on retreating, even as the ball began its near-vertical drop. Realizing his mistake, he stopped so suddenly that his feet nearly slid out from under him and reversed course, charging toward the infield. Then came that fatal half-second of indecision—the ball still falling to earth, Billy seemingly frozen in mid-stride. He made a final, desperate lunge. As his knees hit the ground, he reached out his glove like a mendicant, but the gods ignored his plea. The ball hit the turf, bounced high over his shoulder, and rolled on past. The crowd shrieked in ecstasy as the stunned outfielder lay prone on the grass. By the time Billy picked himself up, retrieved the baseball, and flung it wildly in the general direction of home plate, all three Yankee runners had scored. In an instant, sweet victory had curdled into the bitterest of defeats.

"Was the sun in your eyes?"

"Nah, it wasn't the sun," he answered, his voice curiously flat, as though he were describing an event he had heard about secondhand. "Can't blame the sun. Jackson took a big swing, but he got under the ball. Popped it up. Only I thought he hit solid. I thought it was going over my head. Nine hundred ninety-nine times out of a thousand, I catch that ball. But the one time I didn't…." He shook his head and exhaled a plume of smoke. "Am I gonna get paid for this?"

The couple in the next room had, perhaps, begun to exhaust themselves; their screaming had become intermittent. In the distance, I could hear sirens, car horns, and tires thumping over the rutted pavement of the Cross Bronx Expressway. I rifled through my archival folder until I found the printout I'd sought.

"After the game, your manager told the press—I'm quoting here—'He just quit out there. A little pop fly. First he misses it. Then he just lays there.' It's pretty unusual for a manager to speak that way in public about one of his players, isn't it? I imagine that must have hurt."

Billy's jaw clenched, and he bit his lower lip. He stubbed out his spent cigarette butt against the wall behind him, adding another to the constellation of burn marks on the yellow paint. Only his voice betrayed no emotion. "The man was a fool," he said. "I could tell that even then. I never paid attention to anything he said."

"It must have bothered you the way the fans reacted, though. I understand you got a lot of hate mail. Some death threats."

Suddenly, the memory of my shredded poster made me want to

squirm.

"That was a long time ago. Life goes on."

"Has it, though?"

Rising abruptly, he said, "Look if I'm not getting paid, then there's nothing more to talk about. We're finished here."

My eyes lit upon an ancient headline: Kapanka Fails to Make Cut.

"The next year, you still went into spring training as the starting centerfielder. What happened?"

Older colleagues who had covered the team that March told me that Billy looked like someone who had forgotten how to play the game. In the outfield, he would stand as if paralyzed while balls flew over his head or bounced in front of him. At the plate, he fared no better, waving feebly at fastballs that had already passed him by and swinging over curveballs by a foot.

"They sent me back down to Pawtucket. Then I got let go. I caught on with the Reds' organization. Got let go there. Then the Pirates' organization. Same thing."

"I knew all that."

"Then why did you ask?"

"What I meant was…" I paused a moment, shuffling my print-outs about as I mulled over the wording of my next question. "Do you ever wonder whether things might have turned out differently if not for that fly ball?"

"No."

"Never?"

He sighed impatiently. "What do you want me to say? That I'd be living in a mansion in Beverly Hills if only I'd caught that ball? You reporter types have some funny ideas about cause and effect." Lighting another cigarette, he blew out three perfectly spherical smoke rings. In the gloom, my eyes began to play tricks on me: I fancied that Billy's ashen face was dissolving into smoke.

Pulling out my handkerchief, I wiped the sweat from my forehead. Though my efforts had yielded little, having pursued Billy for so long, I wasn't quite ready to give up. Maybe, I thought, if I could get him out of that yellow coffin of a room, I would have better luck.

He might relax a bit over a drink and yield up a few usable quotes. Or perhaps a return to the scene of the crime, so to speak, would stir up some memories.

I shut down the laptop and put it back in its case, along with the voice recorder and the printouts. With studied casualness, I asked, "Have you ever been back to Yankee Stadium since?"

"No. Why?"

"Why don't we go check out the game tonight?"

"I'm kinda broke right now. In case you hadn't noticed."

"It'll be Rupert Murdoch's treat."

He gazed out the window. At length, he replied, "How generous of him. Why don't you and Rupert Murdoch go check out the game yourselves?"

"I can understand why it would be difficult for you to return to Yankee Stadium."

"That's bullshit," he answered with a scowl. "You think I'm afraid to go back there?"

"Then why not go?"

"Maybe I don't like the company."

Suddenly, the couple in room 119 resumed their battle with renewed vigor. Something crashed against the wall and shattered. Billy winced as though the object had struck him.

"You prefer the company next door?" Rising, I picked up the laptop case and stepped slowly toward the door. There I lingered, my hand gripping the knob.

Billy's lower jaw shifted from side to side, his teeth grinding audibly against one another. "Fine," he snapped. "Let's go to the damn game."

Knowing I had him securely hooked, I played with him a bit. "You're sure now? After all, I wouldn't want to impose."

He shrugged. The smile upon his lips was a bitter one—the smile of a condemned man. "Anyplace is better than here."

≈≈

Our seats in section 51 of the bleachers looked out over centerfield. In the midst of that vast expanse, plush and green beneath the arc lights as the surface of a pool table, stood the solitary figure of the young Tampa Bay outfielder Rocco Baldelli, his back facing us.

"So you're out here in the centerfield," I said. "It's the ninth inning. Bases loaded. Jackson's coming to the plate. What are you thinking about?"

"I'm probably thinking about getting laid. I didn't think about much else back then."

"What were you thinking? How did you feel when…?" I have asked those questions in one variant or another so many times that they have become like reflexes, and usually they elicit answers of a similarly thoughtful caliber. Billy's response was probably one of the more candid ones I had received over the years, but of course I could not use it.

Billy was draining sixteen-ounce cups of beer at the rate of one per half-inning, courtesy of the Herald, but the alcohol seemed only to make him even less communicative than before. When he deigned to answer the questions I put to him, he mostly did so in grunts and monosyllables.

I decided to let him alone for an inning or two in the hope that I might lull him into lowering his guard. Unfortunately, the game proved even less diverting than my companion. Aided by a series of Tampa Bay misplays, the Yankees ended the suspense early, piling up a 9-1 lead by the fourth inning.

The fans in section 51 took to amusing themselves by tormenting Rocco Baldelli. The jeering began in front of us, in row D, occupied in its inner precincts by seven or eight men in their early or mid-twenties with bulked-up torsos, an abundance of tattoos, and grease-blackened hands. Some of the young men wore Yankee caps and navy blue t-shirts emblazoned with the names and numbers of their favorite Yankee players; others wore sky blue t-shirts that bore the Honda logo beneath the legend "Russ Swift Honda."

"Hey, Baldelli," cried the Russ Swift Honda men in chorus, "you suck!" Behind us, in row F, a sweaty, ruddy-faced, orange-haired woman fairly bursting out of her white cutoffs and pink halter top, interrupted her cell phone conversation to shriek, "Your mother just called, Baldelli. She said you suck." Beside her sat a fidgety little man with a large, round head. He had greasy black hair that, atop his scalp, grew in oddly spaced clumps, an olive complexion, and a flat nose. His face appeared capable of registering only two expressions: a sneer or a smirk. He wore brown Bermuda shorts and a blue and orange flowered Hawaiian shirt. Picking up on the theme developed by the others, he rose to his feet and rasped, "Baldelli, your mother's a whore. She sucks even more than you." Then he sat down again and goosed the orange-haired woman, who, while still cackling into the phone, wriggled out of his grasp and gave him a mock slap on the arm. As the evening sky darkened and the beer flowed—particularly in row D, where the men of Russ Swift Honda were playing an intricate drinking-betting game which had dollar bills and beer cups constantly changing hands—the insults grew more inventive. By the sixth inning, poor Mrs. Baldelli stood accused of having had congress with an entire menagerie. The infuriating refusal of the young outfielder to acknowledge his persecutors only goaded them into redoubling their efforts.

"Do you think he can hear them?" I asked Billy.

"He can hear them, all right," he replied, then gulped down the last of his beer and hailed a nearby vendor for another. "Every filthy word."

Suddenly, I felt a bit queasy—an occasional hazard in my line of work. Like most people, I had had the relative good fortune to experience my worst failures and humiliations in private rather than in front of 50,000 spectators and countless more watching on television. No stranger would knock at my door thirty years after the fact to hound me about slights given and received, displays of pettiness and spleen, broken marriage vows, estrangements from those I had loved. I wondered whether I might better have turned away from the Cross Bronx Hotel and let poor Billy Kapanka be. "Anytime you've had enough," I said, "just let me know."

He shot me a quizzical sideways glance. "It was your idea to come here," he answered.

"Not one of my better ones."

"You're going back to the Marriott. I'm going back to Ida's

Whorehouse and All-Night Crack Emporium. I'm not in any hurry."

He took a hefty swig from his fresh cup and then turned his attention back to the game, which he observed dispassionately but with intense interest. The visitors' many miscues—infielders muffing easy grounders, outfielders throwing to the wrong bases, everyone playing out of position—left him muttering and shaking his head. When a Yankee outfielder made a sliding catch, Billy applauded politely; a half inning later, when the Tampa Bay infield, in a rare display of competence, executed a snappy double play, he did the same.

Such impartiality did not sit well with section 51's self-appointed arbiter of taste and decorum, the loudmouth in row F with the unhealthy fixation on Rocco Baldelli's mother. "Hey, who you rooting for, anyway?" he croaked. "What are you, a friggin' Tampa Bay fan?"

"What's it matter to you?" Billy replied.

In the bottom of the seventh inning, the Yankees loaded the bases on two walks and a hit batsman. The Tampa Bay manager strode out to the mound and raised his right hand, signaling for a new relief pitcher. But section 51 would grant no relief to Rocco Baldelli.

By that time, Billy must have had all he could endure of that little man in row F yelling in his ear, for he suddenly turned around and shouted, "Why don't you leave the kid alone already?"

"Why don't you go back to Tampa?"

The next batter hit a pop fly to centerfield, much like the one Billy had muffed all those years ago. This ball Rocco Baldelli caught—and immediately fired homeward. Waiting on third base, the lead Yankee runner started toward home but abruptly doubled back. The catcher, straddling home plate, caught the baseball on the fly.

"Damn! That was a throw!" cried Billy.

The loudmouth in row F was less impressed. Cupping his hands around his mouth to create a megaphone effect, he hollered, "Too little and too late, Baldelli. You still suck."

Billy stood up, his footing a bit unsteady now, and clapped his hands violently together. "That was a damn fine throw!" he yelled, in a tone sufficiently bellicose to provoke some menacing looks from the Russ Swift Honda crowd. "And anyone who says otherwise is a fool."

"Hey, pal, this is Yankee Stadium," said the man in row F. "We're not in Tampa. We don't root for losers here. Capisce?"

Billy whirled around, and the two men glowered at one another. With his orange-haired paramour anxiously looking on, the little fellow put up a brave front, standing on his toes and puffing out his chest. In the end, though, he capitulated, dropping back into his chair and murmuring about "friggin' Tampa Bay fans."

"'Too little and too late, Baldelli,'" mimicked Billy, as he sat down again. "Idiot. I would have killed to have an arm like that."

"I saw you make an even better throw once," I said. "It was against the White Sox, at Fenway. Probably the best throw I've ever seen, in fact. From way, way back in centerfield. You cut down the tying run at home plate in the ninth."

"I don't remember."

The archival press accounts did not quite square with my recollection either, though it seemed one of the most vivid of my boyhood. One article told of an "accurate" throw to the plate—in the eighth inning. Another reporter had not deemed the throw worthy of any adjective. Had memory betrayed me, transformed "accurate" into superhuman?

"If I ever made a throw like that, it was pure luck. But luck doesn't stay with you, unless you're really good. And I just wasn't good enough."

"For two-and-a-half months, you were as good as anyone."

"I suppose," he murmured absently, his gaze fixed upon the Yankees' preternaturally handsome superstar Derek Jeter, who was standing just outside the batter's box taking some easy practice swings while the Tampa Bay pitcher and catcher conferred atop the pitcher's mound. "Those were the best months of my life. I never had to pay for a meal or a drink in Boston that whole summer. People wouldn't let me. And the women….Everywhere we went…I could tell you stories you wouldn't believe." Biting down hard upon his lower lip, he shook his head. "And then everything went to hell in the blink of an eye."

I heard the thwack of bat meeting ball and saw everyone around me rise in anticipation of snagging a coveted souvenir—a Derek Jeter home run ball. But the baseball, seemingly headed directly for section 51, began to lose altitude in the heavy night air. Ten feet or so in front of the wall, Rocco Baldelli positioned himself to make the catch, unaware of the other object streaking in his direction, hurled at him by one of men of Russ Swift Honda. Just as Baldelli's glove closed around the ball, the silvery, rectangular nine-volt battery struck the outfielder between the shoulder blades. He took an awkward shuffle step. The baseball squirted out of his glove, slid down his forearm, and fell to the ground. Though he alertly pounced on the ball and heaved it back to the infield, two of the three Yankee runners crossed home plate.

Section 51 erupted—no one louder than that noisy little fellow in row F. Thrusting his arms skyward in triumph and dancing a little jig, he bayed, "Nice catch, Baldelli!" Then he surprised his companion, who was speaking into her cell phone again, by grabbing her around the waist and giving her a long, slobbery kiss.

Turning his back to the infield, Baldelli looked about him in bewilderment until his eyes lit at last upon the shiny little object that lay in the grass. He scooped up the battery and gazed at it for a moment, holding it in his open palm. Then, suddenly, he sprinted off toward second base.

Baldelli's discovery appeared to hold little interest for the second-base umpire, who merely shrugged and began walking away. Baldelli, literally hopping mad now, bouncing up and down as if on a pogo stick, quickly overtook him. He thrust the battery in the umpire's face and pointed an accusing finger at section 51. The umpire shrugged again, pivoted about, and walked off in the opposite direction.

"Give it up, Baldelli!" yelled the man in row F. "You wouldn't have caught it anyway."

His powers of speech deserted him, though, when Billy, grabbing two fistfuls of Hawaiian shirt, lifted him off the ground, and held him suspended in the air. Billy's eyes were distended, his entire face contorted with rage.

Gently touching his arm, I pleaded, "Billy, let the man go."

"What are you doing to my boyfriend?" wailed the orange-haired woman, her eyes ringed like a raccoon's, awash in tears and bleeding mascara.

Billy answered with a nerve-jarring laugh—then released his grip on the other man's shirt. The little man's face had turned a sickly white. His legs had gone wobbly and only the frantic embrace of the orange-haired woman held him upright.

Scuttling past me into the aisle, Billy bolted up the steps and through the entryway on the landing above. Half-heartedly, I pursued him into the stadium's vast concrete underbelly. I saw him dash around a bend, and then I lost him.

I would have to think of a new lead. Billy Kapanka, I would inform the readers of the Herald, could not be located.

EVICTION

It happens every time. I lie down in the on-call room at some ungodly hour and close my eyes, thinking that maybe, just maybe, I'll get some sleep for once, and there goes my beeper. I splash some water on my face and slog down the corridor to the emergency room, where, in the nineteenth or twentieth hour of my second overnight call of the week, I find Willie Wilkins, who has come for his usual treatment: three hots and a cot. A couple of years ago, while sleepwalking through the final months of my neurology residency, I had what I regarded at the time as an inspiration: I would be happier in a field in which I could actually do somebody some good. I decided to do a second residency, this time in psychiatry. I did not envision Willie Wilkins in the ER in the middle of the night. A lot of things have turned out differently than I expected.

"What is it this time, Willie?"

A haggard-looking man in his mid-fifties, he responds with a yawn. He sits atop the examining table, his legs hanging over the side, his torso slumped forward, his head down and his hands resting in his lap. Around him wafts the reek of vagrancy: a noxious compound of urine, alcohol, and perspiration. Snow, slush, and mud coat his outer garments—a black sweatshirt, torn at the right elbow, and blue jeans that do not quite reach his ankles—as well as the battered running shoes that he wears without socks. A few snowflakes still adhere to his black stocking cap.

"Doc, I be feeling suicidal," he murmurs, his consonants all blurring together.

"Suicidal? Again?"

"I hear voices. They telling me to hurt myself."

The harshness of my laughter—a rather unfortunate countertransference reaction, unlikely to facilitate an effective therapeutic alliance—surprises me, though the cause is no mystery. One grows to despise patients whom one cannot help.

"Voices telling you to hurt yourself. They don't seem to have much power to persuade, do they?" I massage my right cheekbone, which feels as though someone is slowly driving a railroad spike through it.

The patient lifts his head but still does not meet my gaze directly, staring at some undefined spot behind my right shoulder. He has a long, narrow face, lined with several days' worth of salt-and-pepper stubble, and a complexion that in both hue and texture resembles a baseball glove left out in the rain. His nose is scraped raw at the tip. Dried blood cakes his chin, and a large, purplish welt protrudes from his left cheekbone.

A sudden chirping noise makes me start. From the right side pocket of my lab coat, I draw out my beeper. The display is blank, but the chirping does not abate. I pat myself all over until I locate my cell phone in the front pocket of my shirt.

Only one person would try to phone me in the middle of the night when I'm on call: my soon-to-be-ex-wife, Sue. Like Willie—like most people who don't have to work for a living—she is careless with time, her own and that of other people.

"David's been throwing up all night," she tells me, her voice shrill, accusatory. In the background, I hear the wailing of my son, who turned two last week. "He has a hundred and two temperature."

"Since when?"

"Since Monday."

"Jesus Christ! Have you taken him to see Dr. Roth?"

"No."

"Why not? Are you waiting for him to have a seizure?"

Willie eyes me intently, his calculated unresponsiveness overcome by his curiosity. Pivoting my stool on its rollers, I turn my back to him but still feel his gaze. Through the earpiece, I hear more cries from David and the rapid nasal breathing from Sue that usually presages an explosion.

Springing from the stool, I rush out of the examining room and into the empty hallway, the cell phone still pressed against my right ear and cheekbone.

"Is he tugging at his ear?" I ask.

"No."

"It's probably a virus. But get him seen tomorrow."

"I gave him a dropper full of Tylenol at around eleven," she says in a tone of cold fury. "Can I give him some more now?"

I raise my arm to check my watch and find that my wrist is bare. I do not recall having removed the watch. One night last week I became quite frantic, thinking I had lost my beeper, until I realized that I was holding it in my hand.

"What time is it now?"

"It's almost 3:30."

"Yes, you can give him another dose."

"Is that what you would do?"

"He hasn't gotten sick when I've had him. It's funny how when we go to court you call me a negligent father, but when David's sick you call me up and ask me what to do."

"Asshole!" she shouts and hangs up.

I suppose I had that coming. For weeks now, I have found myself unable even to attempt civility toward her.

I could have settled this nightmare months ago. The lawyers had worked out an agreement that, though painful financially, would have allowed me joint legal custody and ample time with David. At the last minute, though, her attorneys insisted on inserting a clause that they must have known I would not accept, which called for hyphenating David's name. Thereafter, he would have been David Pearlhammer-Wright and ultimately, if the Pearlhammers had their way, David Pearlhammer. In the middle of the settlement conference, I walked out. So Sue and I, who had a June wedding, now have a June trial date.

It shames me now to think of how easily I allowed myself to be seduced into marriage—not so much by Sue as by her father. I was a med student, paying my own way through school and drowning in debt, celibate most of the time, subsisting on Ramen noodle soups and four hours of sleep each night. Jeffrey Pearlhammer wooed me with golf, sailing trips on Long Island Sound, four-star restaurants, parties, cruises to Alaska and Jamaica. One day, Sue and I discussed the possibility of my moving in with her. Within a week, Jeffrey Pearlhammer had bought us a condo in the same development as the one he'd bought for Sue's sister and brother-in-law— and about three miles from his own residence. Jeffrey Pearlhammer bought his daughter a husband; when she grew tired of the husband, Jeffrey Pearlhammer bought her lawyers, private investigators, and expert witnesses. But he will not buy my son.

Returning to examining room, I find Willie reclining on the table.

"So, you've been hearing voices. For how long?"

His body tenses. As I settle onto my stool again, he slowly raises himself. "I don't know, doc," he says between yawns. "Two days, maybe three."

"Did something happen that caused the voices to start?"

"They just start."

"What do they sound like, these voices? Are they loud? Soft? Male? Female? Do you hear them all the time? Just sometimes? Are they inside your head or outside?"

He wipes his runny nose with his sleeve.

"They just voices. They telling me to hurt myself."

"Have you been drinking, Willie?"

"Ain't had nothing to drink in two days, doc. Ain't got no money.

I be wanting to crawl out of my skin."

"Yeah, I know the feeling."

Sliding the stool backwards, the rollers groaning against the floor tiles, I reach for the overstuffed blue loose-leaf binder that I had laid upon the counter beside the sink when I first entered the room, and I begin to flip through the pages. The binder contains the history we have compiled on Willie, a sorry tale of drunkenness, drug use, petty crimes, arrests, beatings, stabbings, a gunshot wound or two, homelessness, psychiatric hospitalizations, illegitimate offspring scattered to the winds—the usual North Philly woes. Previous diagnoses have included antisocial personality disorder, bipolar I, bipolar II, major depression, all with comorbid alcoholism. One could make a good case for any or all of them. Willie is the oldest of the three-hots-and-a-cot cohort that we see regularly. Most don't live as long as he has.

At some point in his wanderings, long before I began my residency here, Willie made the fortuitous discovery that the law obliges us to admit suicidal or homicidal patients. He lives, on and off, with a woman named Loretta Hayes and her two daughters. Every so often, Loretta grows tired of the sight of his drunken carcass lying around the apartment, so she throws him out, and he seeks refuge in the psych ward. The voice in his head that drives him here belongs to her.

"The last time you were in here, Willie, you told me you wanted to quit drinking. I gave you a referral to the day program. Why didn't you ever go?"

He sighs, shakes his head, and eyes me expectantly, as though waiting for me to provide the answer.

Instead, I run him through the Mini-Mental State Exam, and he brightens immediately, for he knows this drill well: What day is today? What month are we in? What year? What city? What state? What country? Who's the President of the United States?

The MMSE tests for disorientation. A depressed or suicidal patient could answer the questions correctly, but his psychomotor symptoms—the slowing of speech and cognition—would not vanish in a heartbeat, as Willie's have.

"Now, I want you to start from a hundred and count back by sevens."

Barely do I finish the sentence, before he begins: "Ninety-three, eighty-six, seventy-nine, seventy-two, sixty-five...."

"That's better than I could do. Get the hell out of here, you faker."

He looks confused. He thought he had done well. "But, doc, I'm homicidal, too. The voices....If you send me back out, I might do something bad."

I cannot suppress another laugh.

"Willie, I've seen homicidal people in here. You are not one of them."

My cell phone sounds again, and I feel a sudden stab of pain above my right eyebrow. I ignore the summons, but after a moment's pause, the sound begins anew.

"Yes?" I hiss into the phone.

"We need to talk about next weekend."

In the background, I can still hear David's cries. "I can't now. I'm on call. I'm with a patient. Goodbye."

I shove the phone back into my pocket. Almost immediately the thing begins to twitter again. A true hatred contains a powerful element of lust. Why else would she keep calling, and why else would I keep answering? Over the last year-and-half before the separation, Sue and I rarely had sex, but those few couplings had a frenzied, even a violent quality.

"Don't you ever hang up on me!" she screams. Pearlhammers, unaccustomed to such treatment, do not react well to it.

"I'm with a patient. Are you trying to get me fired and make my career go down the toilet? Your lawyer won't like that. No future earnings to bleed from me."

I hang up on her again. In another second, my head will explode.

"Sounds like you got woman trouble, doc," says Willie, with, it seems to me, a glint of malice in his eyes. "You need to get a black people's divorce."

"A black people's divorce?"

"You walk out the door, and you divorced."

Through gritted teeth, I answer, "I see."

Needing a moment to compose myself, I leave Willie in the examining room and walk through the ER and down the corridor toward the hospital entrance. Just inside the sliding glass doors sits the security desk, manned on this night by Isaiah Grant, a big man, a very dark-skinned African American with a flattened nose and a hook-like scar on his right cheek. But for a slight paunch, he looks every inch the All City middle linebacker that he was in his senior year of high school. Isaiah's forbidding appearance, which serves him well in his work, is a bit deceiving, though. I suspect that his football career never got any farther because he lacked the requisite meanness. He has four young children, and between his real job as a policeman and his moonlighting here, he probably works more hours every week than I do and handles far nastier situations with far greater equanimity.

I sit down on the corner of the desk.

"Isaiah, you're falling down on the job. You let Willie Wilkins in again."

His basso profundo laugh echoes through the corridor. "I can't keep him out, doc, but I'll be happy to throw his ass out if he's making trouble. Just give me the word."

Gazing through the glass at the swirling snow, I answer, "I haven't decided yet." I have two beds open on the fifth floor, but with four more hours of call to get through, I may yet need them for real emergencies.

"Looks bad out there," I say.

"They saying we might have six inches on the ground by morning."

"I hate the thought of throwing a man out into that. Even Willie Wilkins."

Isaiah frowns and shakes his head. "Willie made his own bed. Now he got to lie in it."

Despite his genial nature, Isaiah has little patience with the three-hots-and-a-cot crowd and seems to harbor a particular animus toward Willie.

"My old man would have thrown him out in a second," I say. "He made his living by evicting people. I worked for him during my summer and winter vacations when I was in school. Usually, the people were gone by the time we came for the furniture. Some of them seemed relieved to have the whole ordeal over with. But there were others..."

There were others, such as the wife of the plastic surgeon who, unbeknownst to her, had made a habit of blowing the mortgage each month in Atlantic City. When we came to evict her, the husband already having flown the coop weeks before, she raged, screamed, and cursed at us, until my father, a man not known for his delicate feelings, pleaded, "Lady, we're human beings." The woman ceased her shouting, cocked her head to one side, as though mulling over his words—and spit in his face.

She was not the worst. Others, undeterred by our unlisted telephone number and use of aliases on the job, called at four A.M. to threaten us with disfigurement, death and eternal damnation. Somebody uprooted a flowerbed in our front yard, spelled out an obscenity on the lawn with weed killer, and cut our garden hose into pieces. Someone else slashed the tires on my father's pick-up and shattered the windshield with a cinderblock. One morning we found our dog hanging by his leash from a tree in the back yard, after which my father brought home a Doberman and began to keep his forty-five beside him on the night table while he slept. A man pointed a shotgun at my face as I approached his house. He may or may not have been the one who fired a shell through our living room window one night a few weeks later.

In my senior year of college, I decided I'd had enough of evicting people. When the dorms closed for winter break, I remained on the campus. On mild nights, I wrapped myself in blankets and slept in my car—a twelve-year-old Ford Escort with a rusting body, a Hefty bag where the passenger-side rear window should have been, and no front grill. When the weather got colder, I slept on an inflatable mattress on the floor in lecture halls or on landings in stairwells, showering and changing in the gym. I hid from the janitors and avoided my acquaintances. My father called me an ingrate, perhaps with some justification. His evictions, as he never tired of point out, were paying for my fancy college education.

"He wasn't a bad man," I tell Isaiah. "But pity wasn't a part of his make-up. Or the world had wrung it out of him. The last thing he did on this earth was to throw some guy's easy chair out on the sidewalk. Then he burst an aneurysm and keeled over and died." Suddenly, I feel embarrassed, and I begin to fiddle with my beeper.

"You look like hell, doc. You need to get some sleep." Isaiah's sorrowful expression belies the slightly strained jocularity in his voice.

"I wish I felt half as good as I look."

In the john I remove my lab coat and douse my face and, inadvertently, my hair and the front of my shirt, with water. A glance at the mirror bears out Isaiah's assessment: I do look like hell. One might think I have worn these hospital greens for a week, with all their creases and folds. My face is doughy, my eyes, red and puffy, with dark circles beneath. My mouth hangs open, fish-like. Tufts of whiskers sprout from the places that I missed while shaving. Each day my bangs and my temples grow grayer. Each day I look more like my father.

The cell phone twitters again. I turn the thing off. At least I will not have to hear Sue's voice again tonight. The issue that she wishes to discuss with me at four in the morning when I'm on call and David is ill concerns the christening of her nephew, scheduled to take place nine days from now in Greenwich, Connecticut. She wants permission to take David, but I have a restraining order in place to keep her from transporting him out of Pennsylvania. She dragged him back to her parents' house in Greenwich the first time we separated. It happened right around the time he learned to turn himself over in his crib. I came home to find a note and didn't see David again for three months. The second time we separated, I moved out, but I made sure to have the order in place first.

Sue never wanted to come to Philadelphia and never forgave me for accepting a residency position here rather than the one I could have taken in Connecticut. But in my second year of marriage, I had already come to the realization that I needed to put some distance between the Pearlhammers and myself.

Halfway up the corridor, I switch the cell phone back on and scroll to Sue's number. The kid has had a temperature of 102 for three days. She should take him to the emergency room tonight. But I decide not to call her. She'd do more damage by dragging David out into the snow now than by doing nothing. Morning will come soon enough. Kids can withstand high fevers, I tell myself. I'm overreacting.

When I reenter the examining room, I find Willie lying on his back, snoring away.

"Hey, what the hell is this?" I shout. "You think this is a God-damn hotel?"

Slowly—so very, very slowly—he pushes himself back up into a sitting position, muttering under his breath all the while. I settle myself on my stool once more and gamely try to assume a professional demeanor, less, perhaps, out of regard for Willie than to show myself that I still can, despite him, and despite Sue, and despite my fatigue and disgust.

"Look, Willie, I would like to help you if I could, but, frankly, I have no idea how anymore. If you're not willing to help yourself, there's very little I can do. We have a limited number of beds, and we need them for people who are really sick."

No reply. Professionalism quickly yields again to pique. "You can't come running here every time Loretta throws you out."

His head jerks forward, and he glowers, his eyes narrowed, his nostrils flaring.

"Shit! That bitch don't throw me out. Nobody throw Willie Wilkins out. Willie Wilkins comes and goes when he pleases. I'll go back there and beat her ass in a minute."

"Did you hit her, Willie?"

"I didn't hit her. I just push her off me. She be trying to hit me with a bottle."

"You did hit her, didn't you?"

Sheepishly, Willie lowers his eyes.

"In front of the kids?"

"Wasn't no more than a push."

"Were the kids there, Willie?"

The cell phone startles me once more. I hit "ignore." I should switch it off again. My hands begin to tingle, and I feel a sudden light-headedness.

"Why did she try to hit you with a bottle?"

I can think of a hundred reasons, but Willie only shakes his head.

Again the cell phone. I try to press "ignore" again, but my twitchy thumb cannot find the right button. Over the noise, I shout again, "Why did she try to hit you with a bottle?" and wait for an answer that does not come. I should turn the damn phone off again. But of course I do not, and when it sounds again for the third time within a minute, I answer.

"Are you going to let me take David up to Greenwich next weekend? I need to know now." David, at least, must have fallen asleep, for I no longer hear him. Sue's voice has a brittle edge. At any moment she might begin throwing knick-knacks around her bedroom and yanking hairs from her scalp. I had regarded the latter as a particularly unpleasant little quirk, until I discovered that the DSM-IV had a name for it: trichotillomania.

"The kid is sick. You ought to be worrying about getting him to a doctor, not about dragging him up to Connecticut so Mr. and Mrs. Pearlhammer can show all their friends their little trophy grandson."

Willie, smirking, quickly turns his head when I look up at him. I should hang up or leave the room again but can summon neither the will to do the former nor the strength for the latter, so, toad-like, I remain perched on my stool.

"You leave my family out of this."

"I wish we had, from day one."

"Are you going to let me take him?"

"No, I'm not. I'm not giving up any more of my time with him. Next weekend was to be a make-up for the visitation you decided to cancel three weeks ago."

"It was dangerous. There was ice on the roads."

"It was fifty degrees out. There was no ice on the roads."

"I'm his mother. I have to think of his safety."

"He's safer with me than he is with you."

"I acted within my rights as the custodial parent."

"You violated the visitation order."

"Are you going to give me permission?"

"No."

"Then I'll take him anyway, with or without your permission."

Willie grins, no longer troubling himself to conceal his Schadenfreude. Damn him, and damn her, and damn this life!

"You'll take him without my permission? You think the law doesn't apply to Pearlhammers? If you so much as take him one foot over the state line, I will have you charged with kidnapping. Do you hear me? I will have you charged with kidnapping!"

"Asshole!"

I wind up and fling the cell phone. It smacks against the wall and breaks apart. A piece of the casing ricochets back at me, narrowly missing my left eye. Light splinters; floor tiles stretch and bend. I shake my head from side to side, close my eyes, and breathe deeply.

"Willie," I say, but then stop. I can no longer remember what I wanted to ask him. My eyes are tearing.

He sits wide-eyed and ramrod straight, his hands gripping the edge of the examining table. "That ain't right, doc, what she doing to you. Keep you from seeing your kid. That ain't right."

The one thing I cannot abide from Willie is pity. I feel a burning in my esophagus, followed by a hot, bitter, faintly metallic taste. Fighting back the urge to vomit, I wait, without daring to breathe, for the episode to pass, then reach for the wall phone and page Isaiah. Later, when I have had a good night's sleep, I might even convince myself that I have acted not out of exhaustion and spite but have made a sound medical decision based upon my best clinical judgment, in accordance with established practice guidelines and ethical standards, hospital policy, mental health law, etc., etc.

Barely have I put the receiver down when Isaiah's massive form appears in the doorway. With his jaw set and his eyes narrowed, he appears uncharacteristically grim. Isaiah and I do not require words, just a look and a nod. He grabs Willie's wrist with one hand, a handful of sweatshirt with the other, and yanks him off the examining table. Keeping Willie at arm's length as though fearing contamination, Isaiah swiftly steers him toward the door. Willie gazes at me beseechingly. I avert my eyes.

SOMETHING SMALL

The mutton, the kidneys, and the goat ribs had all been eaten long ago, but the coals in the grills still sputtered and hissed, and the smoke spiraled toward the sapphire sky. A score of children and a few quite tame German shepherds, all yelping with delight, gamboled about an expansive yard bounded by white stone walls lined with crimson bougainvillea. Less energetic, the adults settled into lawn chairs beneath the shade of two large jacaranda trees that were in full purple bloom and formed two circles, segregated by sex. The women ate chocolate cake and ice cream and talked of weddings and baptisms, of Christine Kuria's engagement to John Kamau, and Mary and Patrick Karanja's acrimonious divorce. The men, swigging from bottles of Tusker beer, spoke of politics, business, legal affairs, and the murky places where the three intersected.

Maina Waithaka, the host, crowed about how he had prevailed in a lawsuit against an estranged business partner. Tall and lithe, Maina had the build and the face—long, narrow, bony, and dusky, with fierce black eyes—of a Masai warrior but the dress and attitude of the prosperous Kikuyu that he was. Clad in charcoal trousers and a slate-blue shirt with black stripes that was crisply pressed but open at the collar, he sprawled lazily in his chair, grinning with satisfaction as he recounted the tale. "Luckily for me," he said, "the judge assigned to the case was Humphrey Wainaina, Dad's old golfing buddy. Well, I just had to invite Humphrey out to Windsor to play a round or two for old time's sake. It was the polite thing to do, after all. I told him if he beat me, I would cater his daughter's wedding at no cost to him. I let him win, of course. It cost me a small fortune, but it was well worth it. It's the price of doing business in Kenya. If I had lost that lawsuit, I would have been ruined."

"Another triumph for our justice system," huffed Mwangi Wacira.

"You don't like my story, Kabiro? Maybe you'd like to tell your own. The one about how they stole your shoe shop downtown."

Mwangi scowled. "It's something I'd prefer to forget. And I'm sure everyone here has heard about it by now."

He was a short, thickset, very dark man—darker even than Maina, who had christened him Kabiro, or "Little Soot." Like soot, the soubriquet, which Mwangi despised, had stuck. He wore a brown and white flannel shirt with a frayed collar, and his right knee showed through a horizontal gash in his baggy navy-blue trousers. With his cloudy, puffy eyes, his bald crown, and hair turning to gray at the temples, he looked much older than his thirty-four years.

"Not everyone. Paul hasn't heard the story. I don't think Stephen has either."

Eagerly, the men leaned forward in their chairs, but Mwangi did not speak.

It was Maina who broke the uneasy silence. "It happened when Moi was still in charge. Some KANU MP, one of Moi's cronies, came along with a phony deed, an eviction order, and a bunch of goons and stole the building right out from under the landlord. They ransacked Kabiro's shop, chased him and all the other tenants out, and then changed the locks. The landlord went to court and got an order from the judge telling Moi's friend to let the tenants back in and vacate the premises. All well and good, except that the landlord couldn't get the police to enforce the court order. They still haven't, have they, Kabiro?"

"No."

Rising from his chair, a tad unsteadily, the spidery Paul Waihenya proclaimed, to a chorus of laughter, "We've created a new species here in Kenya: Homo corruptus." He and Maina clinked beer bottles.

Mwangi snorted in disgust.

"Kabiro doesn't like our jokes. He's an honest man," said Maina.

"As honest as most," Mwangi answered coldly. "And more than some people here."

The laughter suddenly ceased.

"An honest man. The only honest man in all of Kenya. But our honest Kabiro has three mouths to feed and another on the way. Even working two jobs, it's a stretch to make ends meet—without a little chai on the side. I bet even honest Kabiro knows how to work the tourists at the airport. He does a little favor here, turns a blind eye there. And when the grateful traveler slips him something small, he doesn't turn it down."

"You'd lose your bet," Mwangi answered. Rising abruptly, he strode off toward the women's circle.

"Muthoni," he whispered to his wife, "we need to be on our way soon. I have to go to work."

Muthoni nodded. A petite woman, eight months pregnant, with a frame that appeared barely able to support her protruding belly, she had high cheekbones, a chin that came to a point, and a close-cropped, masculine haircut that accentuated the angularity of her features. She had the haggard look of one who had not slept the night before. Upon her lap sat plump little Kui, teary-eyed and sobbing, her pink party dress stained with grass and dirt. Muthoni was dabbing at the torn and bloody skin of Kui's right elbow with a wet handkerchief.

Kneeling before the child, Mwangi asked, "What happened, my little angel? Did a grasshopper trip you?"

"I falled down," answered the three-year-old sadly.

"You falled down? Well, it's a good thing you didn't fall up."

Hoisting the girl high into the air, he whirled her about. In a moment, she had forgotten all about her recent misfortune and was laughing and shrieking with joy.

Maina Waithaka then escorted Mwangi, Muthoni, and little Kui around to the front of the house, a massive gray stone structure arrayed with pilasters, balconies, turrets, and heavy russet doors with black iron handles and knockers. "You know I like to kid you, Kabiro," said Maina, draping his arm over Mwangi's shoulders. "But I don't mean anything by it. We can kid one another because we're family."

Maina, who sometimes suffered from sudden attacks of sentimentality when drunk, now launched into a long, disjointed soliloquy on the joys of family life, a topic on which he had acquired much firsthand knowledge, having sired three children by his wife and three more by his mistress. "You're a lucky man, Kabiro," he said. "You have a wonderful wife and such a beautiful little girl." Still hugging the squirming Mwangi to his side, he began to weep.

The watchman, who, upon seeing the party approaching, had sprung from his stool at the bottom of the driveway and opened the front gate, discreetly averted his eyes.

≈≈

The little blue Peugeot, a holdover from Mwangi's more prosperous days as a shoe shop proprietor, stalled twice during the drive back to Nairobi. The second time, it happened at the entrance to a roundabout, and when Mwangi tried to start the car again, the engine refused to turn over. He banged his fist against the steering wheel and flung open the door. With dozens of suddenly immobilized cars, trucks, and matatus—the ubiquitous passenger vans—hooting at him in rage, he searched frantically under the Peugeot's hood. He jiggled and yanked at the ignition wires, finally fastening a particularly recalcitrant one in place with the masking tape that he kept in his glove compartment.

Doused with sweat and coughing furiously, his nostrils and throat scalded by exhaust fumes, his eyes red and tearing, he reentered the Peugeot. He crossed himself before turning the ignition key.

This time, the car started, and he let out a deep, prolonged sigh of gratitude and relief.

Both his gratitude and his relief proved short-lived, though, for, whenever he had to bring the Peugeot to a stop, the feeble, arrhythmic idling of the engine caused his hands to tighten involuntarily around the steering wheel. The fainter the sound of the motor grew, the faster his pulse raced.

"I need new ignition wires," he muttered, "but that's the least of it. The engine is burning oil. It won't last much longer. We can't afford another car now. When this one goes, we'll be without. What then? Will we ride to the delivery room in a matatu?"

"Don't worry, Mwangi. God will provide. He always does."

"He provides heartache."

Mwangi downshifted into second gear as the gray, bunker-like three-story edifice that he called home came into view. A concrete wall, topped with jagged shards of broken glass, fronted the building. Mwangi pulled up before the iron gate and sounded his horn. He sounded it three more times before the gate finally swung open. The attendant, a gaunt young man, dressed bizarrely for such a warm day in a long white cloth coat and a white wool cap, snapped to attention and saluted—a show of respect belied by his mocking grin.

Mwangi carried the now sleeping Kui up the three flights to the family flat. Entering first, Muthoni flicked the light switch. The tiny living room, its dingy off-white walls adorned only with a crucifix and outsized portraits of Jomo Kenyatta and the late Pope John Paul II, remained swathed in gloom.

"Did you pay the electric bill?" asked Mwangi, crossly.

"I paid it on Friday, Mwangi. I had to wait until you got your check. The power must be out again."

"If we don't pay the bill, we have no electricity. And if we pay the bill, we have no electricity. It makes no difference." He laughed mirthlessly. "You should have married someone like your cousin. Someone who could have given you a better life than this."

Muthoni gently stroked the back of his neck. "I would never have wanted to marry a man like Maina Waithaka. He's a crook. You're a good and decent man. You're worth ten Maina Waithakas. He knows it, too. That's why he makes fun of you."

"He laughs at me because I'm poor. The whole world laughs at you when you're poor."

"We're not poor, Mwangi. We have a roof over our heads. We live in a secure building. We have a car. So many people in Kenya don't have what we have."

"What a country," he murmured.

Gently, Mwangi laid Kui down in her bed alongside her furry, pop-eyed Elmo doll—a hand-me-down from one of Maina's girls. Removing the child's shoes, he covered her and Elmo with her blanket, and kissed her forehead.

As he stepped into the bathtub for his shower, he opened the frosted glass window to allow in the day's fading light. He gazed downward upon a rutted street where battered cars and matatus, blasting their horns and churning out great black thunderheads from their exhaust pipes, threaded their way among throngs of pedestrians shopping for produce, meats, and secondhand clothes at the make-shift plywood stalls that lined the curb. The vehicles, the shoppers, the merchants, the stalls—all looked as though covered in grime. Farther off, hundreds of wind-tossed blue plastic grocery bags skittered about a weedy field strewn with broken glass.

Lukewarm one moment and freezing the next, the water trickled feebly from the showerhead. Mwangi, shivering, threw the soap aside, having managed to lather only his upper body, and began to rinse himself off as best he could. Reaching for his towel, he slipped, and only a desperate grab at the towel rack saved him from falling. The room began to spin, and he closed his eyes and gripped the metal bar tightly with both hands.

Like Kui, Muthoni had fallen asleep. For a moment, Mwangi, still a bit lightheaded, flirted with the idea of calling out sick and crawling into bed beside her. Today, Sunday, was his day of rest, when he worked only in the evening. Tomorrow—and countless more tomorrows—would bring fourteen hours of toil, the day spent at a downtown Barclay's branch, where he labored as a teller, handling other people's money, and the evening at the airport. It seemed to him that he lived only to work—to work without end and without reward, save the ability to sustain himself so that he could work some more. At thirty-four, he felt utterly wrung out.

Necessity, though, kept him upright. He groped in the closet for his uniform and dressed by the half-light of the bedroom window. Bending low over the bed, he kissed Muthoni on the cheek

She stirred, yawned, and abruptly sat up. "Oh, Mwangi, your dinner," she cried in alarm. "I forgot. I'm so sorry."

He took hold of her hands. "Rest, Muthoni. Don't worry about me. I ate so much at Maina's party that I couldn't possibly eat anymore."

Cocking her head to one side, she eyed him skeptically.

He kissed her again, this time on the mouth, and stroked her hair. "Rest, my dear. I'm fine."

Again, Mwangi crossed himself before starting the Peugeot. The engine backfired and sputtered but, mercifully, did not cut off. This time, two beeps sufficed to rouse the attendant, who had retreated into his booth beside the front gate. As he emerged, still grinning, he snapped off another salute.

≈≈

London-bound flight 1109, which ought to have departed an hour before, had yet to begin boarding. For the third time in the last week, the terminal's ventilation system had failed, and even as the temperature outside had plummeted, the heat of the day had lingered on within the building. Through the dim, close corridors, a line of sweaty, grumbling travelers slowly snaked its way toward the metal detectors at the threshold of the departure lounge.

Mwangi, stationed just inside the lounge, behind one of the metal detectors, wiped his brow with his sleeve, took a glance over his shoulder at the digital clock above the information desk, and frowned. His feet ached, his head and limbs felt as heavy as if he were standing on Saturn, and he had nearly four-and-a-half hours remaining on his shift.

Suddenly, the metal detector flashed red and shrieked with rage. A traveler had carelessly attempted to pass through while composing a message on his BlackBerry. The man's second attempt, sans Black-Berry, proved no more successful than the first. This metal detector, Mwangi knew from long experience, was not the forgiving sort.

"Oh, bloody hell!" the man cried, looking thoroughly aggrieved. A fleshy Englishman of indeterminate age, he had fat, sausage-like fingers with neatly trimmed, glossy nails, a round face with a pinkish complexion, and light-brown hair that grew ever more sparsely as it approached his forehead. He wore a black suit and a red tie with a rectangular gold-weave tie clip. "I already went through one metal detector after I checked in," he complained to no one in particular. "Why do we have to go through another one here?"

"Please step this way, sir," said Mwangi, picking up an electric wand from the table beside him. "Open your jacket, please. Arms out, feet apart. Thank you."

Swiftly, he traced the contours of the Englishman's body with the wand. As the tip of the device grazed the man's right hip, there came the telltale chirping. Setting the wand down on the table again, Mwangi began to frisk him.

"Oh, please. Do I look like a terrorist?"

"I wouldn't know, sir."

"It's not enough that I've been waiting in this damn queue for nearly an hour."

"So has everyone else, sir."

"Well, we wouldn't have to if you knew how to organize things. I do business on four continents. This is one of the worst airports I have to fly through. It's hot. It's dirty. It's chaotic. It's an absolute hell-hole." As he spoke, the Englishman's face darkened until it matched the hue of his tie. Beads of perspiration glistened on his forehead.

"I'm very sorry that our airport does not meet your high standards, sir. May I see what's in your pocket, please?"

"It's my wallet. What do you think I have in my pocket?"

"May I see it, please?"

The Englishman drew out his wallet and angrily shoved it at Mwangi. A traveler's wallet, made of soft, smooth black leather, it had a leather-encased metal clasp for fastening to an inside jacket pocket or the top of one's trousers. The trouble, Mwangi realized at once, lay with this simple, functional, utterly benign clasp. Nevertheless, his curiosity got the best of him; he opened the wallet and peeked inside.

From his post behind a second metal detector, ten feet or so to Mwangi's right, the bald, hulking Daniel Njoroge observed the scene with keen interest. Not a subtle man, Daniel by now would have ushered the traveler into a nearby storeroom sometimes used for strip searches and likely have emerged shortly afterward several thousand shillings richer.

Thus far, Mwangi had resisted such temptations, but as he counted up the 1,000-, 500-, and 100-shilling notes he had pulled from the wallet, his heartbeat quickened. He felt a sudden, unwonted giddiness. From down the hallway, the door to the storeroom, hanging halfway open, beckoned him. Nearly half a minute passed before he could summon the willpower to avert his gaze. "Have you declared this currency, sir?" he asked the Englishman.

"What?"

"This is Kenyan currency. You can't simply take it out of the country. You're supposed to declare it at Customs."

"Well, it's a bit late for that, isn't it?"

"I could send you back there right now."

"You must be joking. If I have to go all the way back to Customs now, I'll miss my flight. For what? A handful of shillings I forgot to change? I doubt if there's even £200 worth. It's pocket money."

"Pocket money," Mwangi echoed softly, his eyes drawn again to the storeroom door. The Englishman's pocket money could provide a month's rent and groceries. But how would he explain the windfall to Muthoni, who, after seven years of marriage, still believed him to be a good and honest man and could not conceive that he might harbor the same desires as a Daniel Njoroge? Her illusions, her primary-school notions of right and wrong, fettered him and kept him poor. A sudden acidic eruption seared Mwangi's gullet, but as quickly as it had come on, his anger gave way to shame. He slipped the notes back into the wallet and was about to return it when the Englishman provoked him once more.

"I don't have time for this nonsense. Missing this flight is simply not an option. I have a meeting tomorrow morning in London that I absolutely have to attend."

"You should have thought of that before," Mwangi answered sourly.

A second man tripped off the metal detector. While the remaining guard at Mwangi's station employed the wand on this new unfortunate, the line came to a complete halt. The mutterings and wailings of the waiting travelers grew louder.

"Look," said the Englishman, lowering his voice almost to a whisper, "I made a mistake. I was running late, and I didn't think I had time to stop at the Forex. Of course, I travel enough that I should have known better. But there must be some reasonable way to resolve this situation without going through all the bureaucratic formalities. After all, we have some common interests here. You want to get the plane boarded and out of the gate. I need to get on board. That's far more important to me than the notes in that wallet." Smiling insinuatingly, he fiddled with his tie clip. "I'm sure we can find some, shall we say, mutually satisfactory solution."

"Ah, a mutually satisfactory solution. You mean a seat on the plane for you, in exchange for…?"

"Well, ah, perhaps, a, ah…" The Englishman hesitated a moment, tugging nervously at his sweat-stained collar.

"A little of your pocket money?" Mwangi's eyes narrowed and his nostrils flared. "That may be the way you're accustomed to doing business, sir. It's not the way we operate here. If you think our airports are hellholes, wait till you see our prisons." He slapped the wallet down upon the table.

The color drained from the Englishman's face. "Please, please," he pleaded. "I never meant to imply anything underhanded or illegal." He held his hands out in front of him as if to ward off such an evil thought.

Daniel Njoroge, unable to restrain himself any longer, deserted his post and came strutting over to Mwangi's, frowning gravely. "Is there a problem here?" he asked the Englishman. "Maybe I can be of help." To Mwangi, he whispered, "This Mzungu is ripe for the picking." His eyes were red and distended, and his hot, moist breath reeked of whiskey. Mwangi turned away in disgust.

Warily, the Englishman queried, "Are you this man's supervisor?" Daniel nodded.

"No, he isn't," said Mwangi.

The Englishman looked from one to the other in bewilderment.

"So, you have some undeclared currency with you," growled Daniel, stepping up close to the Englishman and glaring menacingly.

"Well, I…," the other stammered, retreating a step. "You see, I didn't know…"

"Ignorance of the law is not an excuse," Daniel interrupted. Edging his way in reverse toward the table, he reached back with his left arm, his fingertips groping for the wallet.

"It's nothing, Daniel," said Mwangi stiffly, as he snatched the wallet away. "A matter of a few shillings that the man forgot to change. Too small an amount to worry about. You should go back to your station. Your queue is stopped."

Daniel glowered at him with hatred, he responded in kind, and, for a moment, the two men stood rigid, chests inches apart, like boxers meeting at the center of the ring prior to the start of a match. Mwangi's partner, having finished his examination of the other passenger, slowly began to approach, then halted as Daniel pivoted about and retreated to his own post.

"Here you are, sir." His hand shaking with fury, Mwangi thrust the wallet back at its owner.

The Englishman's grip proved no more steady, and the exchange was nearly fumbled.

"Go ahead, and have a seat in the lounge."

"Thank you. Thank you," said the Englishman, but he stood frozen in place, still holding the wallet out in front of him.

"Go ahead, please," reiterated Mwangi in a choked, quavering voice, one particularly ill-suited for the delivery of an order by a man in uniform. "We have to get the queue moving again."

Still, he must have sounded sufficiently authoritative to the Englishman, who murmured another "thank you" and then fled to the farthest corner of the lounge.

Had ill luck departed with him? A rare respite followed, with three, four, five, six, seven passengers in succession passing undisturbed through the metal detector. Anger dulled to leaden fatigue. Mwangi took another peek at the clock and noted with dismay how little time had passed since he had last looked. Bowing his head, he covered his mouth with his hand to conceal a yawn.

Suddenly, the metal detector began to squawk again. He winced as though something had stung him.

THE RULE OF LAW

They swear to tell the truth, the whole truth, and nothing but the truth—and that's the first lie. I take it for granted that people will lie in court. But when they lie to you, and then your opponent starts waving bank statements from accounts you didn't know existed, and you want to go hide under the defense table . . . I bet nothing they told you in law school prepared you for that. Too bad your first case had to turn out this way. But it happens. We win some. We lose some. Speaking in my capacity as your mentor, I'd say you learned a valuable lesson today: it's not whether you win or lose that counts. It's the billable hours. What we do now is forget about today and get ready for the Schmidt case. That bad boy goes to trial next Tuesday.

Another pitcher? Ah, come on. It's good for you. It's good for your aura. It cleanses it. Alcohol is the best disinfectant I know. You need a disinfectant, when you swim in a sewer all day long. Otherwise, you'll go home reeking, and people will shun you.

Hey, Ms. Hi-My-Name-Is-Heather, can we get another pitcher over here? Thank you. Thank you. Hey, how would you like to see my copious briefs? No? It would be an experience you'd never forget.

Mm, she doesn't look half bad walking away, either. The way those little shorts ride up her ass. Put a seat belt on me.

Yeah, I'm very conscious of my aura these days. Have been ever since a case I had a couple of years ago. Angelino v. Ostara. Two litigants who had come crawling out of the shallow end of the gene pool.

Ostara. O-S-T-A-R-A. Her real name—I'm not making this up—was Sandra Crapps. But she didn't use that any more. She called it a badge of patriarchal oppression. Or something like that. My eyes tended to glaze over when she started ranting. Of course, she may have had a point. Poor woman. I'll represent her if she ever decides to sue her father. Imagine growing up with a name like that. It'll take a lot of damages to make her whole again.

Anyway, I was representing the former Ms. Crapps—another client who did her best to undo me. Only, unlike this clown we had today, she didn't quite succeed. She was not my type, exactly. I like 'em deep pocketed and docile, and she was neither. She was about five-and-a-half feet tall and must have weighed over 200 pounds. She showed up in my office wearing a kind of faux-Renaissance get up. Black hobnailed boots, a black velvet dress, really low cut, cleavage hanging out to here, rings, bracelets, amulets, a silver neck chain with a crescent moon charm that lodged between her boobs. Her hair—how can I describe it? Teased up the way it was, it looked kind of like a plumed helmet. It was red at the time, but it changed color whenever I saw her after that: black, brown, purple.

No, I didn't like her much. She didn't care for me, either. She gave me an earful that first session, about the system we serve—the "corrupt, adversarial, phallocentric so-called legal system that privileges rich white males and marginalizes women, the poor, and people of color."

I said, "Yeah? So?"

"The point I'm trying to make, Mr. Gierig . . . "

I sang to her: "'Them that's got shall get. Them that's not shall lose. So the Bible says. And it still is news.' Billie Holiday. Now, tell me something I don't know. Something that'll help me win you your case. The clock is running."

She didn't like that. She wasn't used to people cutting her off.

"It's easy enough for you to sneer, Mr. Gierig. But for those of us who don't have a voice . . . "

"Your voice is pretty loud."

"I was speaking metaphorically."

"You couldn't very well have been speaking literally, could you?"

She shot up out of her chair.

"I'm leaving."

"Suit yourself. I have all the business I can handle as it is."

She stayed, of course, because her father, that most patriarchal of patriarchs, had heard somewhere that I was a mean son of a bitch, and he was paying my retainer.

She presented me with a malpractice case of sorts. What, you ask, did she practice? Why, biofield therapeutic healing, of course. A biofield therapeutic healer is someone you take your aura to if it's out of alignment. She will balance it and cleanse it and probably wax it, too, for no extra charge.

Everyone has an aura, you see. You don't see? Well, you have one anyway. Yours is quite a nice one, actually. Almost pristine. I'd like to have an aura like yours. Maybe I did once. I don't know. It was a long time ago, if ever. Keep yours the way it is. If you can.

The ones in this place are not a pretty sight. See that nasty little hatchet face peeking out from behind the potted fern over there? It belongs to Sue Brown, who, reliable sources have told me, has been known to give selected male clients oral services above and beyond what they've contracted for, sometimes right in her office. It seems to work for her. She does things even our firm wouldn't do, like charging for messages she leaves on clients' answering machines—and nobody complains. Her aura's cloudy and foul smelling, full of little swimming things and littered with wadded up Kleenex. Then there's Judge Bowen over there across the room. He once had me spend a night in jail after I suggested during a sidebar that he might take the trouble to acquaint himself with the rules of evidence. You can sniff the brimstone even from here. And you see the old goat with the carpet on his head who's drinking alone? That's that ex-judge Cable, who used to fondle his female clerks. He was forced out finally, but not because of that. It was because of the one time he ever showed any mercy. There was this guy who was convicted of shooting his wife. Cable gave him an eighteen-month sentence. The guy had caught her in bed with another man. A very large mitigating circumstance in Cable's view. The rumor was he'd experienced a similar mitigating circumstance himself once. His aura is composed of drool and bile. You don't want to get too close to it. You don't want to get too close to any of them.

So you see, Ostara's practice involved some risks. When you're working with such toxic stuff, things can get a little dicey.

What happened was our Ostara went to the hospital to perform a healing ritual on a certain Mr. Ennis, who was the husband of one of her friends from her little Wiccan circle. Poor guy. Mr. Ennis had just had his appendix out. He was still groggy, had no idea what was going on. Didn't believe in any of this aura nonsense. But his wife sent Ostara up anyway, apparently figuring that in such a state, he wouldn't put up much resistance.

Ostara went to work and spent about forty-five minutes massaging Mr. Ennis's aura. He kept moaning that he wanted his painkillers, but the nurse said it wasn't time yet, and every time she came in, Ostara shooed her away.

Well, our plaintiff-to-be, another appendix case by the name of Anthony T. Angelino, or Tony A., as his friends knew him, lay in the next bed. He was a big, nasty-looking fellow. And I mean big. This guy made me look petite. Weighed about 320. He'd been arrested for soliciting a prostitute a few months before, and Sue Brown told me in chambers that they had to make a chain out of three sets of handcuffs to get his hands fastened behind his back. I bet even Sue wouldn't service him. His hair was receding. He had a jet-black goatee and a Bell's palsy that froze the right half of his face in a perpetual scowl. Well, he was lying there with—Ostara would testify in her deposition— his hand in his crotch, watching some old Baywatch rerun on the tube. A man after my own heart.

As she went on chanting her mumbo jumbo, he kept turning the sound up. She finally asked him, not very nicely, to shut the T.V. off because it was interfering with her ritual, and, anyway, this iconography of objectification was offending her. He answered by calling her a dyke and a cow and a pig and everything else on Old MacDonald's farm. And Ostara, no shrinking violet, gave back as good as she got.

The nurse, Ms. Bernice Thompkins, heard the shouting, and she came back in. She was about sixty, African American. One of those thousand-watt-smile, kill-you-with-kindness nurses. "Mr. Ennis, it's time for your medicine. Have we eaten anything today, Mr. Ennis? Oh, you can do better than that. Have we had a bowel movement yet? No, Mr. Ennis. It's good that you're feeling frisky today, but I don't think the doctor would want you to put your hand under my dress like that." But Ostara can blow out a thousand-watt smile in no time flat. Bernice and Ostara got into it, and Bernice, who had probably never had a harsh word for anyone in her life, told our new-age Florence Nightingale that she'd better get her fat white butt out of there pronto. This was a hospital, not a freak show. Well, Ostara huffed and puffed, and Bernice went stomping off to get security. Meanwhile, Ostara went on with her little song and dance. By this time, her patient was in tears.

Then the wheels began to turn in the head of Tony A. He was a clever one, all right. Well, at least he knew a thing or two about the legal system. In the last year alone, he'd been arrested for shoplifting and that solicitation business, and he would soon file for bankruptcy.

So Ostara got to the point in the ritual where she was bending down and making scooping motions—scooping off the negative energy from poor Mr. Ennis's aura. And according to Mr. Angelino, she didn't have the requisite lead container to hold all this toxic negative energy. She threw the stuff around the room indiscriminately.

Angelino began to yell: "Hey, whadda ya doin' to me with that negative energy? I was feeling better. Now, the pain is so bad, I can hardly breathe. I got a business. I got a family to support. You tryin' to ruin me? This is negligence. I'm being damaged here. I'm being damaged. Nurse!"

Bless his little black heart. It's people like him who buy me a new

Lexus every two years.

Back came Nurse Thompkins then, with two security guards, and they finally did drag Ostara, quite literally kicking and screaming, and her aura and her prodigious white ass out of the room, out of the building, and off the premises entirely.

So we had what to my knowledge was a first: a case of negligence resulting from the careless handling of negative energy scooped out of a patient's aura by a biofield therapeutic healer. Mr. Angelino was seeking $350,000 in damages. The negative energy, he claimed, had caused him to go bankrupt; caused his live-in girlfriend to leave him, taking her kid, to whom he'd become a surrogate father, with her; and caused him incalculable emotional distress.

Naturally, we went to court, instead of dropping them both out of an airplane as we should have. A case like that makes one long for the halcyon days of trial by ordeal. Of burning at the stake. Of drawing and quartering. Slashing the bastards up and pouring molten lead in the wounds.

We went to court even though Ostara had nothing, the sum total of her assets being about $50 in cash, a bunch of trinkets and crystals and a closet or two full of outlandish clothes and knee-high boots. She didn't own a T.V., didn't even drive. They weren't gonna milk her old man for a whole lot, either. Between his alimony and Ostara's shrink bills, he didn't have much left. I don't know what Angelino thought he would get by suing her. But it didn't matter. Sue Brown, who never met a possibility of a reasonable settlement that she didn't dismiss out of hand, had convinced him that he could win and win big.

We got Judge Carter, also known as "Cadaver," due to the physical resemblance. You'll run into him soon enough. You'll smell his aura. Whiskey and formaldehyde. He's emaciated, has a grayish complexion, a permanent dyspeptic grimace. Mostly bald on top, with a few tufts of hair of indeterminate color that he hasn't brushed since about 1972. He sits hunched over like a vulture, stares into space or out the window. Every time there's a recess, he slinks back into his chambers and takes a nip or three or four. Mean old bastard and totally unpredictable. You don't want to alienate him, especially if he's hung over. But if you're careful, you can get away with a lot, because half the time he has no idea what's going on.

Ostara showed up at court for opening statements with about half a dozen of her Wiccan friends, all as fat and round as she was, wearing leotards and berets and blouses billowing up like sails and dresses out to here. Her hair was auburn, but with a greenish tinge at the edges, and she wore that same black dress again, cut so low it barely covered her nipples. The hair I couldn't do anything about. Fortunately, the cleavage I could. I grabbed a purple shawl from one of her buddies and draped it around Ostara's shoulders.

"Now, we're ready for court," I said.

She, of course, tore the shawl off of her and threw it on the floor.

"I am not ashamed of my body."

"You would be, if you had any shame."

"That's it! I'm representing myself."

"Be my guest. But before you go in there, consider this. In five minutes you're going to go before a judge who, in a very real sense, holds your fate in his hands. Judges don't much care for people who go into court without an attorney. It shows a lack of respect. Most people who do that are off the wall and give everyone a great big pain in the ass. That's what Cadaver will assume about you. He also doesn't happen to like women very much—even less than he likes men and children and dogs. And he certainly doesn't like loud, obnoxious Wiccans who go into court with green hair and their tits hanging out. And you think Sue Brown will take it easy on you in the name of sisterhood? Guess again, sister."

One of the Wiccans piped up, "The goddess will be with Ostara."

I put my face right up against Ostara's. "I'm your goddess, you understand? All 280 pounds of me. I'm the only goddamn goddess that can intercede for you here. So if you wanna say a prayer, you better pray to me."

She hissed at me, "Your jacket looks like a rotten eggplant. You smell. You smell of sweat and nicotine. Don't you ever take a shower?"

She went on like that for a while. About the gap between my front teeth, my physique—she said I looked like a seedy William Howard Taft—and my presumed Nazi ancestry. Which was fine. Better she directed it at me in the hallway than at Sue Brown from the witness stand.

I knew it could be a long day when Cadaver came tottering in forty minutes late, already dead drunk, and it wasn't even 10:00 a.m.

Sue Brown did a creditable job with her opening statement. That nasty little tart can put on the righteous indignation as well as anyone. "My client has been . . . devastated." The little caesura thing she throws in there. "Devastated. He has seen his civil rights violated. He has seen the whole fabric of his life ripped apart. Because of the negligence of this woman."

Then came my turn. I talked for a while about how Mr. Angelino was something less than a saint. About how there might have been other causes for some of his misfortunes than Mr. Ennis's negative energy. About how, for instance, his girlfriend had had to drag herself and her five-year-old down to the city lockup at two in the morning to bail out her wayward Romeo after he'd gone and solicited an undercover police officer. Might that episode, rather the negative energy, have caused Ms. Ruiz to reevaluate her relationship with Mr. Angelino? Might such an incident have had a similar effect on any of the women of the jury?

Next, I went into this whole song and dance about how my client was not negligent but a careful and conscientious practitioner of a venerable healing art that predated Western medicine by hundreds if not thousands of years. Knowing the dangers of the negative energy, she had taken every possible precaution. She had opened the window, so the bad stuff could fly out—never mind that the temperature outside was below freezing, and all Mr. Ennis had on was that flimsy hospital gown with his ass hanging out the back, and the nurse said he was turning blue. And Ostara had opened the door wide for cross ventilation and turned on all the lights, because light and air help to neutralize negative energy.

I took a good look at the jury. It was the usual collection of the lame, the halt, the deaf, the blind, the drunk, the senile, and the terminally stupid. Having to choose between Sue Brown's tall tale and mine, between her sleazebag and my blowhard, they could just as easily go one way as the other. With those blank faces, I couldn't tell.

Then it hit me: I could turn Ostara's charlatanism to my advantage. The old rope-a-dope defense, with apologies to Muhammad Ali.

First, though, I'd get to play a little offense. I knew I could carve Angelino up like a Thanksgiving turkey if Cadaver would only let me. It was getting late by the time I got my shot at cross-examination, and Cadaver, impatient in the best of circumstances, had turned from gray to greenish because he hadn't had a drink since the lunch recess, and instead of his usual nasal whine—"Can we get on with this, puh-leeze?"—he had begun to snarl at us like a Doberman on a leash.

After Sue had taken Angelino through all his losses in direct examination, I started right in with the solicitation thing.

"Isn't it true that your arrest caused Ms. Ruiz to move out temporarily—well before the incident in the hospital room?"

"Yeah, but she was only gone for a few weeks, and then she came back. And we were getting along pretty good. Until that witch over there dumped her negative energy on me."

"My client," I objected, "is an adherent of the Wiccan faith, an ancient pagan religion that predates Christianity by many years. To call her a witch, as this man does, conjuring up images of Margaret Hamilton on a broomstick . . ."

"Oh, who cares?" Cadaver snapped at me. "Just get on with it, will you?"

So I did.

"Okay, so you reconciled with Ms. Ruiz, and you were getting along. I take it you were more careful after that when you went out soliciting."

"Objection!" yelled Sue.

We sat, and we waited, and we waited, and we waited, and Cadaver, who was staring at his clenched fist, said nothing, so I went on: "And isn't it true that the final breakup between you and Ms. Ruiz, which occurred about a month after the incident in the hospital, happened because she asked you to go to the pharmacy to fill her child's Ritalin prescription, and you told her, with your usual charm and tact, 'Hey, the little bastard was your mistake. You want medicine for him, you go get it yourself'?"

"Objection. Hearsay."

"Overruled."

"Hey, she was getting in my face."

"You don't like people getting in your face, do you?"

I got in his face—almost close enough for a kiss.

"No."

His complexion had turned pink, and his skin glistened with sweat. He began to tug at his moist collar, revealing the red crevice it had bored into his neck.

"There were creditors getting in your face then, too, correct?"

"They wouldn't leave me alone. I was getting calls at seven in the morning. Threatening letters every day."

"But that was going on even before you ever met Ostara, wasn't it?"

"Yeah, a little. But it got a lot worse after."

"And you blame my client for that?"

"She threw the negative energy on me."

"But isn't it true that of the $80,000 you ran up in debt prior to filing for bankruptcy, at least $35,000 was accrued in the last three months before you filed? Isn't it true that this three-month spree was quite intentional, that you figured you were getting, among other things. a new dining room set, a new stereo, and a water bed for free? That you had no intention of ever paying off these bills?"

More objections from Sue, which Cadaver overruled without explanation. He had gone into his automatic overrule mode.

"You had gotten used to the good life. You owned a Lexus and a Caddy, a condo in St. Pete. But all that would be gone—even if you were lucky enough to avoid jail. Fortunately, Ostara came into your life. The answer to your prayers."

"Objection"

"Overruled."

"Now, Mr. Angelino, you seem like a regular guy. A hard-headed guy. A shot-and-a-beer kind of guy like me. Isn't that right?"

"Yeah."

"Not the kind of guy who would be taken in by all this negative energy gobbledygook."

"Hey, I wasn't a straight 'A' student or nothing, but I got some common sense."

"Yeah. And so you put that common sense to work, didn't you? You're lying in your hospital bed, and you see this bat brain who calls herself a healer come in, and the dollar signs start flashing before your eyes . . ."

"Objection. Putting words in my client's mouth."

"Overruled."

"And knowing full well that this so-called negative energy, which you never believed in for a moment, had had no effect on you whatsoever . . ."

"Objection!"

"Overruled! Overruled! Overruled!

Sue slammed down her legal pad.

"Your honor, if you're not going to allow me to defend my client . . ."

"O-VER-RULED!"

She turned crimson, started hyperventilating. "Your honor, these proceedings are an affront to the rule of law! I have never seen anything like this in twenty years of practice!"

"Oh, shut up," wailed Cadaver, gritting his teeth and clutching at the knot of hair on his left temple. "You've never seen anything like this in twenty years? Please. There's nothing unusual going on here. It happens every day. You got a case that you should have laughed out of your office? Bring it before Carter. Tie up his courtroom for a week. He has nothing better to do. The jurors have nothing better to do. The taxpayers have nothing better to do with their money."

≈≈

I thought Sue might put Angelino back on the stand the next morning to try to rehabilitate him, but she probably wanted the jury to forget that he existed. She brought on the nurse instead, then the two security guards and the long suffering Mr. Ennis, before resting her case.

After lunch, I had my turn. Ostara strode confidently to the stand in her purple bloomers, with no inkling of what I had in store for her.

Rope-a-dope with a vengeance. I would not just lie back against the ropes and let Sue flail away at me. Hell, I'd do her punching for her.

"What qualifications does a biofield therapeutic healer need?"

"Empathy most of all. And a belief in the healing power of positive energy."

"What is this energy of which you speak? Is it something you can see? Can you measure it in volts?"

"It's something you can feel."

"It produces tactile sensations, then? Does it give you a shock?"

"You feel it in your inner being."

"Is this inner being a corporeal entity? An Ostara within an Ostara? How tall is it?"

Sue objected. She couldn't see where my examination was going.

"Where are you going with this, Mr. Gierig?" Cadaver growled.

"Well, it goes back to Mr. Angelino's testimony concerning the pain he claimed to have experienced when he realized Ostara was dumping the negative energy on him. If, in fact, these sensations could only have been experienced by his inner being, and if that inner being is legally a separate entity, then his testimony ought to have been ruled inadmissible as hearsay. I believe I may have to subpoena Mr. Angelino's inner being to testify for the defense as a hostile witness."

Sometimes I don't know when to stop.

"There has been no ruling by the court that my client's inner being is a separate entity," answered Sue. "Mr. Gierig has not presented any expert witnesses to testify to that effect."

"Why, God?" moaned Cadaver, gazing heavenward.

"Never mind. I withdraw the question."

"Which question?"

"Whichever." I resumed the examination: "Had you ever attempted to heal anyone before you went up to visit Mr. Ennis?"

"Not by myself. But I had observed and assisted at other rituals."

"Now, you got your degree at... What was the name of the school?"

"Frostboro College."

"Frostboro College? What kind of place is that?"

"It's a small women's liberal arts college outside Boston. Dedicated to providing a holistic, multicultural education in a nurturing environment."

"I'm sure. Has Frostboro ever produced a Nobel Prize winner? A Pulitzer Prize winner? A scientist, entrepreneur, inventor, surgeon, elected official, engineer, architect, writer, actor, artist, or composer of note?"

"Prizes and competition are not the objectives at Frostboro. The emphasis is on cooperation and learning in a social context."

"They do give degrees there, though, don't they? What did you get your B.A. in?"

"Women's studies."

"And how long did it take you to get your degree in women's studies?"

"Well, I went for one year, then took a semester off . . . "

"Just answer the question, please."

"Six years."

"Six years. In the course of obtaining your four-year degree in six years, did you ever take any courses in biochemistry?"

"No."

"Pharmacology?"

"No."

"Anatomy?"

"I had courses on aspects of female sexuality in which . . . "

"Yeah, yeah. Did you ever study any other part of the human anatomy?"

"You cannot separate . . . "

"I take that as a 'no.' Did you ever have any formal instruction in any branch of medicine?"

"Not in Western medicine. But there's a lot more to healing than just treating symptoms. The body is not a machine."

"Just where did you pick up your knowledge of healing? From the side of a box of herbal tea?"

I half expected Sue Brown to object that I was badgering my own witness. For once in her life, Ostara found herself speechless. I pressed the attack.

"Isn't it true that you're a total charlatan? That you couldn't heal a paper cut with a Band-Aid? Yes? No? Hello. Are you still there?

"I resent that, Mr. Gierig."

"Isn't it true that you are currently unemployed and have been for most of the time since you graduated from college?"

"I work as a volunteer peer counselor at . . . "

"I'm talking about paid employment. As in earning a living. Something you've never done. Isn't it true that your father still pays your rent and your living expenses, not to mention the astronomical costs of your perpetual therapy? Isn't it true that, peer counselor though you may be, at various times you have been diagnosed with anxiety disorder, adjustment disorder, borderline personality disorder, and just about every other disorder in the book, and that you've been in one sort of treatment or another since adolescence?"

"These are labels that are used to oppress."

"Isn't it true that you could not possibly have affected Mr. Angelino's life, for good or for ill, any more than you could have affected Mr. Ennis's? That as a biofield therapeutic healer, you could neither heal nor hurt anyone? Aren't you, in fact, a person of no consequence whatsoever?"

At that point, she erupted. "I object! I will not be marginalized this way! I will have a voice! I demand to represent myself."

Cadaver, who I think had fallen asleep, said, "What? What's the question? Who's objecting? The client can't object. What's the hell's going on here, Gierig? Can't you control your client? How'd you like to spend a night in jail, missy? You and your loopy cheering section back there. You're giving me a migraine."

I had taken care to place the Wiccans in the last row, counting on Cadaver's nearsightedness, but the way they flapped their arms and clucked like a bunch of chickens over their charms and effigies, invoking fire, air, water, and earth, they could have awakened a real cadaver.

I asked the old stiff for a moment to talk to my client, walked up to the stand, and put my hand on her shoulder. She tried to swat my hand away. Then I grabbed her by the wrist and literally pulled her all the way through the courtroom, past a gauntlet of hissing, shrieking

Wiccans, and out into the lobby. No mean feat.

"Listen, babe," I said.

"Don't you ever call me that, and don't you ever put your hands on me again. You do not own me. Nobody owns me."

"Tony Angelino will, if you keep this up. You'll be working to pay him and Sue Brown for the rest of your life. We're in a court-room here. This isn't your little touchy-feely Wiccan circle where we all make nice and hug one another and bless the four elements and throw rose petals in the air. Those two will take from you every last dime you have and will ever have. And even that won't satisfy Sue Brown. You think I was rough on you? Wait till she gets her turn. She'll cut out your heart and have it for dinner, ground up, tartare style. Not because she's hungry. Just because she loves the taste and the feel of the warm blood running down her chin."

My description of Sue Brown's dietary habits was accurate enough, but what I didn't tell Ostara was that if my little gamble had paid off, she'd probably have to face just a perfunctory cross examination. I would have taken the wind out of Sue's sails.

Ostara gaped at me, her mouth hanging open. Then the tears came—a veritable Niagara Falls. I don't think I've ever seen anyone cry that much. Up until that moment, I believe she had had no idea of what a cruel, savage species Homo sapiens is. For twenty-seven years, her dad, her shrinks, and her dippy friends had protected her from an awful lot. Not from everything, of course. She'd been used a time or two and then thrown away. She had that look about her that I knew so well—that the clothes, the charms, the hair could not quite hide—of forlorn hope mingled with dread. The sweat hog look. In college, we used to call it sweat hogging—latching onto the ugliest girl in the bar when it got near closing time, and you were drunk and horny enough that it didn't matter what she looked like. It was probably the most valuable part of my pre-law curriculum.

For almost a quarter century, I've made a very nice living as a lawyer. A lot of the job I could take or leave—the number crunching, the poring over bank statements and credit card receipts. But to eviscerate a greedy, lying bastard like Angelino or a fool like Osta-ra—that's what gives me the buzz. It's better than a shot of Cadaver's whiskey. Better than sex—at least better than sluggish, middle-aged, married sex.

At that moment, though, I almost felt sorry for Ostara. The situation called for empathy—or a passable counterfeit. I put my arm around her, and she offered no resistance.

"Hey, come on. It's all right. We're gonna beat them. I know what I'm doing. Just let me do my job, and you'll be fine. I promise you."

≈≈

For once, I kept a promise. I didn't call Ostara back to the stand. Instead, I asked that we adjourn for the day, a request that Cadaver happily granted. The next morning, Sue Brown hardly laid a glove on her. When you base your whole case on the destruction of your own client, it doesn't leave your opponent with much room to work. I'll have to try it again some time.

When Ostara stepped down, I called on a couple of the creditors, very briefly, to confirm some of what I'd brought out about Angelino's financial shenanigans. The jury got the case after lunch and took less than two hours to let her off the hook. The Wiccan chorus let out a great big whoop, came rushing up to the front, and just about smothered Ostara with hugs and kisses. Me they ignored. Cadaver thanked the jury, stuck Angelino with the court costs, and disappeared back into his hole, where he could swig away to his heart's content. Sue Brown stormed out of the room. To this day, she refuses to speak to me. If she gets a case against me, she passes it off to her associate.

Ostara and I are pals now—from a safe distance. She sends me a card for winter solstice, and I mail her a Christmas card. Compared to some, her aura doesn't look so bad.

May yours always remain clean and balanced. Cheers!

ASHES

Of all the clients Nick Giannakopoulos had represented in his many years of practicing law, none had demanded as much of his time, his effort, and his spirit as Mrs. Grace Nasrallah.

He had first made her acquaintance in the mid-1970s, when she had come to his office unbidden one afternoon as he was rearranging the folders on his desk, preparing to leave for the day. A fellow parishioner of theirs at St. Anthony's Greek Orthodox Church in East Baltimore had referred her, she explained.

"You help him when he is bankrupt. He says you can help me."

A stout woman with skin the color of burlap, she wore a loose-fitting blue flannel dress and a blue and white flowered kerchief that bathed her blocky features in shadow. Nick offered her a seat, and she immediately launched into a disjointed narrative in halting English peppered with Arabic. Nick, a small, slender man whose hair had already begun its long retreat up his crown and whose hooded eyes gave him a look of perpetual weariness, nodded, smiled, and murmured, "Uh huh." A quarter hour passed before he could grasp what she wanted.

"I don't do divorce," he told her, rising from his chair. "It's the one area of the law I don't touch. It's too dirty."

"Please, you must to help me." She rolled up her right sleeve to reveal three large purple bruises on her upper arm. "He hits me. He is cruel. I have nowhere to go. I will die."

In the end, he had yielded to her blandishments, her entreaties, and her tears. Not only did he take the case, but he would go on to spend the better part of the next decade hounding her ex-husband. Though the stories she spun when she testified sometimes made Nick doubt the solidity of the ground beneath his feet, her immigrant naïf persona played well in court. She invariably got what she wanted: the children, the house, ever increasing spousal and child support. When the spousal support ran out, and Mrs. Nasrallah's found that she could not make ends meet on what she earned as a bookkeeper, Nick first extracted a disability settlement from her employer and then sued to force the hapless Elias Nasrallah to resume the payments on the grounds that Mrs. Nasrallah's poor health rendered her unable to maintain herself. Nick's triumph in the latter case set a precedent in the state.

As a regular babysitter for Nick's daughter, Grace Nasrallah soon became no mere client but a de facto member of the Giannakopoulos household. With her two sons, Stephen and George, in tow, she would arrive on a Saturday night laden with cakes, tins of baklava and candies, and homemade dresses, dolls, and bonnets. For Stephanie Giannakopoulos, Mrs. Nasrallah reserved not only her gifts, but her kisses, her pet names, and the seat of honor upon her lap. Her own boys, who never passed an evening without an exchange of kicks and blows and without breaking a glass or leaving a divot in a wall, gave her far less pleasure. "Look at little Mishmesha, little Amar," she would tell them. "She is good girl. She is never trouble. She does not yell. She does not cry. She does not hit." More often than not, these rebukes only goaded the boys on to more destructiveness.

As the boys grew and became more independent, Grace Nasrallah's appetite for litigation, whetted by her early victories, increased. Nick began to devote far too much of his time to dissuading her from suing. She raged for months over what she viewed as the paltry compensation that Nick obtained for the neck and back pain inflicted upon her by the errant driver who—depending on which version one chose to believe—had either tapped or slammed into her rear bumper at a stoplight. With the dismissal of a particularly ill-advised slander action that she brought against her brother, she broke off all connections with the Giannakopoulos family for more than ten years—an estrangement that Nick viewed more as a deliverance than as a punishment.

≈≈

Poor health and money woes would bring her back into his life. Just as she had many years before, she appeared in his office—the same converted walk-up apartment that he had occupied when she had come to him the first time—without an appointment at the end of the day. She had diabetes and "blood pressure" she explained, and now a failing liver had given her skin and eyes a yellowish cast. Her spousal support had run out again, her Medicare did not cover her prescriptions, and bill collectors harassed her day and night. What she wanted from him this time was a job.

"Please, you are kind man. You help me many times. I will work hard. I will do everything. I know many people. I will bring you more business, God willing."

Though his secretary had quit to have a baby, and each successive temp he had hired had proved more inept than the last, Nick, now a stooped and weathered little man with gnarled, arthritic fingers, who looked much older than his sixty-two years, held out for a week before Grace Nasrallah wore him down. The method of payment he agreed to, in order not to jeopardize her Social Security disability funds, was one he would have advised any of his clients against on financial, legal, ethical, and moral grounds. He paid her salary to her older son Stephen as a "consulting fee." No longer the unruly child that Nick remembered, Stephen had become a psychiatrist, with a burgeoning practice and an office on Manhattan's upper west side.

Nick soon had cause to regret his generosity. Grace Nasrallah lost both paper and computer files and rarely took messages. Seated behind a massive gray metal desk to the right of the door in what had been the living room before Nick had converted the apartment into his office, she spent most of each day raging into the telephone in both English and Arabic at Stephen and George.

Both sons caused her no end of heartache. Stephen had worked his way through college, borrowed his way through medical school, moved to New York to open his practice, and all but forsaken his family. George, having struggled through high school, had remained in Baltimore, living with and off his mother all through his twenties. His predilections for shoplifting, brawling, and driving despite blood alcohol concentrations that would have killed a smaller man had provided Nick with steady business. At long last, though, George had settled into a steady position in the produce section at Giant and had embarked upon a spiritual quest that led him to something called the Holy Apostolic Church of the Risen Lord. His conversion had so impressed Grace Nasrallah that she had followed him there, forsaking the elaborate ritual, and the brown brick façade, Gothic spires and imposing blue dome of St. Anthony's for a new faith of untrammeled emotion and all-encompassing Christian love. Grace's Christian love, though, had not extended to the fellow congregant whom George chose as his bride. Of her, Grace Nasrallah said, "She is no good. She take drugs. She sleep with many men. She only make believe to find God." Even worse, the woman was black. Though Grace had continued to attend the Holy Apostolic Church of the Risen Lord, she had skipped her son's wedding.

Often, her telephone monologues, delivered in a steady whine punctuated by shrieks and glottal stops, disturbed Nick when he worked in his inner office, formerly the apartment's master bedroom. Dim and sparsely furnished, its walls a lusterless off-white, it featured, in addition to his diplomas, such adornments as one might expect from a man who had lived his whole life and maintained his practice in the Greektown section of Baltimore. A large watercolor of a hillside dotted with white stucco houses and domed churches that overlooked a Homeric wine-dark sea hung behind his desk. On the wall to the left, beneath a framed photograph of the Acropolis, its pillars gleaming under a full moon, stood a small console, atop which rested two urns, one depicting a battle, the other, a hunting scene. A bookshelf to Nick's right supported a white bust of Aristotle, and despite Nick's healthy respect for the Golden Mean, the thought often occurred to him that the sculpture could serve very nicely if he found himself unable to resist the urge to brain Grace Nasrallah.

One day, assailed by a pounding headache and Mrs. Nasrallah's incessant and increasingly feral cries, he threw a fountain pen across the office and stormed out the door, determined to excise her from both his practice and his life. He found her in tears.

"I give them everything," she moaned, squeezing both his hands. "All they do is to make me suffer. All the money you give to Stephen, he does not give to me. He is doctor. He has so much. And he give me not one dollar. I am sick. I am dying. And he give me nothing."

Instead of firing her as he had planned, Nick gave her the rest of the day off and all the cash in his wallet. He spent much of the afternoon trying to navigate his way through the maze of voice mail menus and submenus that insulated Dr. Stephen Nasrallah from his callers. On his fifth attempt, Nick got through.

"My mother is delusional," said Dr. Stephen Nasrallah, and then he hung up.

Delusional she might well have been. Still, Nick decided that in the future, he would pay Mrs. Nasrallah directly, in cash.

For a few days, she stopped calling her sons. Morose and unresponsive, she sat at her desk murmuring over and over, "Soon I will die. Then I will have peace, God willing."

Curiously, the consuming obsession that she then developed with the drafting of her will seemed to bring her back to life. The document went through dozens of permutations in the ensuing weeks, though Grace had little to leave but her debts. On Monday, she would leave everything to Stephen, though he still would not relinquish her money; on Tuesday, to George; on Wednesday, she would disinherit both and make the Holy Apostolic Church of the Risen Lord her heir;

on Thursday, she favored Stephen again. In a nostalgic moment, perhaps, she expressed a desire for a grand funeral service at St. Anthony's with hundreds of mourners. Later that day, she reversed herself, opting for cremation followed by a brief memorial service at the Holy Apostolic Church of the Risen Lord. When Nick refused to add some of the nastier provisions she wanted, such as barring her brother and his family and George and his wife from her memorial service and directing Stephen, the son she favored at the moment, to throw her ashes in Elias Nasrallah's face, she scrawled them in herself by hand, in English and in Arabic. Much of the day she now spent scribbling over Nick's drafts and faxing copies to Stephen and George.

A bereaved couple came to consult Nick one day. The woman, pausing frequently to dab her eyes with the tissues Nick offered her, told of how her husband, while trying to parallel park their SUV, had bumped it lightly against the car in front, causing the air bag to inflate—and crush their two-year old son. The husband, a gaunt, expressionless man with a rumpled white shirt, open at the collar, and a three- or four-day growth of beard, slumped mutely in his chair. He had not worked in months, she said, and, after numerous failed attempts, no longer even tried to make love to her. No amount of money could bring their son back, but she wanted someone held responsible. Though a Christian, she wanted some measure of justice in this world. Nick assured her he could get it for her.

"You will get nothing!" Grace Nasrallah's scream pierced the stillness. "And your whore will get nothing, too. I will tell Mr. Giannakopoulos to give you nothing because to me you are nothing."

A deep male voice answered her, bellowing curses and threats. Then something crashed against the wall outside. Down went the plaster Aristotle, hitting the blue-gray carpet with a thud and losing the tip of its nose.

Nick raced outside. In the hallway to his right, the hulking George Nasrallah had his mother backed against the wall, his hands clutching her neck. Her mouth was agape, her eyes bulging, her face purple.

Seizing George from behind in a bear hug, Nick barely held on long enough to allow Grace Nasrallah to inhale before the younger man threw him off and grabbed hold of her throat once more. Nick fell backwards, his head smacking against the opposite wall. The room swayed like a dinghy in rough waters as he pried himself from the carpet.

Able, finally, to sit up, his back resting against the wall, he cried, "Enough! Get out of here you lunatics, you freaks! Get out this minute, both of you, or I'll call the police."

George, who had been well-acquainted with the police during his benighted, pre-conversion days, froze for an instant and then, letting go of his mother's neck, turned and bolted out of the office.

"I am so sorry, so sorry," said the tearful Grace Nasrallah, bending over Nick and offering him her hand. "He hurt you. He is bad man. All his life, he make me to suffer. God will punish him."

"Out!" cried Nick. He pointed toward the door with his right hand and massaged his throbbing scalp with his left. A steady whistling noise, like that of a boiling kettle, filled his ears.

"I will tell him he must not come here again when I am working. I will tell him he must not call me on the telephone."

"Get out or I'll strangle you myself! I never want to see you or your spawn again."

She looked stricken as she slowly backed away and out the door. Long after the couple from the inner office had made their furtive exit, the wife gripping the husband's arm and hurrying him along, Nick remained seated on the floor, his face buried in his hands.

For the next week, Grace called at least two or three times each day, to apologize and beg Nick to take her back. He ceased answering and began to erase her messages without listening to them. The calls stopped suddenly. Then, one morning, he picked up the telephone, and the voice he heard belonged to Stephen.

"My mother is dead. She was walking up Eastern Avenue, on her way to a doctor's appointment, and she just collapsed on the sidewalk. She died before they got her to the hospital."

"Dead?"

Nick, who was standing, suddenly felt light-headed. He placed his free hand on his desk to support himself.

"Listen, I'm driving down to Baltimore on Saturday for the memorial service. I'll pick you up. I need to talk to you about something."

Nick sat for a long time at his desk, his forehead cradled in his hands. Slowly, though, the shock gave way to a sense of relief. He was free at last of Grace Nasrallah! Stephen's second call of the day quickly disabused him of that notion, however. He reminded Nick to inform certain people—George, George's wife, Uncle Ramzy—that Grace Nasrallah had requested their absence at her memorial service.

"I doubt they'll show up anyway," Nick answered, irritably. "But if they want to, I can't stop them. I'm a lawyer, not a bouncer."

Dr. Nasrallah must have decided then to carry out that particular filial obligation himself. The days that followed brought a barrage of telephone calls and messages from Mr. and Mrs. George Nasrallah, who accused Nick of having conspired with Stephen to thwart Grace's true intentions by cutting them out of her will. George's obscenity-laced tirades threatened him with death, dismemberment, and disbarment. George's wife warned of the torments that awaited him in hell.

"I am in hell," he answered.

The Saturday of the memorial service was gray and raw, with a near-horizontal drizzle that bore, like a thousand tiny needles, through Nick's clothing and flesh to the very marrow of his bones. Hunched over in his trench coat, his face obscured by the handkerchief into which he frequently coughed, his bald crown beaded with rainwater and the hair that remained matted to his temples in swirls of gray and white, Nick waited for his ride. He stood at an Eastern Avenue bus stop, before a thrift shop display window that contained a jumbled assortment of women's and girls' dresses, toys, lamps, and a tricycle with chipped red paint. He did not know what sort of vehicle to expect and so did not react immediately when a candy-apple-red Corvette pulled up to the curb in front of him. The passenger-side door swung open. Upon the single passenger's seat in the tiny car rested a bronze urn with jug handles on either side, its surface adorned with reliefs of praying hands, doves, and crosses.

"Get in," said Dr. Stephen Nasrallah, a stocky, swarthy young man with a goatee, black hair thinning slightly on top, and a petulant look about him. He wore a lightweight gray suit that fit his dimensions much better than it did either the weather or the occasion, black patent leather shoes, a white shirt, and a very wide tie with a black diamond pattern set against a gray background. "I hope you don't mind riding with Mom in your lap. She can't hurt anyone now."

"Don't talk about your mother that way."

"I tell the truth, whether people want to hear it or not."

Stephen thrust the gear lever forward. The engine growled, and the powerful little car quickly gathered speed, reaching seventy miles per hour as it zigzagged its way up Eastern Avenue. Nick's hands tightened around the handles of the urn.

"I see Greektown hasn't changed any," said Stephen.

"I like it the way it is."

On I-95 and then on the Beltway, the Corvette cruised effortlessly at ninety. For a quarter hour or more, neither man spoke. Only the sound of the engine was heard,—a full throated, triumphal roar.

"Powerful," said Nick. "Is the car new?"

"I've had it a couple of months. Made it down here from West 59th in just over three hours. And that's with the midtown traffic."

"Stella and I used to take the train up to New York a couple times a year. See a play, go to the shops. We saw the Rockettes at Radio City. We saw Aida at the Met with Pavarotti and a cast of thousands. They had a live elephant on stage for the march scene. But I haven't been up there since she passed. It's going on three years now. She loved the city. In a way it's almost a blessing that she didn't live to see the planes hit the towers." Turning to the window on his right, he let out a long sigh, clouding the glass. "These are bad times we're living in. Awful times."

"I get a lot of funny looks in New York these days. Even the psychotics have become noticeably more hostile. I was doing morning rounds in the hospital the other day. This patient—a seventy-two-year-old woman—starts screaming at me. 'Murderer! Poisoner! Filthy Arab scum! How many Americans have you killed today?' I said, 'I can see we haven't had our meds yet this morning, Mrs. Hardesty.' She threw her slippers at my head."

He smiled wanly and chuckled to himself. "But Medicare makes her easier to bear. Eighty dollars for five minutes with her, and then on to the next room and another $80. Ka-ching!

"How many Americans have I killed? Shit, I'm more American than most Americans. I've lived in this country since I was seven. I'm much more fluent in English than in Arabic. I've even volunteered my services to the rescue workers at Ground Zero. It's a great way to get referrals. What could be more American than combining business and patriotism?"

Nick answered with two resounding coughs.

"I don't even like my fellow Arabs. My mother was a typical Arab."

"Your mother wasn't a typical anything."

"All I ever wanted to do was get away from them. Unlike George, I had the strength to do it and make a life for myself."

"George is planning to challenge the will. I can't seem to make him understand that there's nothing there to fight over."

"George always thinks someone's trying to put something over on him. Most of the time, he's right. He's such an easy target," Stephen concluded, with a satisfied grin.

≈≈

The Holy Apostolic Church of the Risen Lord was housed in a long, rectangular conference room in a suburban office building with a façade of tinted glass and beige concrete. The room had white walls and white floor and ceiling tiles, the latter with recessed light fixtures. Rows of plastic chairs stretched from front to rear, but most remained unoccupied. Seven or eight mourners, all women in their twenties and thirties, all plump and plain and shrouded in black, clustered in the forward rows. The smell of bug spray permeated the air. Though Nick kept his trench coat on, he could not stop shivering, nor could he restrain his coughing.

Upon a riser at the front of the room stood a squat man with a ruddy face and a shiny, bald pate. He wore no clerical garments, just a pale blue suit and matching tie, and looked, thought Nick, more like a car salesman than a clergyman. Fixed to the wall behind him, a large wooden cross, stained the color of dried blood, loomed above his head. On a small table to his left sat Grace in her urn.

He told of a dream he'd had, in which he had found himself in a dusty room full of manila file folders—the files that contained the record of his life. He saw files labeled "Friends," "Marriage," "Family," "Comfort I Gave," and "Jokes I Laughed At," and other, fatter ones titled "Friends I Betrayed," "Lies I told," and the immense "Lustful Thoughts." The smallest file of all was "People I Shared the Gospel With." He wanted only to obliterate those files so no one could ever see them. But when he took a match to them, he found that they would not burn. In his shame and despair, he fell to his knees and wept. And then, to his horror, he saw Jesus enter the room and begin to read the files. But Jesus did not grow angry. No, Jesus only looked at him with infinite pity.

"And then Jesus walked over and fell to His knees and put His arm around me. He didn't say a word. He just cried with me."

Just as in the dream, he dropped to his knees, and on cue, the tears flowed. Sweat gleamed atop his head and darkened the collar of his jacket. The flush on his cheeks deepened.

The women of the congregation wept and trembled with him and moaned for Jesus. Nick shuddered violently. Nausea seized him, and he slumped forward in his chair, resting his forearms in his lap and holding his breath.

The minister in the blue suit then popped back onto his feet and called upon the Lord to bless Grace's ashes. Lifting his arms over the urn, he sang:

> *There's a new name written down in glory,*
> *And it's mine, O yes it's mine!*
> *And the white robed angels sing the story,*
> *"A sinner has come home."*

Next, Stephen stepped up onto the riser. He delivered his eulogy in a lugubrious monotone, developing, at great length, several variations on the theme of how Grace, as both mother and father to him, had helped him through his many tribulations and made his achievements possible: "She was there for me when my father abandoned us. She was there for me when he reneged on his promise to put me through medical school."

He had wanted to sue his father over that broken promise, until, after much arguing, Nick had convinced him of the impossibility of winning. Nick shifted his weight from one side to the other and then back again. The hard chair had become a torment. He longed only to crawl into bed and stay there, but Stephen droned on and on and on.

≈≈

The late afternoon sky had grown preternaturally dark. The rain that smacked against the windshield of the Corvette obscured all but the white lines of the highway and the tail lights of the car in front, though at times Stephen approached so closely that those lights vanished too.

"What a fitting memorial," chortled Stephen.

"It just about made me sick. Your mother was a piece of work, but she deserved better than that."

"You mean you didn't enjoy my performance? I'm hurt."

"How can people act like that? Like animals! Was that a church or a lunatic asylum? Why in the world did she leave St. Anthony's, a good Greek church, for that zoo?"

"To take your questions in order, we are animals after all, and there are a lot of very primitive subspecies out there. Second, it's hard to say just what kind of a place that was. On the one hand, the behavior we saw is about what you would expect from some of the more florid psychotics in the hospital. On the other, these people can come and go as they please, while the psychotics can't. As for my mother…"

He shrugged and fell silent. Only when Nick had ceased to expect any other answer from him did Stephen speak again.

"My mother was a lot smarter than George. I wouldn't have thought she'd go in for that. But she was a borderline, among other things. Rigid, paranoid, self-righteous, emotionally labile, histrionic, prone to magical thinking and primitive defense mechanisms. Such a habitual liar that she lost the ability to distinguish between her lies and the truth. Filled with grandiose delusions one minute and utter self-loathing the next. And just as changeable toward those around her. One day, I was her only son. The next, I was a curse on her. I was the devil. Most borderline patients end up as treatment failures. When you add in religion—and it doesn't matter which one—it only makes things worse. Then you have God blessing the pathology. Then you have what it takes to fly a plane into a building. Maybe the Church of the Holy Snake Handlers was a perfect match for my mother after all. It sanctified her viciousness."

"You need to get over this, kid. It's not healthy."

Scowling, Stephen pressed the accelerator to the floor. With mere inches separating the nose of the Corvette from the bumper of the massive tractor-trailer in front, he cut the steering wheel hard to the right and sped on past the larger vehicle. He then zigzagged his way around two more trucks traveling directly ahead of the first, undeterred by the blasts of their horns and the flashing of their bright lights.

"You may have a point," Stephen answered finally. "Her life isn't worth thinking about anymore. It's her death that concerns me now. She was taking a cholesterol drug that was withdrawn from the market last year because there were documented cases of hepatic toxicity. I think I might have a pretty good case against the manufacturer. You think you'd be interested?"

The recollection of what had become of his "consulting fees" blunted whatever interest Nick otherwise might have had. Supporting the urn in his in his lap with his left hand and holding his handkerchief in his right, he blew his nose, still unable to shake his chill.

"Are you sure it was the liver that killed her? She had diabetes. She had lots of problems. If you wanted to build a case, you shouldn't have had her cremated. You should have had an autopsy done."

Stephen frowned. "I can always find someone in New York if you don't want the case."

"I wouldn't be so sure. New York lawyers worry about their reputations too."

Veering suddenly to the right, across two lanes of traffic, Stephen exited the highway. The tires squealed as he whipped the Corvette around the sharply curving ramp. Nick closed his eyes and hugged the remains of Grace Nasrallah to his chest.

They rode without speaking down Eastern Avenue until Stephen made a sudden turn onto a side street and brought the car to a stop outside a convenience store. Behind the window, a man with a large round head and an even rounder body, and with his belt pulled so tightly around his middle that it seemed to bisect his enormous girth, tottered like a circus dancing bear as he traversed the floor with a broom. Slowly, the realization came to Nick that he knew the man: Elias Nasrallah. Then he knew why they had come.

"You're going to do it, aren't you? You're going to throw the ashes in his face."

"It's what she wanted."

Stephen reached for the urn, but Nick pulled it away, twisting his body to shield the vessel.

"How can you be a shrink when you're crazier than any of your patients? She was a sick woman. She was in pain. She couldn't think straight. If you ever had any feeling for her at all—never mind for him—you wouldn't do this."

"I'm her son and sole heir. I have to honor her wishes."

"You never gave a damn about her wishes when she was alive."

"I don't have time to argue with you. I have to drive back to New York. Give me the damn thing."

He grabbed one of the handles of the urn. Nick held fast to the other.

"Just answer me one question, O.K.?" he sputtered. "One question, and then I'll let go, and you can do whatever the hell you want—kill each other for all I care—because I've had all I can take of the whole lot of you. Why did you have to steal from her? Stealing from me is one thing. I've been a lawyer for thirty-five years. If I couldn't see it coming, then I deserved what I got. But why did you keep her wages from her when she couldn't even pay for her medicines? It couldn't have been the money because what I was paying her was pocket change to you. Just for the hell of it? Just because you could? Did you enjoy doing that to her? What kind of creature are you?"

Stephen's eyes narrowed, and his nostrils flared.

"When you make accusations like that, you'd better be prepared to back them up in court."

Stephen yanked at his handle and Nick, at his. The urn tilted sharply to the right, the heavy lid dropping onto Nick's right thigh and then rolling off and falling to the floor. Ashes spewed from the urn, landing in a heap in Nick's lap. A choking gray cloud filled the car.

Releasing his grip on the urn, Nick flung the car door open and staggered out into the rain. Though he swatted furiously at his coat, the ashes still clung to him.

DEPARTURE

"When are you coming back here to stay?" Wherever Mary Kamau went, it seemed, the question would arise.

She lightly attempted to deflect such talk: "You mean you don't mind having the electricity going out every couple of hours? Or turning on the tap and having the water trickle out if it comes out at all?"

"Oh, you get used to it," someone would reply with the usual Nairobi insouciance. "You start to think it's normal."

Not surprisingly, Auntie Margaret, the self-appointed clan matriarch, proved more persistent than the others, and, try as Mary might to wriggle out of her vague promise to visit sometime, she could not do so indefinitely. The dreaded summons to the house in Langata came by telephone one afternoon.

"I'd love to come for tea," said Mary. "I really would. But I have no way to get there."

"Nonsense!" snapped Auntie Margaret. "I'll send my driver. He can pick you up in half an hour."

Auntie Margaret lived in a lime-green structure of Brobdingnagian proportions, fronted by a curving stone stairway and fluted columns. She greeted Mary on the porch with a prolonged and crushing embrace and then escorted her niece inside, where Moorish arches, cornices, and wrought iron sconces abounded.

Mary followed Auntie Margaret into an expansive, high-ceilinged sunken living room that lay to the right of the main hallway. The walls were of the same lime-green hue as the exterior of the house. To the right, there hung a large wood and alabaster crucifix. A gauzy portrait of the late Pope John Paul II—a poor likeness—adorned the opposite wall. Uncle Joseph's medical reference books vied with Auntie Margaret's Bibles and hymnals for space on the cherry wood shelves, which also held decades' worth of family photographs.

Mary seated herself on a leather sofa, the pope looming above her right shoulder and Auntie Margaret perched on the love seat to her left. A servant brought the tea and quickly disappeared. It was the usual Kikuyu concoction—the sort that tempted Mary to ask, "May I have some tea with my milk?"

"I think you know what I want to talk to you about," said Auntie Margaret, a diminutive, walleyed woman with an ever-present smile, but a terror nonetheless.

Mary knew. A couple of years before, on Christmas Day, when Mary, alone in her apartment, had polished off a bottle and a half of Merlot, Auntie Margaret had called to offer her holiday greetings. Why, she asked in alarm, did Mary sound so despondent? Where was the boyfriend? In a moment of weakness that Mary had regretted ever since, she had confessed the truth: "He's with his wife and kids."

Now, leaning close, Auntie Margaret said, "I won't even discuss the morality of it anymore. Yours is a generation for which such considerations simply don't exist. But look at what this is doing to you. You can never go anywhere with him in public. You spend your holidays alone. It's been four years. He'll never leave his wife and daughters for you. And God help you if he did."

"I don't expect him to leave her," Mary conceded, for her lover, a sweet man but a weak one, several years younger than she, had, in addition to two beautiful young girls, a spouse whose wild mood swings, private and public tantrums, and suicide threats had turned his life into a hell that he dared not try to escape. "We don't even talk about it anymore."

Auntie Margaret threw up her hands. "Then why do you let it continue? I've never understood you. How can such a bright person, such an accomplished person, be so utterly lacking in common sense? Can't you see that you're throwing your life away on this man? You can do so much better. You're a very attractive woman."

Mary shrugged. Plump and dark-skinned, standing just over five feet tall, she had a round face, a wide mouth and nose, and severe-looking black eyes. Of her attractiveness, she had always had her doubts. "I like things as they are," she answered at last. "I have him as much as I want. I couldn't bear having him around all the time. I couldn't bear having anyone around all the time."

"What utter nonsense! This is what comes of living in America," scoffed Auntie Margaret, who had never set foot in America. "It's a cold place. It's made you selfish and lonely and unhappy. You have nothing to go back to there. Why don't you come to your senses and come home? Everyone who loves you is here."

"I have my job."

Auntie Margaret snorted contemptuously. "Is it really worth that much to you?"

"I have friends. I have a life there."

"Friends who leave you alone on Christmas Day? Look at you. You're almost forty, and you're miserable. Come home. Start a family of your own while you still can."

Later, Mary would take some small solace in having summoned the strength to hold back her tears until her return to Nairobi.

She began to find excuses to avoid family functions, hiding herself away in her childhood home on the outskirts of the city. The sprawling white stone house, uninhabited now and sparsely furnished, sat on a large, lush plot of land where flowering eucalyptus, jacaranda, and flame trees proudly displayed their dazzling colors and gave refuge from the blazing sun. Beds of azaleas, roses, and lilies surrounded the house. A high stone wall, topped with razor wire, bounded the property. A gardener and a domestic servant came during the day and a watchman at night. Neither the gardener nor the watchman ever entered the house, and the servant, a young country woman who wore a purple head scarf and listened to religious songs on the radio all day long, spoke no English and only fragmentary Kiswahili with a heavy Kamba accent. Entire days passed without Mary exchanging a word with another human being.

Having lived without servants for so long and finding the efforts of this one sadly wanting, Mary immediately began to expropriate many of the woman's duties: hanging curtains, scouring the bathtub, unclogging the drain in the washroom sink with bleach, mopping the floors, making the place livable again after years of neglect. It did not escape her notice, though, that when she put on the faded blue housedress that she had found hanging in the laundry room and began to scrub and mop, while the tall, slender Kamba woman sat idle and bewildered in the kitchen, servant and mistress appeared to have reversed roles.

The strident off-key singing on the radio and the barking and baying of the guard dogs at all hours of the day and night soon began to grate. The thought began to gnaw at Mary that, having traveled thousands of miles, traversing an ocean and two continents, she had somehow contrived—and not for the first time—to miss out on her own holiday. She would go to the coast, she decided, and spend the remaining days before her return to Washington lounging by the indigo waters of the Indian Ocean.

She would not fly, for she spent too much of her life waiting in airport lounges and vainly trying to sleep in cramped airplane seats, and she needed a holiday from that, too. Instead, she would take the slow overnight train from Nairobi to Mombasa—a less efficient means of transportation, certainly, but a much more comfortable and pleasant one. At least it had been twenty-five or thirty years ago.

The evening before her planned departure, her younger brother Patrick flew in from Kampala, where he now resided, for a meeting with a developer. At breakfast the next morning, Mary learned just what her brother, already dressed for business in a charcoal pinstriped suit and maroon tie, planned to develop. It made no sense, he argued, to pay gardeners, watchmen, and servants to maintain a crumbling, empty house. Better to raze it. He could build two low-rises on the property, each holding half a dozen luxury flats, with plenty of room left over for a car park and a swimming pool!

Lighter-skinned than his sister, with thinning hair, narrow eyes, and a reedy voice, he had the build and the fidgetiness of a grasshopper. His spindly arms whirled through the air as he spoke, and often he punctuated a thought by slapping his palm against the tabletop.

Mary, still in her bathrobe and lost in a pre-coffee fog, listened with growing alarm. "But it's my home," she wailed. "You want to destroy my home."

Patrick gaped at her in astonishment. "Your home? You haven't lived here in more than twenty years. You have no intention of ever coming back."

"How do you know what I intend to do?"

"You do have a point there. With someone as flighty as you, it's not always easy to guess."

"You're just the kind of Kikuyu I detest. Crass as can be. You let the house you grew up in go to rot because it meant nothing to you."

"I let the house go to rot? Where were you?"

"Now you want to tear it down and put up a block of flats. Never mind that Mum and Dad would be turning over in their graves."

"At least I was around to see to it that they had proper burials."

"Never mind that you're destroying the character of the neighborhood. What does any of that matter when there's money to be made?"

"I keep forgetting that you work for the World Bank. It's your job to keep Africans poor."

Many hours later, as the little silver-gray Peugeot sport coupé that Patrick had hired upon his arrival in Nairobi inched its way through evening rush-hour traffic along the city's rutted streets, the mutual hostility had not abated.

"Why in the world do you want to take a thirteen-hour trip—if you're lucky and nothing goes wrong—in a dirty, noisy, bumpy train when you can fly to Mombasa in an hour?" asked Patrick, breaking a silence that had persisted for most of the drive.

"Not for reasons you could understand."

In front of the railway station, a dusty, brown-brick edifice dating from colonial times, cars, taxis, and matatus, horns howling, stereos blasting hip-hop, exhaust pipes spewing clouds of soot that stung the eyes and clawed at the throat, jockeyed for scarce parking spaces. Peddlers, seated on frayed blankets, hawked trinkets and produce. Glass fragments, plastic water bottles, and soft-drink cans littered the pavement. Plastic grocery bags flitted hither and thither in the breeze.

"My God!" Mary cried. "What happened to this place? It was never like this."

"It's been a dump for as long as I can remember."

"Rubbish! It used to be immaculate."

"Only your memories are immaculate."

As Patrick inched the coupé forward, a police car entered the parking lot from the opposite side and began a slow cruise along the perimeter. A dozen or more peddlers—country women in headscarves and long, tattered skirts—frantically stuffed their wares into large rubbish bags and began to run.

The spectacle caused Patrick to snicker. "I guess they couldn't afford the bribe. The only time the police enforce the law in Kenya is when you don't pay them not to."

"This is not the Kenya I left," Mary murmured, shaking her head.

No sooner had the police car exited, than the peddlers began to reemerge and take up their former stations.

"I used to love riding the train out to the coast when we were young," she said softly, speaking more to herself than to Patrick. "It seemed like such an elegant way to travel. You'd enter the dining car, and you felt as if you'd been transported back to another age. Brass light fixtures. Waiters in starched white jackets. Bone china, crystal, polished silver cutlery. You almost expected to see Cary Grant and Eva Marie Saint at the next table."

Patrick shrugged. "I just remember that the trip took forever." He eased the coupé into the vacant parking space reserved for the station master.

Mary glanced at him questioningly.

"He's not using it."

"And you've never been one to pass up an opportunity."

"No. That's a luxury that, unlike you, I never could afford." He turned off the ignition and sat silently for a moment, his left hand still gripping the gear lever and his right fiddling with the key. "Look, about the house…I'm sorry about it, too. It's not an easy thing. I know I shouldn't have sprung it on you this way."

Her mouth constricted as if she'd bitten into something sour. "I'm only surprised that you told me at all. But I suppose you had no way around it. Legally."

"I'm being completely above board with this," answered Patrick stiffly. "There'll be a full accounting. You'll get everything that's coming to you."

"Oh, bloody hell! What does it matter? It's just a house. It can't stand there forever. Do with it what you want."

Indeed, with each passing year, she had less and less reason to return. The past decade had seen the deaths of her parents and of more aunts and uncles than she could count, while such nuisances as Auntie Margaret had endured. Friends and cousins had scattered across four continents and no longer wrote. Those who had welcomed her back home so eagerly would forget her the moment she had gone. Still, the thought of the house reduced to rubble caused her eyes to fill with tears, and she reached inside her purse for a tissue.

He touched her shoulder lightly. She shuddered, and he withdrew his hand. "Shiru and the boys are always asking about you. They'd love to see you. Do you think you'll have time to get to Kampala before you go home?"

How like him, she thought. He'd cleave your skull, then put away the axe, and expect you to behave as if nothing untoward had happened. "I'd have wanted to see them, too, but it won't be possible," she replied and quickly stepped out of the coupé.

≈≈

She had a sleeping compartment to herself. Otherwise, she found little in her surroundings to cheer her. The fan affixed to the wall opposite her berth did not work. A wad of chewing gum clung to the window screen. The grimy seat covering had several long horizontal gashes, as though someone had methodically sliced it up with a knife.

A wobbly walk through the corridor brought her to the stuffy, dimly lit dining car. At one table sat four well-dressed Kenyan men, probably off-duty railway employees, for most locals rode third class. The men kept up a loud conversation in English, Kiswahili, and Kikuyu, sometimes employing all three languages in the same sentence. Westerners had occupied most of the other available tables. These were not the stylish tourists of a generation ago, when the train was an obligatory part of a Kenyan safari, but lean and unkempt young backpackers wearing torn jeans, t-shirts, and bandanas. A high-spirited lot, they prattled away merrily in German, Dutch, and Australian-accented English and took turns mugging for photographs.

Neither tourist nor local, Mary sought out a corner table, away from the others. The waiters, still wearing the white jackets she remembered, albeit ones that sorely needed washing and ironing, ladled out the food with an indifference that bordered on sullenness. First there came a brackish soup with no discernable flavor, followed by the main course, a beef stew served over rice.

The stew, though of a higher caliber than the soup, lost some of its savor when one of the waiters placed another passenger at Mary's table. A squat, balding, bulbous-nosed man in his fifties who wore a light-brown sport jacket and a yellow shirt with an open collar, her new dining companion did not in the least resemble Cary Grant.

"Jambo," he said, as he sat down, evidently taking her for a tourist. He smiled ingratiatingly, revealing a set of teeth marred by the telltale brownish deposits built up over a lifetime of drinking the iron-rich water of Kikuyuland.

"Hello."

"My name is Simon."

She answered with a perfunctory "nice to meet you" and resumed eating.

"Is this your fahst visit to Kenya?"

The accent made her cringe. Why did her fellow Kikuyus embarrass her so?

"Hardly. I grew up in Nairobi."

His eyes grew wide. "I don't berieve it. You talk rike a Mzungu," he cried, gesturing toward a table full of Australian backpackers.

"I'm a Nairobi Kikuyu."

"I don't berieve it. Where did your fathah come from? Where was his virrage?"

"Muranga, I suppose." Then, hoping to put an end to the conversation, she added, "He and my mother are buried there."

"I'm from Muranga," Simon replied cheerfully, and then he uttered something in rapid-fire Kikuyu.

She shook her head.

"You don't understand Kikuyu?"

"I've forgotten most of what little I once knew. I'm a very bad Kikuyu."

"I asked you what subdivision you come from in Muranga."

"I don't come from any subdivision in Muranga," she answered sharply. "I have never spent a night in Muranga in my life. I have no ties to any living person there."

Shamefaced, he managed a weak smile and then turned his attention to his dinner, which he consumed noisily and with great gusto. Just when she had begun to hope that she might have silenced him for good, though, he asked, "Ah you married?"

She frowned as she pondered her reply. A yes would likely prompt this nosy fellow to question her ad nauseam about her putative husband, and she would have to spin out a whole skein of lies. A no might send an unwanted message of encouragement. In the end, she said nothing.

"I was married for thahty-four years. Next Tuesday, it will be two years since my wife passed away."

"I'm sorry to hear that."

"She was just seventeen when we married. I was nineteen. All we had then was a little shamba. We wahked it togethah. We grew maize. God was good to us. He saw to it that we prospad. He gave us five children. They ah all grown now." He reached into his wallet and drew out several photographs, which he handed Mary one at a time. "This is Samuel, my oldest. He's in Cape Town now. He's a hotel managah. Here's my daughter Muthoni, her husband Joshua, and my grandson Mwangi. He just turned two. They rive in Mombasa. I'm going to visit them."

Mary smiled and nodded as appropriate, though viewing family pictures of strangers, whose bonds she would never share, always left her feeling a bit dejected.

"It's best to staht a famiry when you're young. That's when you have the energy to do it."

"So I've heard. I enjoy being around children, but not twenty-four hours a day. I'm probably better suited to be an aunt than to be a mother."

"Children give you great joy. Great joy. And when you ah old, you have someone to take care of you."

"Yes, I suppose it works that way," she replied absently. "For some people. When my parents were dying, I was thousands of miles away." She furtively brushed away a tear from the corner of her left eye.

"Great joy," repeated Simon, gazing past her. "But they nevah stay put."

≈≈

A search through the shadowy corridors of several cars for a usable toilet proved futile. She found one washroom locked and two others outfitted with Eastern toilets—mere holes in the floor. The two Western toilets she discovered were both clogged, reeked of excrement, and lacked seats. Defeated, she trudged back to her compartment. Though it was scarcely nine o'clock, she undressed, put on a white nightgown, and lay down. From the corridor came the sounds of Dutch merrymaking.

Salama, Sultan Hamud, Emali—the little station houses sprang up outside the window and vanished just as quickly. In between stops, the night revealed nothing—not a human form or dwelling or even the outlines of a landscape. Sitting up in bed and peering into the blackness, Mary felt a floating sensation, as if the train had somehow slipped the Earth's gravitational pull.

Trying mightily to ignore the pressure of a full bladder, she rolled from her back to her side, to her stomach, and then over again. Sleep came at last, but the screech of metal on metal soon woke her. The train shuddered so violently before it stopped that she was nearly thrown out of bed. Doors slid open and closed, whining for lubricant. Men shouting in Kiswahili stomped up and down the corridor, carelessly tossing about crates or suitcases that thudded against the floor.

Wheels thumping, engine rumbling, the train began to move again, steadily gathering speed. Rummaging through her valise, Mary, to her great relief, found a full box of tissues. She threw on her bathrobe and, tissue box in hand, made her way up the corridor to the toilet, for she could hold out no longer. Fighting back nausea all the while, she thickly papered over the toilet rim with tissues. The stench in the room seemed to have become a solid mass, pressing against her chest.

Back in her compartment, she quickly fell asleep, but again her slumbers proved short-lived. She heard a horn and then a piercing metallic shriek and felt herself beginning to roll.

The sign above the door to the station house said Makindu. For an hour—a twitchy, sleepless hour—the train sat still. Then, groaning wearily, it began to pull away from the station. After a few minutes, the engine fell silent, but the train rolled onward, slowing gradually, until its momentum could carry it no farther. Another half hour passed, during which the engine started up and sputtered out at least a half-dozen times. Sometime later, Mary awoke to find the train slogging backwards toward Makindu. Or was she dreaming it?

Sunrise saw the train stalled again between stations, somewhere in the Tsavo, with more than a third of the journey still ahead. Mary lay in bed until the last call for breakfast, then threw on a t-shirt and her skirt from the night before and, without making herself up, stumbled out the door and up the corridor toward the dining car.

The waiters' jackets appeared to have acquired a whole new layer of filth overnight. No one had thought to set or even clean the table at which the headwaiter seated her. Coffee stains and crumbs covered the table cloth. The half-melted remnants of a stick of butter lay upon an uncovered butter dish in the center of the table. At the far corner, a butter knife and a slice of toast with a corner bitten off rested upon a small plate.

She asked a waiter, a tall, thin, blank-eyed man of indeterminate age, for coffee. He nodded, walked off, and returned a few minutes later with a glass of orange juice, which he set down in front of her. She asked him again for coffee. He nodded again and brought her a grease-coated plate of eggs, bacon, and fried potatoes, as well as a knife and fork, but no napkin and still no coffee.

Simon, dressed now in a white polo shirt and khakis and look-ing thoroughly rested, entered the dining car. He strode jauntily up to Mary's table, bypassing several unoccupied ones along the way. "May I join you?" he asked and then sat down without waiting for an answer. "How ah you this morning."

"Fine," she answered, staring listlessly at her untouched break-fast, her stomach gurgling. A painful cramp made her wince.

When his food arrived, he set upon it greedily. "Why ah you not eating?" he asked, holding his fork aloft, a large slice of bacon im-paled upon the tines.

"Look at this," she snapped, gesturing at the tablecloth. "How can you eat off of this?"

"Well, the sahvice is not what it used to be, but there ah wass ways to travel. In thad crass, they ah given nothing to eat and they ah jammed in rike cattle. I don't know how they can stand it."

"It's what they're used to, I suppose. It's the Kenyan disease. We can get used to anything." Rising, she added, "I'm sorry. Please excuse me."

"Ah you unwell?"

"Very." She walked a few steps up the aisle, then turned about and added, "Please don't think me rude, Simon. It was very good to have met you. I hope you have a wonderful visit with your daughter in Mombasa."

Outside the window of her compartment lay a flat expanse of high, tawny grass and widely spaced thorn trees, some with vultures perched on top. The sun, a vast, incandescent disk, hung low in the sky, its light and heat suffusing the little room. Something was bob-bing in the grass a short distance from the train. Shading her eyes with her hand and peering through the filmy windowpane, Mary spied three golden lion cubs. They were wrestling, tumbling, cuffing one another about. Nearby, a lioness lay stretched on her side in splendid repose.

Mary reached into her carry-on bag and hurriedly drew out her camera. Squinting into the viewfinder, she waited, waited, waited as the cubs flitted into and out of the frame. An instant before she snapped the picture, the train lurched forward.

The photograph came out as an amber blur, with no cubs to be seen anywhere.

A VIEW OF THE FIREWORKS

From the hallway, there came the whine of gurneys on the move, the squeak of rubber shoes against linoleum, murmurs, shouts. Then he heard a laugh, quick and light—an arpeggio. It sounded eerily like Gilda's. But it had to have come instead from one of the legion of Stacys and Heathers and Kims that populated the ward and seemed to multiply daily.

Professor Thomas Venuti did not respond to the knock, and when the door of his room swung open, he covered his face with his arm to shield his eyes from the light. He did not rise from the bed to greet the three figures that strode into the room.

"There is no God," he muttered, with an exaggerated weariness.

"Good morning, Professor Venuti," called Dr. McKay, a cheerful, ruddy faced Canadian in bow tie and tweeds. "How are we doing today?"

The doctor sat down in the chair against the opposite wall, the only chair in the room. One of Professor Venuti's least favorite resident physicians, a gangly, sallow, rather officious young man with acne-scarred cheeks, immediately stationed himself by Dr. McKay's left shoulder. On the opposite side, not quite as close, stood someone Professor Venuti did not recognize: a very tall stoop-shouldered young woman, the sleeves of whose lab coat fell perhaps two inches short of her wrists.

Without rising, the professor answered, "I eat—as much as I find edible. The food here is not a fair test of appetite. I sleep, except when people wake me up to ask me how I've slept. I'm not suicidal. My mood is lousy, and my concentration abysmal. I see no hope for the future. Does that cover it?"

"Just about," answered Dr. McKay. "Going to watch the fireworks tonight?"

"What fireworks?"

"The ones they shoot off at midnight over the harbor. You can see them from the top of the building."

"No thanks. I can make my own fireworks. Just stick my finger in a light socket. I'll light up the building. The top of my head will blind you."

"Ah, yes. That is something we need to talk about."

"The top of my head?"

"No, your treatment."

"Let's not. I'll tell you, though, I'll never look at jumper cables the same way again."

"Specifically, the treatment that you should have had this morning."

"I see you've brought someone else to observe the patient today, in addition to your usual lapdog," said the professor, sitting up and fixing upon the young woman the glare that had cowed countless undergraduates over the years. "You're here to see what a . . . What's the politically correct term for it? Loonie? Nut ball? You're here to see what a nut ball looks like. Note the blunted affect," he said, in a slow monotone.

"The lack of eye contact." He looked down at the floor.

"The poor grooming." He ran his fingers through the scraggly growth of what had once been a neatly trimmed Van Dyke beard and through the gray-black hair, now hanging halfway over his ears, which surrounded his bald pate.

"The motor retardation." His palm facing the young woman, he moved his left hand slowly in an arc, from left to right.

The woman, fading back into the corner as far as she could, seemed to shrivel in front of him like a bug caught under a magnifying glass beneath a hot sun. Remorse gripped him as he watched her, just as it often had in the classroom when he had allowed his spleen to get the better of him. In vain he groped for some words that might ease her distress. He had always found the undoing of damage much harder than the doing.

The lapdog resident with the acne scars cast a sidelong glance at Dr. McKay, but did not receive the cue he sought and so remained silent and impassive.

"She's here to see a recovering nut ball," piped Dr. McKay.

"You don't miss a beat, do you? What do I have to do to really piss you off?"

"A little show like that won't do it. The more obnoxious you are, the better I like it. Your sarcasm requires a pretty high level of cognitive functioning. What you have to do to piss me off is to refuse to go through with your ECT treatments, as you did with the one you should have had this morning."

"I was afraid I'd create an atmospheric disturbance when I walked out of here."

"You'll walk out of here a lot sooner if you don't refuse the treatments."

"Something would walk out of here, but would it be me? Linda brought me my manuscript the other night. I was working on it. For the first time in six months. I can't recall quotations I should know. Used to know. I can't even call up the words I need a lot of the time. Simple words."

"You certainly don't seem to be at a loss for words this morning. And the difficulty in remembering could just as easily be due to the illness. In any case, the memory loss with ECT is almost always temporary."

"It happens sometimes, even in ordinary conversation. I want a word, and I don't have it."

≈≈

When he had at last rid himself of the invaders, he arose, stretched out his spidery six foot frame, threw a bathrobe over his hospital pajamas, and headed out for breakfast.

He wandered slowly through the day room, a large, open area bounded on three sides by lines of sofas and chairs right-angled to one another and on the fourth, by a set of cabinets and shelves, one unit of which supported the television. He noted with some surprise the bright crepe paper streamers taped up high on the walls, the Happy New Year posters done in silver and gold glitter. The eating disordered girls must have put those up the night before; no one in his group would have had the desire or the initiative. What a strange place to be on New Year's Eve. A little over a year ago, during Gilda's last stay, he had frequented this room as a visitor, never imagining that he'd return as a patient.

To his right, the pay phone was ringing, as it did all day long, for the use of cell phones by the girls with eating disorders was severely restricted by the staff, and his fellow depressives felt little inclination to answer theirs. He walked on past the phone. No one would be calling for him at this hour; no one else in the day room showed any interest; and the eating disordered girls were already seated at their table, from which they could not rise until they had consumed every bit of food on their trays. Also, it was too early in the morning to try to navigate his way around Peter Campanello, who, as usual, had parked his padded wheelchair directly in the path of anyone seeking access to the phone. A cadaverous looking man with a concave chest, thinning, disheveled hair of no definite color, a week's worth of whiskers, and a mouth that hung wide open, Campanello hammered away at the bell on the little plastic table attached to the arm of his wheelchair. Every few seconds, his tinny ring punctuated the equally disagreeable bursts from the phone.

Professor Venuti had nearly reached the dining area when, struck by a pang of conscience, he abruptly reversed his direction, squeezed behind Peter Campanello into the little alcove that housed the still jangling pay phone, and picked up the receiver. Putting a finger in his free ear, he struggled to make out the words of the speaker amid the static and the sound of Campanello's bell. The voice, a shrill one, belonged to the mother of one of the eating disordered girls.

"No, Mrs. Hudson," he explained. "I don't think Kim can come to the phone now. They're not allowed. I'll tell her you called."

Kim Hudson, at thirteen, was the youngest of the Kims and Stacys and Heathers. She had an upturned nose and large, lucent brown eyes, very much like Gilda's. The same tawny hair, almost—perhaps just a shade lighter—hung to her shoulders. Flat chested, large boned, and thin, though not emaciated like some of her peers, she had a boy's build, hiding whatever roundness she might have possessed in the grossly oversized jeans and sweatshirts that she hoped would conceal her imagined fat.

"Kim," the professor yelled across the room.

"Which Kim?" responded three Kims in unison.

"Kim Hudson. It was your mother. I told her you were eating."

"What did she say?" asked the girl, rolling her eyes.

"Good!'"

He resumed his trek toward the dining area but progressed only a few feet.

"Professor," called the nurse he knew, as he knew all the others, by her first name only: Valerie. Over the past few weeks he had grown quite fond of this short, plump, dark haired woman, despite her unrelenting cheerfulness, a quality that, in almost anyone else, would have nauseated him. "I'm your nurse today. I need to get your vital signs now. And give you your morning meds."

"Save yourself the trouble. I have no vital signs."

He followed her to the nearest sofa, sat down, and offered her his right arm, around which she quickly slipped the blood pressure cuff while placing her fingers on his wrist to check his pulse.

"Let's make this quick. If my powdered ersatz eggs get cold, I'll be playing handball with them instead of eating them."

"I hate to ask you this, but you think you can rate your mood for me this morning on the old one-to-ten scale? You didn't think you could get through a morning without it, did you?"

"There is no God. I would say...pi, 3.14159265. And on and on. It goes on just about forever, doesn't it?"

"I think so."

"Just like my mood."

"Well, it's better than Tuesday's absolute zero, anyway."

Patients drifted, one by one, through the day room toward the dining area. The television blared, but no one watched. And Peter Campanello continued to hammer away on his bell.

Suddenly, a chorus of anorexics and bulimics burst into song: "You can ring my be-eh-ehll, ring my bell."

Professor Venuti gestured angrily toward Campanello.

"What's Quasimodo doing here, anyway? Shouldn't he be on a stroke ward or something?"

"What are you worried about, professor?" replied Valerie, with an impish smile. "You're thinking, 'There goes the neighborhood?'"

Try as he might to appear offended, he could not stifle his laughter.

"That's it. Have your fun at my expense. Everyone's a comedian here."

"We try."

"Valerie, Valerie, how is it that you're always so happy? I see you here at eight in the morning and you're smiling. And eight at night and you're smiling. How do you do it?"

"I love my job."

"How can you stand listening to people like me day after day after day?"

"Well, you're a challenge, I admit. But what makes it all worth it is seeing people get better."

"Must be nice. I used to love my job. But it's not what it was. Each year we have to dumb down the reading lists a little more. I get up in front of a class now at the beginning of the school year, and I appraise my eager, young scholars..." Grimacing, he shook his head. "The leather, the body piercings, the studded dog collars, tattoos, purple hair…And I feel as though I'm in a foreign country. They come in in the middle of a lecture, rattle desks around, eat and sleep in the classroom, sit listening to their iThings with the ear buds jammed halfway down their ear canals, take calls on their cell phones, get up and leave halfway through. And if you try to suggest that their behavior may not be quite appropriate for a university classroom, they look at you as though you have two heads. In a hundred years, we'll all be communicating in grunts."

"Let's worry about the here and now," she answered, raising a thermometer to his lips.

He held up his hand to block her. "All my adult life, I've tended to think of words as my currency, as it were. Only in the last year have I realized just how worthless they are.

"The other night, one of the eating disordered girls…It's hard not to think of them as girls. Even the thirty year olds look and act fifteen. One of them had asked for a priest. And she was sitting there talking to him out here in the day room. And when they finished, and he got up to go, I asked him if I could speak to him for a few minutes. I haven't had much use for creatures of that sort over the last thirty, thirty-five years. Not since my near-death experience in the Navy, when I was almost done in by an aspirin, of all things. But just then I thought I did. So we sat down. He looked to be about half my age. Except for his collar, you might mistake him for one of the medical students. I asked him, 'Why is it that a bright, beautiful, multi-talented fourteen-year-old girl with everything to live for goes and starves herself to death? And how is her father to live with that fact for the rest of his life?' And the helpful priest answered, 'You'll look at it differently once you're feeling better.' I wanted to grab that collar of his and strangle him with it."

Valerie nodded and slipped the thermometer into his mouth. He heard Kim Hudson wailing, "It was a piece of fat! It was a piece of fat!"

"It's true," said Valerie, "that he didn't put it very well, but there is some wisdom in what he said. Without minimizing the loss, you have to live with it because you have no other choice. Not on my shift, anyway. And you have to get stronger if you're going to live with it.

I admit I don't have answers to those questions, either. Fortunately, that's not part of my job description. I'm just here to try to get you back to your ornery old self. The rest is up to you."

"It's funny," he said, when she had removed the thermometer, "how it lies dormant for a while. And then, you hear a laugh that sounds like hers. Or see the back of a head, a pony tail. Or go to the house of a colleague for dinner, and lying on the sofa is a book you used to read to her when she was a toddler. It never goes away. You carry it along with you, and it just gets heavier and heavier."

"That's why you have to learn to find ways to lighten that load."

"Such as?"

"Such as fireworks. That's another reason I'm always so cheerful: I never pass up a chance to see fireworks. I'll be down there at the harbor tonight, but you might get just as good a view from the top of the building."

"It'd be pretty cold up on the roof, wouldn't it?"

"Not the roof. The eighth-floor lounge. You think we'd have you people on the roof? We'd have to put nets down below first." She punched him lightly on the arm.

He let out a rueful laugh. Kim Hudson, still loudly insisting that she had left only a piece of bacon fat on her plate, was being dragged away, most likely to the isolation room, by two nurses. The woman who clutched Kim's left arm wore an expression of barely suppressed fury, while the usually genial Percy, an African American male nurse of massive proportions, who held the girl's right arm, looked infinitely weary. Eight o'clock in the morning, said his expression, still in the first hour of a New Year's Eve double shift, and Kim's begun her shenanigans already.

"I don't think I'll stay up," said the professor. "Last year, the three of us...Marie and I...It was our last attempt at reconciliation. I don't know what got into us to try that, but we did. And Gilda had just gotten out of here a little while before. We took the train up to New York, and we went to Times Square to see the ball drop and the fireworks afterward. I wasn't that anxious to do it. I'd seen enough drunkenness and mayhem in the Navy to last me one lifetime. But Gilda wanted to go so badly, and I wasn't going to refuse her anything then. So we went, and we did have a nice time. A happy family again for a night. Of course, within a month, Gilda was...gone. And a couple of weeks later, no more reconciliation."

As Kim disappeared from view, her cries echoed through the ward. She let loose a volley of obscenities and then was heard no more.

"My God. She's thirteen? She could make my old shipmates blush. What can you do with her, short of violence?"

He gazed absently at the posters. "No, I don't think I'll go to-night. A year that begins with reconciliation, however misguided, and Gilda coming home and fireworks in Times Square, and then to close the circle a year later with everything gone and fireworks seen from the psych ward..."

"These fireworks have nothing to do with last year's or anything that's happened in between. You can't weigh everything down like that. You wouldn't see the fireworks even if you did go."

"Maybe old Plato had it backwards. It's the examined life that's not worth living."

"The life examined to the point of paralysis."

"At my next buzzing session, I think I'll bribe the tech to give me five times the usual voltage. Then you can put me down here on the sofa, turn on the soaps, wipe the drool away every once in a while, and I'll be happy."

"Go see the fireworks."

≈≈

After breakfast and a shower, he went down with the others to relaxation group, the one activity in which he participated regularly. Too stiff and creaky to perform the preliminary stretching exercises, and rarely able to attain or maintain the desired focus on breathing during the meditation sessions (his attempts to do so inducing anxiety rather than calm), he did like the darkness and the quiet. On occassion, he would fall asleep and, so his fellow patients told him, snore loudly, much to the amusement of the eating disordered girls. Upon awakening, he might entertain them further by tweaking the nurse-instructor when, inevitably, she asked him to rate his anxiety level on the one-to-ten scale before the exercise—two—and afterwards—497.

Today, though, he could not sleep, so he tried instead to call up words, as many as he could retrieve from storage in as short a time as possible. He began with the mat upon which he lay: mat, pat, sat, bat, rat, fat, hat, vat, cat, hat, cat in hat...But The Cat in the Hat evoked a snapshot: Gilda as a toddler, with puckered lips and furrowed brow, purple ribbons in her hair, a white party dress and white shoes. He started over with the color of the mat: blue, azure, cerulean, ultramarine, aquamarine, sky blue, ocean blue, ocean waves, currents, undertow, depth, darkness, gloom, obscurity, murkiness, duskiness...

In the physical activity session, he sat on a bench at the side of the gym, having grown tired in the last week of his erstwhile favorite pastime of pummeling the heavy bag. No longer could his imagination transform that mass of leather and stuffing into the likeness of his ex-wife's lawyer. He ignored the admonishments of the staff escort to find something to do until Kim Hudson approached and, as she often did, challenged him to a game of Ping-Pong.

With her, he played only defense—just as he once had with Gilda, until the latter had developed enough skill to force him to get serious. Gilda had thrown tantrums when she lost, but she could not abide an opponent who condescended to her by handicapping himself, even if that opponent happened to be her father. Kim, however, could—or did not notice. After one interminable volley, which ended when she hit an easy shot into the net, she asked, "Mr. V. don't you ever make a mistake?"

"Why do you think I'm here?"

Without breaking a sweat or even focusing more than intermittent attention on the games, he won easily three straight times, and on the walk back to the elevator that would take the patients back up to the ward, she gushed, "Mr. V., you're so good."

"Unofficial champion of the USS Iowa City in 1973 and unofficial affective disorders champ here. The two proudest achievements of my adult life."

In occupational therapy, he did no new work on his never-ending trivet project, opting instead to linger outside in the little courtyard with the smokers. Though wet snow, slush, and water covered the ground, the day's brightness and warmth held out a hint of April. Closing his eyes, he turned his face upwards, letting the sun bathe it. What a strange, cloistered existence he had led for nearly a month now. He had gone outside perhaps half a dozen times, mostly at night, had seen little of the daylight and, in all this time, not a single sunrise or sunset.

Another nonsmoking patient, Joy Carswell, stood nearby, absolutely still, her feet close together, her arms frozen at her sides, and her gaze, as always, turned toward the ground. A thickly built woman, she wore her usual gray sneakers and sweat suit. Her hair, too, was gray, and even her complexion had a grayish cast. Observing her, Professor Venuti sometimes had the feeling that he was witnessing a human being undergoing petrifaction. A one-time teacher but now more or less permanent patient who must have known little joy in her life, she had undergone, over the past several months, a series of perhaps thirty ECT treatments or more, without any noticeable success. Professor Venuti had tried, on occasion, to converse with her, but had had to speak volumes to pry from her a syllable. Now, he entreated her with ECT jokes, and to his immense gratification, he did win from her a faint smile—the first she'd ever shown him.

Strange: it seemed that the only people whose company he could abide now were his fellow patients, Valerie, Percy, and a handful of other nurses, and, for short periods, the annoying but well-meaning Dr. McKay. The daily visits of Linda, his—just what was she? he could hardly call her his lover anymore— brought him as much annoyance as solace, consisting as they did primarily of interminable chronicles of the misadventures of her ne'er-do-well son. Just the day before, the professor had driven her away in tears by suggesting that the boy might have a bright future as a crash-test dummy or an organ donor. The drop-ins of his colleagues had ceased to exhaust Professor Venuti only because he had discovered he could hide behind his condition. No longer feeling obliged even to feign interest in departmental gossip, he gaped at the floor or out the window and saddled his guests with the burden of making conversation with themselves, until the strain of it drove them out. The ward was a protected environment, with peers who could understand and nurses who catered to his every need. Had he, though, grown too comfortable? Perhaps the jump from professor to career patient was not such a big one after all.

≈≈

Back in his room, he lay down in his bed and dozed off—but only for a moment, before a burst of light, the clack of heels against linoleum, and the sense of a hovering, brooding presence awakened him. That presence belonged to Marie, a heavy-set woman with a swarthy complexion, filmy, unfocused eyes, a jaw perpetually clenched, and a mouth set in a hard, bitter line. The heavy parka that she kept on despite the warmth of the room—for she always felt cold, no matter the temperature—did not conceal the weight she had gained; she now bordered on obese. The tears that flowed down her cheeks, he knew, might just as soon signify rage as sympathy or remorse, or, most likely, a highly combustible compound of the three. Clasping his hands behind his head and gazing up at the ceiling, he spoke first.

"'And what rough beast, its hour come round at last...' It doesn't surprise me that you would let yourself into my room when I'm sleeping and turn on the light. Respecting boundaries has never been one of your strong points. But why are you here at all? To gloat? Do you enjoy seeing me like this? Or do you want something? You're already living in the house I spent twenty years paying for, while I'm living in a shithole of an efficiency. What else do you and that slime ball lawyer of yours imagine that I have to give you?"

"What I want, I'll never have. All I ever wanted was for you to be a husband. And a father. And you never were either."

"I was as good a husband as you were a wife. And as good a father as you were a mother. We both did our part. Classic eating disorder parental profile." He pointed at her. "Overbearing mother." Twice, he pounded on his chest with his fist. "Aloof father."

"I was a good wife. And I was a good mother. I stayed up nights typing your great manuscript that no one wanted to publish and no one will ever want to read."

"And then tossed 300 or so pages of it into the fire."

"I stayed up night after night!" she shouted. Her tears, as of old, now spilled in torrents, soaking the collar of her parka.

"Even after I went back to work, and I had to run Gilda to school in the morning and then get to my job all the way across town. I stayed up nights because it never occurred to me not to. Because that's what you do for your husband. But you have no sense of family, and you never will. I'll never take you back, Thomas Venuti. It might be harder without you. I might be alone. I might feel sorry for you because you're here, but I'll never take you back."

"O. K., you'll never take me back. Fair enough. Have I ever given any indication since you last threw me out that I wanted to come back? Have I?"

He sat up and faced her. "All these years, and I still cannot fathom how you think. Or if you think. Do you imagine I'd ever want to come back after what you did to my manuscript? After that bogus restraining order? After the things you and your hired character assassin called me in court?"

"Everything that happened in court was by God's hand."

"You mean God suborns perjury?"

"God is punishing you."

"God is punishing me. Well, next time you speak with Him—and I know you often do—tell Him I'm flattered that He's giving me such close personal attention, but enough of a good thing is enough."

"You always mock everything. But look where you are."

"It's true enough. I mock everything. And here I am. But that does not imply the causal connection between the two that you assume. It's a nonsequitur—a logical fallacy to which you, like most ignorant and superstitious people, are particularly prone. You make God in your own image. The Marie God. The Marie God is powerful. She can change the past just by wishing. She's not a conventional liar; she honestly believes the preposterous tales she tells in court. The truth, for her, is what she wishes to be true.

"But not even the Marie God can resurrect a daughter. Not even the Marie God can take away that pain. The best the Marie God can do there is to grant Marie absolution. The fault always lies with someone else. The husband. The doctors. Always someone else. And that, at least, gives her comfort."

She spat in his face. He shot up to his feet, his fists clenched. Glowering, he stood over her menacingly.

"You want to hit me?" she wailed. Panting now, she placed her hand upon her chest. "I'll get the police in here. I'll have you arrested, Thomas Venuti."

"No. You've already pulled that trick on me once."

He slipped around her, opened the door, and, his quaking hand still grasping the handle, turned to face her again.

"Get out!"

"I'll never take you back, Thomas Venuti!"

"Get out of here. Now!"

She stood rooted, though, the tears still pouring down, until Percy stuck his head inside and asked, "Is there a problem here?"

≈≈

Professor Venuti meandered through the day room. Though the figure of Kim Hudson, standing in front of the television, registered only at the periphery of his awareness as he passed, he nonetheless dutifully performed his part of their long-running call-and-response routine.

"Sit down, Kim," he growled at the girl, who never did unless forced, even as he settled himself in a chair.

"Mr. V., did you eat everything on your plate at lunch? You don't want Percy to throw you in the isolation room."

"Kim Hudson!" bellowed the long-suffering Percy, from somewhere in the vicinity of the nurse's station. "Sit down! Now!"

Sit the girl did, but after a minute or so, when she thought it safe to do so, she popped right back up.

Besides Kim Hudson, another Kim was crocheting, and a Stacy and a Heather were making bead bracelets of clay. Joy Carswell faced the television, but with her eyes directed at the floor; Peter Campanello hammered away at his bell; and another patient, a lean and gnarly septuagenarian named Sam Bowen, paced up and down in his baggy blue sweat suit, sighing loudly, grimacing, and picking at his nails.

Every day at this time, the flaccid, unscheduled hour between occupational therapy and dinner, the ebullient Oprah! Invaded this place of sadness. Out of sheer boredom and an inability to concentrate enough to read, Professor Venuti, like the others, had become a regular viewer of sorts, though one who paid such scant attention that if asked immediately afterward who had appeared on the show and what subject or subjects it had covered, he could not have said. But today, something caught his eye: an enlarged photo of a skeletal young girl—the guest, explained Oprah, before her tenuous victory over anorexia. He shot up from his chair.

"Kim, isn't there something just a little incongruous about watching a TV program on anorexia while standing because you think it will burn off an extra calorie or two?"

She gaped at him, uncomprehendingly.

"Damn it! Can't you see what you're doing to yourself?"

She drew back, her eyes moist, a stricken look upon her face.

Suddenly, Sam Bowen stood still, and Campanello's bell grew silent. All the eyes in the room, it seemed to Thomas Venuti, had fastened upon him, and he felt his face grow hot. He stroked his beard several times, stared hard at the floor, shook his head.

"I'm sorry, Kim. I didn't mean to yell. I know you get enough of that as it is. But are you going to go through life breaking the heart of everyone who cares for you? Trouble can always find you, Kim. You don't need to go looking for it."

He slunk out of the room and did not return for dinner.

On his windowsill, he found several envelopes and a message on pink stationary written in green ink, in a large, rounded script:

> Stopped in earlier but they said you were in occupational therapy. Will come by again after dinner. I got your mail and checked your messages. Bonnie Butler called. Wanted to know how you are doing with the revisions on your book. Also wished you happy holidays.

> Love, L.
> xoxoxo

He could not say for sure what impelled him to crumble the

note into a ball and slam-dunk it into the wastebasket: the ex's and o's or the mention of Bonnie Butler. That lizard-like creature with the beady eyes and the darting tongue. It had to be fed within six weeks' time—a lean, tight manuscript of 400 pages tops, though what it really would have preferred was for him to scrap the whole thing and give her instead 200 pages or so, in large type, about the masturbatory muse in the oeuvre of Madonna, sans bibliography or citations. What he had for her was a tome of nearly 1,100 pages that he had toiled over, on and off, for the better part of eighteen years, first on a creaky manual typewriter and then, when he could no longer find replacement ribbons, on an IBM Selectric. Some combination of perversity and technophobia had led him to shun most of the gadgetry developed in the last thirty years or so. To him, a computer seemed suitable for cranking out departmental memos or letters of recommendation but not for serious work.

From the bottom shelf of the little wall cabinet near the foot of the bed, he retrieved two formidable stacks of paper that rested in two separate halves of a cardboard box and set them down on the mattress. As often happened when he tried to read now, the black marks on the white page refused to coalesce into sentences or ideas. He would reach the end of a paragraph and, no more enlightened than when he had begun, would immediately return to the top. Now his gaze fastened upon the chapter heading on page 291: "'I Have No Way and Therefore Want No Eyes': A Dark Vision on the Heath."

He picked up the smaller stack and flung it across the room. From the larger pile, he grabbed handful after handful and did the same, until he had emptied the box. Heaps of erudition flew through the air, hit walls and ceiling, and scattered. Single sheets swirled, hung suspended, then slowly fell, covering the linoleum floor like fresh, soft snow. He swatted away the two empty box halves, then lay back on the bed.

Though he heard the knock, he acknowledged neither it, nor the opening of the door, nor the eyes that peeked around the edge, nor the faltering "Tom?" The second "Tom?" he answered with a grunt, and Linda emerged from behind the door. Tall and well-proportioned, she had a small mouth but fleshy lips, a nose with a graceful upward arc, and straight chestnut hair held back from her face by a pink hair band. A strong clove-like scent wafted about her. She wore pointy-toed beige boots, tight-fitting blue jeans—Marie would have had some choice words for those—a black fake-fur jacket, and glasses with large, tinted lenses that, in the right light, swathed her entire face in pink and made her seem, somehow, a thirty-nine-year-old waif. He saw her through Marie's eyes—as precisely the sort of woman that his ego demanded.

"I would have been here sooner," she said, "but Jason got detention again. He couldn't get the bus home, and I had to go pick him up. He never turns in his work. He's failing English, math, and social studies. The doctor took him off the Ritalin, and he put him on Prozac. But that's not working, either. So now he's talking about trying him on both together. I don't know what to do anymore."

"I don't know, either."

"Do you think maybe you could have a talk with him?"

"Why, sure. Just bring him up here. Preferably when I'm stretched out on a gurney, drooling, after ECT. I'll make a fine picture of a role model."

She irritated him. The situation irritated him—the trite and unseemly involvement between department chairman and department secretary seventeen years his junior and the knowledge that this hapless underling was perhaps the one person remaining on this earth to whom his existence truly mattered. He had shown her ordinary kindness, but that was far more than her ex-husband ever had done, and she had mistaken it for love. Her hunger had frightened him, and the burden of feigning a passion he did not feel had become too heavy to carry. For at least two months before he'd entered the hospital, he had found himself unable to perform in bed. Viewing his incapacity as a judgment on her, she had become ever more desperate to please.

Her eyes scanned the floor.

"Tom, what have you been doing in here?"

"Waiting for death. Something better done in the dark. Would you mind turning off the light?"

She removed her jacket, folded it, and set it down upon the chair, revealing a pink and blue flowered blouse, opened at the neck to display a gold chain and the circular brown beauty mark just beneath her throat.

"Tom, your manuscript!" Dropping to her hands and knees, she began to collect the pages he had strewn all around.

"Yes, my manuscript. It was supposed to justify a life. What was I thinking? There is no justifying this life. Would you please stop that? I will pick it up myself later. Or let housekeeping take it out with the rest of the trash."

She continued, though, to gather, pausing only to dab with a handkerchief at the tears that came coursing down her cheeks.

"Please. I mean it. I don't want you to pick up after me. I'll speak to Jason if you'd like."

She gazed at him through fogged, pink lenses. "Would you? He might listen to you. His father doesn't want anything to do with him."

"Yes. But don't expect a miracle. You talk till you're blue in the face, but they'll do what they will."

He blinked back the tears that filled his eyes. "All you want is to take it upon yourself. Whatever the thing is that's gnawing at her."

"At who, Tom?"

"That's causing her to starve herself to death. Let me waste away instead of her. You'd sell your soul to the devil. But the devil isn't buy-ing."

≈≈

When Linda, after first gathering and collating all the pages—in defiance of his repeated demands that she stop—had finally gone, he turned off the light and lay down again. He would sleep through New Year's, or so he hoped. But try as he might to beckon it, sleep remained beyond reach. He tried to focus on his breathing, but each inhalation brought the terrible question, "When would come the last breath?" He rested his hands upon his protruding ribs. How much weight had he lost over the past two months, when even eating had come to seem as pointless as any other activity? The slight burning in his stomach that had begun after Marie's visit and worsened when he took his medication unaccompanied by the customary evening meal had become an inferno.

When he was in the Navy, his ship anchored off San Diego, an aspirin had lodged in his esophagus. Awakened by a searing pain, he had somehow risen from his bunk and staggered to the sink. In the mirror, he had seen blood pouring from his mouth. The thought had gripped him then: "I am going to die now. I am alone, and I am going to die." To keep from losing consciousness, he had sung out loud, over and over again:

Sing a song of sixpence,
A pocket full of rye,
Four and twenty blackbirds
Baked in a pie.

He had stayed awake just long enough to crawl out of the cabin and grab the leg of the startled Ensign Garcia, the first man passing.

The four-and-twenty blackbirds had saved his life. Had they blessed or cursed him? He had honored them in Gilda's babyhood by singing of them while rubbing her back when he put her to bed. But they had not saved her when he'd found her curled up at the bottom of the stairs, a near skeleton in a pink nightgown, blue veins showing through almost translucent skin. A scream rose to his lips, but at the last instant, he stifled it.

The faint light of a veiled moon filtered in through the windowpane. He held his hand up to the glass, stretching the fingers wide apart. How insubstantial, how fragile, the hand seemed; it might have been a leaf, with the bones as the petioles, the flesh as the blades.

Letting his hand drop back onto the bed, he peered out at the night sky. A sudden and very powerful longing seized him. If only he could soar into that charcoal sky, leave behind this botched life, this aging, decaying body. If only he could soar.

He heard a soft knock at the door.

"Mr. Venuti?"

"What is it?" he barked.

"It's me, Kim. Kim Hudson."

"Oh, I'm sorry, Kim. I thought you were one of the nurses, checking up on me."

"Are you going up to the eighth floor to see the fireworks?"

"I don't think so."

"You get a really good view from up there."

"I'm sure. I take it then that you've watched the fireworks from there before?"

"On the Fourth of July."

"Jeez!"

"What?"

"Nothing. Nothing. I'm sorry I lost my temper before in the day room."

"That's O.K. Are you all right, Mr. V.?"

"I'm fine, Kim. Listen, I'll come along—if you promise me one thing."

"What?"

"That the next time you see fireworks, it'll be somewhere else."

"O.K. I promise."

"And not another psych ward, either," he murmured under his breath.

≈≈

He dressed and joined the gathering in the day room—Kim Hudson and her two namesakes; various Stacys and Heathers; Sam Bowen, still sighing, grimacing, and picking; Peter Campanello in his wheelchair; and, perhaps most surprisingly, Joy Carswell. As they ascended in the elevator, the eating disordered girls began to giggle, to groom one another, to jump up and down, and when the door opened on the eighth floor, they spilled out and scurried off toward the end of the hall.

"Ladies, ladies," cried Percy from behind, pushing Peter Campanello's wheelchair. "Let's slow it down up there. We need to stay together. Or else we'll turn right back around."

Their enthusiasm, though, had infected even Joy Carswell, the curve of whose lips hinted at a smile. Professor Venuti, who upon leaving the darkness and the solitude of his room had ceased musing on his mortality and felt his stomach pain ease, turned to the burly nurse and whispered, "Look at that little Kim Hudson. She's just dying to break into a sprint."

Percy's guffaw resounded through the hallway. He shook his head. "Sixteen hours of Kim Hudson duty today. And the last just has to be the hardest. Lord, get me to the end."

At that moment, Kim Hudson did, in fact, break into a sprint, and all her cohort followed, leaving the professor, Sam Bowen, Joy Carswell, Peter Campanello, and Percy far behind.

"Ladies! Ladies!" shouted Percy, but then, with a wave of his hand, he signaled his capitulation.

Taking his place before the eighth-floor activity room window, flanked by Joy Carswell and Sam Bowen, Professor Venuti looked out upon the metallic skeleton of the new hospital wing under construction. A harsh, brassy light outlined the dingy streets and the crumbling row houses that surrounded the medical complex. In the middle distance, where the grid of crossing streets began to blur, he discerned Little Italy, an area of brighter light streaked with neon. Farther down, a pearly string of headlights illumined the expressway, and still farther, beyond the downtown lights, lay the dark waters of the harbor.

He heard a rumble, and saw orange tendrils fill the sky. Then there came silver swirls and globes of green, blue, and purple that fragmented in all directions, the foremost offshoots poised to touch the building, until, suddenly, they faded. Peter Campanello hammered at his bell.

"Happy New Year!" yelled Kim Hudson.

"Happy New Year!" chimed in all the Kims, the Stacys, and the Heathers.

MATTERS OF THE HEART

Father Anthony Stanco yanked off his glasses and tossed them onto the desk, where they came to rest upside down atop a stack of pages in an open manila folder. Leaning backward in his chair, he raised his burning eyes to the ceiling and shut them, and the lassitude that had plagued him all morning stole over him once more. His large head sank slowly forward, and his arms fell from the armrests.

He shook himself back into wakefulness. Pulling at the edge of his saturated collar, he drew a handkerchief from his pocket and dabbed at his jowls, his forehead, and his neck. From the pitcher that sat on the shelf behind him, he poured himself a glass of ice water and took a long draught. Rarely, outside of his nightmares, had he felt so parched, so heavy, so weary, so weak.

He stood up, raised his arms above his head and stretched his massive frame. A sudden pain in his chest made him wince. His hands grew numb and his balance unsure. Gripping the edge of the desk, he lowered himself back into his chair. He closed his eyes, pressed his hand against the hurting spot, and inhaled deeply—once, twice, three times.

When the pain had ebbed to a level at which he could safely assume that he was not about to die, he took another sip of water and reached for his glasses, his folder, and the translucent glass letter opener with which he habitually fiddled while reading. He resumed where he had left off:

> Dr. Ryland's manner of acting during these annulment proceedings offers evidence that lends some plausibility to the descriptions of Mrs. Ryland and her witnesses of his extreme volatility. On numerous occasions Dr. Ryland contacted the offices of the Tribunal by telephone, fax, or e-mail, or appeared in person to demand that his petition be expedited, often making reference to the cost of initiating this inquiry and to his unsolicited donations to the diocese above and beyond that amount. Staff described his demeanor in the office as threatening at times, though no specific verbal threats were made.

≈≈

Father Stanco finished his glass and filled another. There came a faint tapping on the door—a timid, forlorn sound that a less attuned ear might not have picked up at all.

"Yes, come in, Mrs. Peterson," he bellowed, jabbing at the pad of his index finger with the point of the letter opener.

The door opened slightly, and a yellow shaft of light pierced the dimness. The outlines of a face peeked around the edge of the door.

"Father?"

Amid the wheezes and gurgles of the air conditioner set into the wall to his left—the death rattle of a dinosaur—her voice barely reached him.

"I said come in, Mrs. Peterson. You have nothing to be afraid of. You can show yourself. In this world, the meek shall inherit only heartache."

Slowly, a slight, dark-haired woman of about sixty, with a wattled neck, deep creases in her face, and downcast eyes emerged from behind the door.

Why, he wondered, did this harmless little creature—who asked nothing of him other than that he allow her to donate her time and efforts to the rectory—so provoke him? Did God create the Mrs. Petersons of this world to test one's compassion? If so, Father Stanco had failed miserably.

"What is it, Mrs. Peterson?"

"It's Dr. Ryland and Miss Barnett," she squeaked. "They're here for their pre-Cana classes."

"Pre-Cana classes. Is that what they're expecting? Close the door behind you, Mrs. Peterson. Would you please? Thank you. I've been reading all about Dr. Ryland. It seems that he's made himself quite a presence down at the archdiocese, though nobody bothered to inform me until today. Tell me, Mrs. Peterson, have you ever heard of a case in which a petition for annulment was granted because of the petitioner's unfitness?"

Facing him at an oblique angle, her left shoulder raised to obscure her face, she replied, "No, Father. I don't think so."

"Nor had I, until today. But I suppose anything goes nowadays. Maybe one day soon we'll have no-fault annulments.

"In seven years, when I was in Mexico, I never had one annulment. There it was always last rites, last rites, last rites. Last rites on the dirt floors of squatters' huts. Last rites on the sidewalk. Last rites in a public toilet. Last rites for the old, the not-so-old, the young. Conditional baptisms for babies who died before I could get to them. And I always got to them too late."

He paused for a gulp of air and another of water.

"Father, should I tell them to come in?"

"The funny thing was, despite my impotence, people seemed to need me in Mexico. But here... What need do you have of a priest in Greenvale, New Jersey, where you can write a check and annul all your troubles away? Father Anthony Stanco: the Maytag repairman of the soul. That's why I've grown to be such a fat, bilious, old toad, Mrs. Peterson. In case you were wondering.

"Tell the happy couple I'll be with them in about ten minutes. I haven't finished my reading yet."

"Oh, and…and…" she stammered.

"Yes?"

"Dr. Carlson called before, while you were out."

"Doctor Carlson himself? On a Saturday?"

"He said it was urgent. He wanted you to call back as soon as possible."

"But I already know what he's going to tell me."

He held the blade of the letter opener up to the bulb of the desk lamp. White light splintered into rainbows.

"Contrary to what you may think, Mrs. Peterson, it's not true that I have no heart. Mine is actually bigger than most. It's enlarged. And it's causing me a great deal of trouble.

"It's a curious thing. In all the patient literature I've slogged through, I've never seen a description of how the surgeon opens up the chest. A rather telling omission, in my view."

"Father, if there's anything I can do to help."

He put down the letter opener. When he looked up at her, she met his gaze head on.

"Thank you, Mrs. Peterson. That's very kind of you."

As she opened the door to leave, he called her name once more. When she looked at him, he suddenly found himself at a loss and could only stammer out the words, "Thank you."

The white golf shoes of Dr. Ryland and his fiancée click-clacked against the hardwood floor of the study as the two approached Father Stanco's desk. Both visitors wore identical white shorts and white baseball caps that bore the logo "Chantilly Manor" in maroon script. He wore a canary yellow knit shirt, and she, a lavender one. Dr. Ryland was tall and deeply tanned, bulky in the arms, chest, and shoulders. He had a bald crown, a sharp nose, a small, tense mouth, and dark, piercing eyes. Ms. Barnett, though she appeared younger than her fiancé—early thirties, Father Stanco guessed—had a haunted look that her ready smile could not conceal. She was all bone, sinew and sharp angles, with concave cheeks and sunken eyes.

Without rising, Father Stanco beckoned them to sit and turned his attention back to his folder.

"It's dark in here," said the woman, nervously.

"Yes, I like it that way. In the seminary, I was known as 'The Mole.' As long as I have enough light to read by, I'm fine. Planning to get some golf in today?"

"Never miss a weekend," answered Dr. Ryland, grinning.

"Now he's got me hooked, too," added his fiancée. "Do you play, father?"

"No. No, I don't," he answered, irritably. "I never could quite see why otherwise sensible, intelligent people would want to chase a little ball around for miles."

"You should try it, father," said Dr. Ryland. "It's great exercise, which is essential, even for a man your age. It's not good to lead a sedentary life."

Father Stanco grunted, reached for his handkerchief and mopped his face. His crudely clipped hair, which, though gray as the hull of a battleship, hung as thickly as it had in his youth, was soaked at the temples. Of the three people in the room, he alone was sweating. Breathing had become a labor.

"Tell me, Dr. Ryland, why is it…?"

"Jeff."

"And I'm Sue," added the woman.

"Right. Jeff and Sue. Is it very important to the two of you to marry in the Church?"

The doctor's head jerked back, his mouth tightened, and his eyes narrowed.

"Where else would we get married? We're both Catholics. We go to Mass. Maybe not as often as we should. But we go."

"I understand that. But is it of great importance to you to marry in the Church?"

"Of course it is, father," answered the woman. "To both of us. Why do you ask?"

"Well, I'm afraid we have a bit of a problem. I've been doing some reading this morning, Dr. Ryland. About you and the former Mrs. Ryland. When you spoke to me on the phone, you neglected to tell me that you'd been married in the Church before."

"Oh, that. I got the final annulment decree three months ago at least. That's all behind me."

"That seems to be a common expression these days. Things get put behind one very quickly. What's that line from Hamlet about the leftover funeral meats furnishing the wedding tables?

"Well, as a procedural matter, you are correct. It is behind you. Mrs. Ryland has decided not to appeal. And far be it for me to question the legitimacy of annulling an eleven-year marriage that produced three children. I guess that's just the way things are done now. Still, it's not a good idea to mislead the priest who's giving you your pre-Cana instruction."

The doctor bristled.

"I didn't mislead anyone. You never asked about it when I spoke to you on the phone. I didn't know it would be a problem."

"He would have told you if he'd known it was important," added Ms. Barnett.

"No doubt, no doubt. Still…"

"Look, can we get on with this?" interrupted the doctor.

"In due time. Did you happen to read the decision of the Tribunal, Dr. Ryland?"

"No. I'm sorry, father. I know I should have, but I'm a busy man. I don't have time to dwell on the past. What's done is done."

"True, but…."

"Then what's the problem?"

"The problem is that while annulments may not be what they used to be, we still like to limit them to one per customer. The Church regards—or used to regard—marriage as a fairly serious business. Jesus spoke quite clearly on that. God does the joining, not man. Marriage is a sacred bond. It's not something to be set aside lightly."

"Lightly? The divorce cost me two years of my life and $70,000, at least."

"I think you're missing my point."

"Father, with all due respect," said Ms. Barnett, "I don't see how

God could want a person to suffer all their lives for a mistake they made when they weren't mature or experienced enough to know better. Or would want three beautiful children like his to suffer for their parents' mistakes. I work in family mediation. I have cases every day where there's been so much conflict that getting separated or divorced was the best thing the parents could have done for the children. Most of the studies I'm familiar with on children of divorced parents confirm that. It's not divorce per se that causes adjustment problems for the children. It's the level of conflict between the parents."

"That may be. Still, there were some pretty troubling issues raised by the former Mrs. Ryland that I think may have implications for your future together. Perhaps, Dr. Ryland, you and I might want to discuss some of them in private, initially."

"I have nothing to hide."

"He's told me everything, Father Stanco," added Ms. Barnett, taking hold of her fiancé's hand. "We have no secrets from each other."

"No secrets, Dr. Ryland?"

The doctor glowered at him.

"O.K., then. There was an allegation of adultery, for one."

"Oh, come on. All through the marriage she was accusing me. If I so much as looked at another woman she'd start throwing dishes around the house. That woman persecuted me. My home was like a prison."

"To be perfectly fair, Dr. Ryland, the Tribunal couldn't resolve that one. It said—I'm quoting here—'The allegations of adultery against Dr. Ryland, while credible, are not proven to the degree required by this Tribunal.' What I want to know..." Father Stanco broke off in mid-sentence. Short of air, he breathed in avidly, like one who had just emerged from the bottom of a pool. He picked up the letter opener and pointed it at the doctor. "What I want to know, Dr. Ryland, is can you look me in the eye right now, in front of your fiancée, and tell me that you didn't cheat on your wife?"

"I did not commit adultery," replied Dr. Ryland, his gaze firm and his voice brimming with indignation.

How many times had he rehearsed that line? Father Stanco's mouth contracted into a pinched smile.

"There were also accusations of emotional and physical abuse. Of her and the children."

"Oh, please. I have never hit my kids. Never. I'm a good father."

"If anything, he's too modest," said Ms. Barnett. "He's a wonderful father. "I've seen how he interacts with those children. He loves them, and they love him. They're sorry when it's time to go back to their mother. So many men just pay their child support and think that's all they have to do. He does so much more."

"I'm not questioning that, Miss Barnett. He may well be an excellent father. But the Tribunal…"

He coughed twice, and before he could resume, Dr. Ryland seized the opening: "They gave me the damn annulment, didn't they?"

"Yes, they gave you the damn annulment," answered Father Stanco, icily. "But the grounds were 'lack of due discretion in the man.' I'm quoting here from the decision:

The petitioner is presented as lacking in due discretion because he was grossly lacking in the internal freedom and judgmental discretion to appreciate the nature of the communitas vitae and to establish such a relationship with his wife in the marriage. It is the judgment of this Tribunal that the extreme volatility on Dr. Ryland's part amounts to an inability to appreciate the nature of marriage as an intimate partnership.

≈≈

"In other words, Dr. Ryland, the marriage was not legitimate because of your unfitness. In receiving the sacrament of holy matrimony, before, God, before your wife, and before the whole congregation, you lied. It was not…" For a moment, he found himself without sufficient breath to complete the sentence. "It was not in your heart."

"What are you, a psychic or something? You know what was in my heart when I got married? How do you know that?"

"I was not a member of the Tribunal, Dr. Ryland. What I have to determine is whether you're ready to undergo a Catholic marriage ceremony now."

"Look, I don't deal in uncertainties. I don't have the time. Are we moving ahead on this or not?"

Father Stanco tightened his grip on the handle of the letter opener.

"If you insist on an answer now, I'll give you one. No. I cannot allow this marriage to go forward."

"Fine. Then I'll get someone who will."

Dr. Ryland rose abruptly and turned toward the door.

"Not in this diocese, you won't. Not in any diocese, if I have anything to say in the matter. I'm sure you're used to getting what you want. But in this instance, the Church is not going to oblige you."

"But Father Stanco," said Ms. Barnett, with a look of utter incomprehension, "we've already sent out the invitations."

"I'm sorry," he sputtered, between coughs. "But I cannot give my approval for a Catholic wedding ceremony."

"Let's go, babe. Now!" ordered the doctor, his meaty hand squeezing the doorknob.

"Father, please," begged the doctor's fiancèe. A single teardrop shimmered for an instant in the corner of her right eye, then slid down her cheek. "He's made mistakes in the past. But people change. You of all people should know that."

"People do change, Miss Barnett. But I see no indication that Dr. Ryland has."

"How can you decide that in the few minutes you've spent with him? You never gave him a chance." Her cheeks were now bathed in tears.

"Sue, let's go!"

Now she was the one straining for air, gasping like an emphysemic as she rose from her seat. When she glared down at Father Stanco, he saw in her eyes a scalding hatred. He marveled at how, even now, so late in his life, people could still confound him. Just a moment before, he could not have imagined Sue Barnett, the professional conciliator, capable of harboring such fury. Hers was a rage that, the priest suspected, would smolder on long after Dr. Ryland, so blessed with the gift of selective amnesia, had forgotten this day. Perhaps no less than she, the good doctor would have some unpleasant surprises awaiting him, and, in the not-too-distant future, would regret this union just as bitterly.

"Father," she said, in a voice as caustic as ammonia, "I think you need to look into your own heart. You're a cruel, hateful person."

"It would not be an act of kindness on my part to allow this marriage to proceed, Miss Barnett. This gives me no pleasure. It's true that I've never been known for my tact. But when I see someone about to step off the curb into the path of an eighteen-wheeler...."

Out of breath, he left the sentence hanging in the air.

"Come on, Sue. Now!"

When they had gone, Father Stanco dipped his handkerchief into the ice water and rubbed down his face and the back of his neck. With two fingers pressed tightly against the brachial artery in his right wrist, he grimly counted out the heartbeats in a minute.

WANDERERS

When Peter Dolan's daughters, having reached mid-adolescence, decided that no matter what the court had decreed, they would no longer live with him forty percent of the time, he sold his house in the suburbs and purchased an aging duplex that stood in the shadow of his alma mater, Johns Hopkins University. He traded in his Ford Explorer for a Mini and began having flings with his receptionists. As in his undergraduate and law school days, Peter once more became a habitué of the Charm City Pub, a dark, roomy establishment where a team portrait of the collegiate national championship lacrosse team for which he had starred decades before hung from the paneled wall opposite the bar alongside autographed pictures of such Baltimore sports deities as Johnny Unitas, Brooks Robinson, and Cal Ripken, Jr.

His ex-wife mocked him for imagining that by returning to his old haunts he could recover something of his youth. Events proved her right. Now more than twice the age of most of his fellow drinkers at the Charm City Pub, he no longer found there the comradeship he remembered. The affairs with the receptionists invariably ended with firings and recriminations. The right knee that he had shredded during the season that followed the national championship had grown so arthritic that climbing the stairs to his second-floor apartment— he rented out the first floor—had become a torment. He had nearly resigned himself to the knee replacement that his doctor had urged upon him for so long.

One dank Sunday night in early April, when Peter had wearied of sitting at home alone with his pain, he hopped down the stairs and limped his way over to the Charm City Pub—a short but agonizing journey, for anything more than the slightest flexing of his bad knee produced a sensation like that of a hammer blow to his patella. With the Hopkins students away on spring break and the bar nearly empty, Peter, carrying on a half-hearted flirtation with the bartender, lingered longer and drank more than a man with a conference call scheduled for 7:30 the next morning should have. It was, he recalled, a year to the day since he had last seen his daughters, but the anniversary evoked in him only a mild melancholy. He had grown accustomed to the girls' absence as he imagined one must grow accustomed to life with a missing limb. One could get used to anything.

The bartender, a cheery brunette in her mid-twenties, dressed in tight blue jeans and a black, short-sleeved blouse that left her flat midriff exposed, regaled him with tales of her recent trek through Nepal.

"And as soon as I've saved enough," she confided, "I'll quit this job, and I'll be off again. I never work a day longer than I have to."

"Where will you go next?"

"Africa."

"Africa. Cool!" Draining his shot glass, Peter rapped it against the surface of the bar. "I always wanted to go on safari. See some lions and tigers in the wild."

Deftly scooping up his glass, the young woman answered, with a teasing smile, "There are no tigers in Africa."

His gaze remained fixed upon her nicely rounded buttocks as she sauntered away.

The front door swung open, and a slight, stooped, elderly man came stumbling inside as if blown there by the blast of frigid night air that suddenly filled the room. The man stood for a moment, tottering slightly, looking about as if trying to puzzle out where he was. Then he shuffled up to the bar, just to Peter's left, and leaned against it. Beside Peter, a burly six-and-a-half footer, who, since his lacrosse-playing days, had acquired a salt-and-pepper beard and a bit of a paunch, the man looked tiny. His rumpled trench coat hung open, and the black and green flannel shirt that he wore beneath it was soaked. His white hair was matted to his temples. He wore black square-framed glasses, their clouded, oversized lenses concealing his eyes. His blanched complexion, labored breathing, and slack, unshaven cheeks gave him the look of someone who had just risen from a sickbed.

"Maybe I should go to Africa," said Peter to the man, whom he felt sure he had seen before. "And not come back."

The man gave Peter a puzzled look and began inching away to the left.

"I wish it had occurred to me that I could have lived the way she does."

"Who?"

"Instead, I had a family. Emphasis on had. And I became a lawyer. Speaking as a lawyer myself, I think Shakespeare had the right idea about us. 'The first thing we do, let's kill all the lawyers.'"

"People who use that line to denigrate lawyers," answered the man sharply, "understand neither the play from which it comes nor the judicial system." Scowling, he removed his glasses and lay them down upon the bar.

The scowl startled Peter, who felt certain he had encountered it before. "Professor Whitfield?"

"I'm sorry. I don't think I know you."

The bartender returned, handed Peter a newly filled shot glass, and set a coaster down on the bar in front of her new customer.

"Do you know who this is?" Peter asked the bartender. Leaning far to his left, he draped a beefy arm over the shoulders of the older man, who tried in vain to wriggle free.

She studied the man for a moment and then, shrugging, replied, "Not really. Should I?"

"This is Professor Lawrence Whitfield."

"It's been a long time since I've been Professor Whitfield."

"This man was the best professor I had in law school by far. He didn't just teach me constitutional law. He taught me how to think." With the stereo muted, Peter's alcohol-fueled baritone resounded through the barroom.

"The extent to which I succeeded appears to be an open question."

The bartender chortled and gave Peter a playful punch on the arm.

"God, this man used to terrify me," said Peter. "He'd pace from one side of the classroom to the other, smoking his pipe. And then he'd stop and ask a question it had never occurred to you to think about, and he'd point at you with the stem of the pipe. You felt like you were being skewered."

But the once imposing Professor Whitfield appeared to have shrunk to half his former size—an impression that Peter found profoundly unsettling. The ache in his knee, tolerable for the last hour or so, began to intensify once more.

"I spent many a night in here trying to forget about how I'd made a fool of myself in class in the afternoon. I never thought I'd run into you here, Professor Whitfield."

"Yes, well, you wouldn't have, except that I got a bit lost. I was out running some errands. The weather's bad, and I seem to have missed a turn somewhere."

"Where are you going?" Peter asked.

"Where am I going?" Professor Whitfield suddenly looked flustered. "I'm going…I'm going home. Lutherville."

"Lutherville? How did you end up all the way down here?"

Professor Whitfield answered with an irritable sigh.

"Well, it's not hard to get back to the highway from here," said Peter.

The confusion in Professor Whitfield's eyes belied his repeated assurances that he understood Peter's directions perfectly well. Borrowing a pen from the bartender, Peter drew a map on a napkin.

"I hope you'll forgive me for not remembering you," said Professor Whitfield as Peter handed him the improvised map. "There's a lot I don't remember these days." With his head bowed and his eyes fixed upon the map, he shambled out the door.

"He shouldn't be out driving on a night like this," said Peter to the bartender. "I suspect he shouldn't be driving at all. But people are stubborn that way. My father wouldn't give up the car until a couple of months before he died. I fought with him for years about it. He could barely see. The only way he could tell that the light had changed was when the guy behind him started honking. It's a wonder he didn't kill himself or someone else."

"My grandmother's the same way," answered the bartender with a yawn. "Drives my parents crazy." Opening the tap above a bifurcated metal sink behind the bar, she squirted a stream of green dishwashing detergent into one of the basins, filling the other with clear water. From the counter beside the sink, she snatched up several glasses, immersed them in the sudsy water, and then plucked them out one by one, giving each a quick going over with a bottle brush.

Peter gulped down his whiskey and handed the young woman his glass. "One more. Last one."

No sooner had she returned with his drink, than he finished it off. He peered into the empty shot glass as if it were a telescope

"The older I get, the less I understand. Parents become like children. Children disown you." He shook his large head mournfully.

"Mm," murmured the bartender in a vaguely sympathetic way, and then she turned her attention back to the glasses in the sink.

"One more," said Peter, holding out his shot glass again. "This is really my last one."

When he had finished his drink, he reached for his wallet and tossed several bills onto the bar, without bothering to check their denominations. Gingerly, he lowered himself from his stool and made his way to the door.

As he stepped onto the sidewalk, he immediately regretted his carelessness in having left his apartment clad in only a t-shirt and jeans, for now he faced a four-block slog home through a wind-driven downpour. Hunched over, his arms folded across his chest, he started forward. Despite all he had drunk, he suddenly felt sober—far too sober. The last two shots of whiskey had deadened the pain in his knee, but now it returned in full force.

He had not gone far when he heard a loud thump. A wheat-colored Toyota Corolla, sandwiched into a parking space between two large, black SUVs, had backed into the bumper of the one in the rear. The Toyota then inched forward, its front end angling away from the curb, only to bump against the vehicle in front.

Peter knocked against the passenger-side window.

Professor Whitfield lowered the window a couple of inches. "Yes?" he snapped.

"Are you O.K., Professor Whitfield?"

"I'm fine. Thank you."

"Do you still have the map I gave you?"

"The what? What map?"

"The one I drew for you in the bar."

"You drew me a map?"

"In the bar. On a napkin."

Professor Whitfield sifted through the array of fliers, envelopes, and magazines that covered the passenger's seat. Leaning far to his right, he opened the glove compartment and groped inside it. Then he reached into his coat pockets, shrugged, raised the window again, and gripped the shift lever. But the car did not move.

Positioning himself behind the Toyota, near the curb, Peter turned an imaginary steering wheel sharply to the right and then beckoned with his hands. He had to hop out of the way, landing painfully on his bad leg, when Professor Whitfield missed his stop signal and backed the right rear wheel of the Toyota up onto the curb.

Peter limped around to the driver's side and tapped on the window.

"Yes?"

"Why don't you let me pull the car out for you?"

Again, there came the familiar scowl. "I hardly think that's necessary. Besides which, you're obviously quite drunk."

"I've driven in worse states than this."

"That's very reassuring."

"I'll have you out of here in thirty seconds, and you'll be on your way."

Professor Whitfield let out a long, sibilant sigh. Shifting the Toyota into park and engaging the emergency brake, he stepped outside, ignoring the hand that Peter proffered him, and walked around to the rear of the car. Bracing his left hand against the trunk, he mounted the curb and stepped onto the strip of wet grass that separated the road from the sidewalk. There, wobbling and wheezing, he halted and gazed about as if he had just alighted in a strange country.

"I can manage it all right," said Peter, throwing his right arm around Professor Whitfield's shoulders and deftly steering him toward the passenger's seat. "No need to stand out here in the rain directing me."

Professor Whitfield slid backwards into the seat, settling himself atop the mass of paper. On the floor by his feet lay a month-old Sunday New York Times and several issues of The Economist, all of which looked as though they had been left out in the rain. There was also a portable urinal, which Professor Whitfield hastily covered over with the newspaper.

Peter, finding the steering wheel nearly flush against his chest, pushed the driver's seat backward as far as it could go. Though the odometer had yet to register its first thousand miles, the car's interior smelled of mildew and—more disconcertingly—of urine.

"I suppose I've become something of a pack rat in my dotage," said Professor Whitfield, who, Peter remembered, had maintained a punctiliously ordered office at the university. "Which, in turn, has driven my wife toward the opposite extreme. If I'm not watching her, she'll throw out the mail before I've had a chance to look at it. That's why it all ends up here."

"Mine only threw me out. She kept everything else."

After adjusting the mirrors and turning on the defogger, Peter carefully steered the Toyota away from the curb and out onto St. Paul Street. Then he kept going.

"What do you think you're doing?" Professor Whitfield demanded.

"I'm driving you home."

"What? Who are you? What gives you the right?"

"The way I see it, there's a 'duty of reasonable care' standard that applies here. A duty to prevent the foreseeable harm that's likely to result from letting you drive yourself home on a night like this."

≈≈

Professor Whitfield's face shone red as a traffic light. "You've taken it upon yourself to decide this? What else do you recommend? Should I stop driving altogether? Should I crawl into a corner and die? It's not enough that I get such advice from my children. Now I'm hearing it from total strangers. From drunks I meet in bars."

With an empty highway and a pitch-black night before him, Peter pressed hard on the accelerator. The Toyota gradually gained speed—too gradually for Peter's taste—until the needle edged past 80. For several minutes, neither man spoke, and the only sounds to be heard in the car were the murmuring of the engine—too quiet for Peter's taste—the pattering of the rain upon the roof, the swishing of the windshield wipers, and the panting of Professor Whitfield as he stared out his window at the rain.

Perhaps, Peter reflected, many of his troubles stemmed from having given insufficient attention over the years to the qualifier *reasonable* when exercising his duty of reasonable care. Once, while driving on I-95 at 2:00 AM, he had seen a burning car on the shoulder and a woman frantically waving for help. He had pulled her baby from the flames and, because she could not retrieve her handbag from what remained of the front passenger's seat, had given her one of his credit cards. Three months later, with fresh charges still appearing on his statements, he had finally closed the account. Perhaps the experience should have taught him something. Perhaps he should have let Professor Whitfield drive himself into oblivion. He should forget the daughters who no longer wanted to see him and cease raging at the woman whom he blamed for turning them against him and the crooked lawyers and biased judges who had abetted her.

The highway began to blur, and the Toyota drifted to the left. Peter shook his head violently to rouse himself, turned down the heat, and cracked the window open.

"The law can be a blunt instrument sometimes," said Professor Whitfield, "especially where children are concerned."

"Huh?" answered Peter, who did not realize that he had been ruminating out loud.

"I'm sure your girls will come around, though. They always do."

Peter shrugged. "That's what people tell me. I'll believe it when I see it."

"You said you were a student of mine?"

"Yes, and a devoted one, by my standards. Yours was the one class in law school I found worth attending."

"When were you in my class?"

"Oh, it must have been about twenty-five years ago."

"What are you doing now?"

"Wills and trusts. Pretty mundane stuff, mostly. But it's a decent living."

"And an honorable one. It's certainly nothing for which you need to apologize."

"Sometimes, I even manage to do a little good—when I'm able to temper my clients' greed, rage, and spite."

Removing his glasses, Professor Whitfield wiped the lenses with a handkerchief. He put the glasses back on and blinked several times.

"You were a student of mine, you said?"

Peter shook his head. This was vintage Professor Whitfield: the deadpan mockery like a knife between the ribs. But was it mockery? Professor Whitfield looked genuinely perplexed. Could he really have forgotten that he had asked the very same question just moments before?

Leaving the highway, Peter drove along unlit side streets, until directed by Professor Whitfield to turn left into a short cul-de-sac. He brought the Toyota to a stop in the driveway of a modest, gray-shingled Cape Cod house—the only house on the block with its lights on at this hour. In the glow of the headlights, he noticed several chipped shingles.

Turning in his seat and reaching for the door latch, Peter felt not the customary ache in his knee, but a pain like the thrust of a carving knife. He cried out in anguish.

"Are you all right?" asked Professor Whitfield.

"Bad knee," Peter answered, cupping his kneecap in his hands. "I need to get a replacement. It's something I should have had done a long time ago, but I've kept putting it off. It's not a pleasant thing when you think about it. It involves having your leg cut into three pieces and then put back together again."

"Most medical procedures—and, by this time, I believe I've endured most medical procedures—are rather grotesque."

"I had my knee operated on once before, when I was twenty-one. I almost died afterwards. A blood clot floated up to my lung. They had me in a pediatric ward because they had no other place for me. I'm lying in a bed that's way too small in a tiny room with pictures of giraffes on the walls. A priest is giving me last rites, and I'm gasping for breath and thinking about how undignified it would be to die there."

Professor Whitfield, turning his face toward the window, let out a harsh, clipped laugh. "You were expecting something more dignified? I do envy the young their expectations."

"The strange thing was that when I got out of the hospital, everything seemed brighter, clearer, more vivid. Colors, tastes, smells. But that only lasted a day or two, and I've never had that feeling since."

"Interesting. Death recedes, and one finds clarity. Conversely, for me, the fog grows thicker each day."

A queasy silence ensued, until Peter, unable to endure it anymore, eased himself out of the Toyota. Standing in the rain, holding the car door open for Professor Whitfield, he spied through the living room window a ghostly female form—a diminutive, bent woman dressed in white pajamas and a white terrycloth robe. She had a pallid complexion, a puffy, careworn face, and hair of white ringlets. Perched upon the edge of a plush, dark-blue sofa that sat behind a low coffee table, she repeatedly dabbed at her eyes with a tissue.

"May I have my keys back, please? If you don't mind."

Grinning sheepishly, Peter handed them over.

"Eunice," said Professor Whitfield, turning his own gaze toward the living room window, "is a worrier. The last couple of years have been hard on her."

Haltingly, he made his way up the gravel path to the front door, beside which a pale yellow bulb, enclosed in a cracked glass cylinder, emitted a sickly light. Peter stood frozen in place. In the living room, Mrs. Whitfield had risen from the sofa and begun pacing rapidly back and forth across the room, just as her husband had once paced at the head of the classroom.

"Aren't you coming in?" Professor Whitfield asked. He had the door open now and one foot over the threshold.

Peter hesitated. "Well, maybe just for a few minutes, while I wait for a cab."

"We have a guest room. You're welcome to stay the night."

Peter answered with a noncommittal shrug, though soaked and weary as he was, the prospect of sinking into a warm bed seemed quite enticing. He followed Professor Whitfield inside and found himself in a gloomy, overheated hallway illuminated—barely—by a brass chandelier with eight tear-drop-shaped bulbs, only two of which were lit.

The shadow that Eunice Whitfield cast on the wall preceded her as she came charging down the passageway, eyes distended, cheeks dripping tears, hands balled into fists, the right one clutching a tissue. "Where have you been?" she cried. "You said you were going out for a container of milk."

Professor Whitfield rolled his eyes, then calmly removed his coat and hung it on the coat tree beside the door. "I knew I forgot something," he muttered.

"You think it's a joke? You've been gone for seven-and-a-half hours. I called the police."

"I just got a bit lost. That's all. There was no need to call the police." Nodding in Peter's direction, Professor Whitfield added, "This man was kind enough to help me find my way back. He's a former student of mine. I'm sure he'd appreciate a cup of hot tea and a little less hysteria, though I suspect he's too polite to say so."

"Please don't bother," said Peter.

"A bit lost? A bit lost? What have you been doing for seven-and-a-half hours? Where were you? Do you even know where you've been?"

"I'm here now, am I not? There's no need to get so upset." Sidling past his wife, Professor Whitfield trudged up the hallway.

Despite his head start, she needed just a few strides to catch him. "How many times are you going to do this to me? You promised not to drive anymore at night."

"It was still light out when I left."

"It was raining. You shouldn't have gone out."

"No, I should be entombed here."

Left alone, Peter yawned loudly, slumped against the wall, and reached into his pocket for his cell phone.

From the living room, there came a despairing plea: "Will you please leave me alone?"

"No, I won't leave you alone. Look at what happens when I leave you alone. Next time, I'll hide the key."

"The address? I don't know the address," said the sleepy-voiced Peter to the sleepy-voiced taxi dispatcher. "No, I don't know the name of the street either. Hold on a minute." He took a few tentative steps toward the living room and peeked inside.

"Professor Whitfield?"

Professor Whitfield sat slumped upon the sofa, his right elbow perched on the armrest, his hand braced against the side of his head. His brow was creased; his mouth, a taut, colorless line. Eunice Whitfield, gesticulating wildly with her arms, hovered about him, now on his right side, now on his left, weeping, accusing, admonishing.

"I feel like a prisoner in my own house!" cried Professor Whitfield.

"I'll call you back in a minute," said Peter to the dispatcher. "As soon as I find out what the nearest intersection is. I'll wait there. Yes, I know it's pouring."

Peter slipped out the door as quietly as a burglar. Dragging his right leg, he lurched up the street toward the corner, the wind and the rain at his back, goading him onward.